BLAKE'S

Guide to Maths Problem Solving

Acknowledgements

I have been an enthusiastic mathematics educator for almost 40 years and interested in mathematical problem solving my entire life. As a young Mathematics Consultant in 1978, I was especially influenced by the work of George Polya, a Hungarian-American mathematician who wrote *How to Solve it* in 1945. Another influence was the 1977 research by Anne Newman, an Australian language educator who analysed errors made by Year 6 students when solving 1-step mathematical word problems. Her key findings, now called *The Newman Prompts*, are used by many schools to help teachers identify specific errors in problem solving.

I hope this *Blake Guide to Maths Problem Solving* proves to be another useful tool, designed specifically to help Stage 2 and 3 students become successful maths problem solvers.

Bev Dunbar
Maths Matters
December 2016

Blake's Guide to Maths Problem Solving

ISBN: 978 1 92549 010 7

Published by Pascal Press
PO Box 250
Glebe NSW 2037
www.pascalpress.com.au
contact@pascalpress.com.au

Author: Bev Dunbar
Publisher: Lynn Dickinson
Editor: Tim Learner
Design, illustrations & cover: Janice Bowles
Typesetter: Ruth Schultz

CONTENTS

AUSTRALIAN CURRICULUM CORRELATIONS

YEAR 4	
Mathematics Content Descriptions	**Problem Solving Proficiency / Pages**
Number & place value	
• Investigate and use the properties of odd and even numbers (ACMNA071) • Recognise, represent and order numbers to at least tens of thousands (ACMNA072) • Apply place value to partition, rearrange and regroup numbers to at least tens of thousands to assist calculations and solve problems (ACMNA073) • Investigate number sequences involving multiples of 3, 4, 6, 7, 8, and 9 (ACMNA074) • Recall multiplication facts up to 10 × 10 and related division facts (ACMNA075) • Develop efficient mental and written strategies and use appropriate digital technologies for multiplication and for division where there is no remainder (ACMNA076)	**Formulate, model and record authentic problems involving number operations** Pages: 15, 21, 24, 27, 28, 31, 33, 35, 36, 38, 55, 63, 65, 66, 67, 68, 70, 71, 72, 78, 79, 81, 89, 100, 127
Money & financial mathematics	
• Solve problems involving purchases and the calculation of change to the nearest five cents with and without digital technologies (ACMNA080)	**Solve simple purchasing problems using coins and notes** Pages: 24, 77, 80, 90, 117, 118
Patterns and algebra	
• Investigate number sequences involving multiples of 3, 4, 6, 7, 8, and 9 (ACMNA074) • Explore and describe number patterns resulting from performing multiplication (ACMNA081) • Solve word problems by using number sentences involving multiplication or division where there is no remainder (ACMNA082) • Find unknown quantities in number sentences involving addition and subtraction and identify equivalent number sentences involving addition and subtraction (ACMNA083)	**Use properties of numbers to continue patterns** Pages: 62, 68, 76, 81, 100, 101 **Solve problems using number sentences** Pages: 47, 63, 64, 68, 88, 89
Using units of measurement	
• Use scaled instruments to measure and compare lengths, masses, capacities and temperatures (ACMMG084) • Convert between units of time (ACMMG085) • Compare objects using familiar metric units of area and volume (ACMMG290)	**Formulate, model and record authentic problems using measurements** Pages: 11, 12, 15, 29, 30, 31, 35, 36, 43, 44, 45, 46, 47, 48, 49, 55, 78, 88, 90 **Solve problems using time durations** Pages: 11, 12, 43, 55, 88

AUSTRALIAN CURRICULUM CORRELATIONS

Mathematics Content Descriptions	Problem Solving Proficiency / Pages
Shape	
• Compare the areas of regular and irregular shapes by informal means (ACMMG087) • Compare and describe two dimensional shapes that result from combining and splitting common shapes, with and without the use of digital technologies (ACMMG088)	**Formulate, model and record authentic problems using 2D shapes** Pages: 13, 14, 22, 26, 27, 28, 29, 30, 31, 68, 70, 83, 107, 126 **Formulate, model and record authentic problems using 3D shapes** Pages: 15, 16, 17, 18, 107
Location & transformation	
• Use simple scales, legends and directions to interpret information contained in basic maps (ACMMG090) • Create symmetrical patterns, pictures and shapes with and without digital technologies (ACMMG091)	**Solve simple map problems** Pages: 16, 23, 73, 94, 96 **Solve simple problems related to symmetry** Pages: 13, 14, 22, 30, 109
Data representation and chance	
• Select and trial methods for data collection, including survey questions and recording sheets (ACMSP095) • Construct suitable data displays, with and without the use of digital technologies, from given or collected data. Include tables, column graphs and picture graphs where one picture can represent many data values (ACMSP096) • Evaluate the effectiveness of different displays in illustrating data features including variability (ACMSP097)	**Formulate, model and record authentic problems using statistics and probability** Pages: 32, 37, 43, 44, 45, 47, 50, 52, 69, 76, 85, 101, 128, 129, 130

AUSTRALIAN CURRICULUM CORRELATIONS

YEAR 5	
Mathematics Content Descriptions	**Problem Solving Proficiency / Pages**
Number & place value	
• Use estimation and rounding to check the reasonableness of answers to calculations (ACMNA099) • Solve problems involving multiplication of large numbers by one- or two-digit numbers using efficient mental, written strategies and appropriate digital technologies (ACMNA100) • Solve problems involving division by a one digit number, including those that result in a remainder (ACMNA101) • Use efficient mental and written strategies and apply appropriate digital technologies to solve problems (ACMNA291)	**Formulate, model and record authentic number problems using a variety of strategies** Pages: 33, 64, 65, 68, 71, 76, 77, 81, 82, 106, 112, 113, 133, 134
Fractions & decimals	
• Investigate strategies to solve problems involving addition and subtraction of fractions with the same denominator (ACMNA103) • Add and subtract decimals, with and without digital technologies, and use estimation and rounding to check the reasonableness of answers (ACMNA128)	**Solve problems involving fractions** Pages: 78, 79, 80, 113
Patterns and algebra	
• Describe, continue and create patterns with fractions, decimals and whole numbers resulting from addition and subtraction (ACMNA107)	**Solve problems involving number patterns** Pages: 81, 85, 101, 102, 106, 123
Using units of measurement	
• Choose appropriate units of measurement for length, area, volume, capacity and mass (ACMMG108) • Calculate perimeter and area of rectangles using familiar metric units (ACMMG109)	**Formulate and solve authentic problems using measurements** Pages: 15, 35, 36, 44, 46, 48, 57, 59, 62, 78, 90, 91, 95, 119, 122, 126
Location & transformation	
• Use a grid reference system to describe locations. Describe routes using landmarks and directional language (ACMMG113) • Describe translations, reflections and rotations of two dimensional shapes. Identify line and rotational symmetries (ACMMG114)	**Solve problems using a grid reference system** Pages: 16, 73 **Solve problems involving flips, slides and turns** Pages: 108, 109
Data representation and chance	
• Pose questions and collect categorical or numerical data by observation or survey (ACMSP118) • Construct displays, including column graphs, dot plots and tables, appropriate for data type, with and without the use of digital technologies (ACMSP119) • Describe and interpret different data sets in context (ACMSP120)	**Formulate, model and record authentic problems using statistics and probability** Pages: 38, 54, 113

AUSTRALIAN CURRICULUM CORRELATIONS

YEAR 6	
Mathematics Content Descriptions	**Problem Solving Proficiency / Pages**
Number & place value	
• Identify and describe properties of prime, composite, square and triangular numbers (ACMNA122) • Select and apply efficient mental and written strategies and appropriate digital technologies to solve problems involving all four operations with whole numbers (ACMNA123)	**Formulating and modelling authentic problems using number operations** Pages: 62, 82, 92, 102, 106, 122, 123
Fractions & decimals	
• Solve problems involving addition and subtraction of fractions with the same or related denominators (ACMNA126) • Find a simple fraction of a quantity where the result is a whole number, with and without digital technologies (ACMNA127)	**Solve problems involving fractions** Pages: 26, 55, 56
Money & financial mathematics	
• Investigate and calculate percentage discounts of 10%, 25% and 50% on sale items, with and without digital technologies (ACMNA132)	**Solve problems involving percentages** Pages: 80, 92, 122
Patterns and algebra	
• Continue and create sequences involving whole numbers, fractions and decimals. Describe the rule used to create the sequence (ACMNA133)	**Solve problems involving number patterns** Pages: 104, 105, 106
Using units of measurement	
• Convert between common metric units of length, mass and capacity (ACMMG136) • Solve problems involving the comparison of lengths and areas using appropriate units (ACMMG137) • Interpret and use timetables (ACMMG139)	**Formulate and solve authentic problems using measurements** Pages: 57, 58, 59, 62, 63, 91, 93, 124, 125, 126
Data representation and chance	
• Interpret and compare a range of data displays, including side-by-side column graphs for two categorical variables (ACMSP147) • Interpret secondary data presented in digital media and elsewhere (ACMSP148)	**Formulate, model and record authentic problems using statistics and probability** Pages: 50, 51, 52

SUMMARY OF TYPES OF PROBLEMS AND STRATEGIES

MATHEMATICS CONTENT	TYPES OF PROBLEMS					
	1 step	2 step	More than 2 steps	Multiple choice	Open ended	Puzzles
NUMBER and ALGEBRA						
Whole Numbers	118		70, 100, 103, 132			101, 127, 132
Addition & Subtraction		79, 89, 123	24, 64, 65, 70, 71, 77, 78, 81, 85, 93, 100, 101, 102, 103, 106, 127			71, 72, 76, 101, 127, 133
Multiplication & Division	54, 119, 122	21, 123	27, 31, 33, 49, 62, 66, 67, 68, 82, 100, 101, 104, 105, 115	115	134	
Fractions, Decimals & Percentages	122	26, 29, 79, 123	48, 55, 56, 80, 92, 113			
Money & Financial Mathematics	112, 117, 118, 134	90, 134	24, 80, 113, 134	134	134	134
Patterns & Algebra			44, 45, 46, 69, 81, 83, 85, 100, 101, 102, 104, 105, 106, 123			
MEASUREMENT and GEOMETRY						
Length	119		35, 44, 95, 116	116		
Area	122		36, 116, 124	116		
Mass	122		45, 57, 62, 63, 78, 90, 125	125	62	
Volume & Capacity		126	15		126	
Time	11, 88	12	34, 43, 57, 58, 59, 91, 93, 124			32, 34, 134
3D Objects	107	16	15, 17, 18			19
2D Shapes	13,14, 107	30	22, 68, 69, 83, 108, 109			73, 126
Location & Transformation		94	16, 23, 32, 35, 73, 96, 114			32
STATISTICS and PROBABILITY						
Chance			113			
Data Representation & Interpretation		128	37, 38, 39, 47, 50, 52, 53, 54, 55, 56, 57, 58, 59, 64, 129, 130			128, 129, 130

	MATHEMATICS CONTENT	Visualise the problem	Draw a table or graph	Guess and check	Break it into smaller parts	Work backwards	Look for a pattern	Eliminate it
		STRATEGIES						
NUMBER and ALGEBRA	Whole Numbers			70	127, 132		100, 101, 103, 106	118
	Addition & Subtraction	24	85	64, 65, 70, 71, 72, 133	76, 77, 78, 79, 81, 85, 123, 127	89, 93	81, 100, 101, 102, 103	133
	Multiplication & Division	21, 27, 31, 33	49, 54	62, 66, 67, 68	82, 123		100, 101, 104, 105	115, 119
	Fractions, Decimals & Percentages	26, 29	48, 55, 56	113	29, 79, 80, 123			113
	Money & Financial Mathematics	24	92		80, 134	90, 112, 134		112, 113, 117, 118, 134
	Patterns & Algebra		44, 45, 46, 69, 83, 85				44, 45, 46, 69, 81, 83, 85, 100, 101, 102, 104, 105, 106, 123	
MEASUREMENT and GEOMETRY	Length	35	44		95	95		116, 119
	Area	36			124			116
	Mass		45, 57	62	78	90		125
	Volume & Capacity	15			15			
	Time	11, 12, 32, 34	43, 57, 58, 59, 91			88, 91, 93, 124		
	3D Objects	16, 17, 18, 19, 109					107	
	2D Shapes	13, 22, 30, 109, 123		68, 69, 73, 126	73, 83		107, 108, 109	
	Location & Transformation	23, 32, 35, 114		73		94, 96		114
STATISTICS and PROBABILITY	Chance				113			113
	Data Representation & Interpretation	37, 38, 39	44, 47, 50, 52, 53, 54, 55, 56, 57,58, 59		128, 129, 130, 132			

HOW TO USE THIS BOOK

Mathematics is a way of thinking. It helps you understand how the world works. *Blake's Guide to Maths Problem Solving* helps you see mathematics all around you. It helps you talk about, draw and record it. It will give you the tools you need to be a successful mathematician, able to solve a wide variety of real-life problems.

Throughout this Maths Guide you'll be reminded about personal skills and strategies demonstrated by an effective problem solver. Plus there is a model to follow that helps you solve mathematical problems. And the explanations are clear, concise and written in friendly language.

Practise some of the strategies yourself in TRY THIS and CHALLENGE sections. These help you put the maths ideas inside your head, with detailed answers included at the back of the book.

This Maths Guide is a vital tool for any primary student who wants to be successful at solving mathematical problems.

ABOUT THE AUTHOR

Bev Dunbar is a highly respected mathematics educator, whose website, Maths Matters Resources, is used by primary teachers all over Australia and the world. For over 40 years, Bev has worked extensively with primary teachers, students, pre-service teachers and parents at universities, public and Catholic departments of education.

Bev is the author of many mathematical resources, including *Times Tables 1 and 2* (for primary students), the *Exploring Maths* series (16 books for primary teachers), the *Excel Early Skills Maths* series (10 books for preschool students) and the *Blake Maths Guides* (3 books for primary students, parents and teachers).

Bev is dedicated to helping you understand, enjoy and experience success at solving mathematical problems.

WHY SOLVE PROBLEMS?

Everyday problems are all around us. But if you already know what to do, or what mathematics to use, then it is NOT a problem for you.

Problem solving is where you use a variety of strategies to find at least one solution to something you don't yet know how to answer. Everyone can solve problems like these, once you put in a bit of effort.

Of course a mathematical problem is one you can solve using mathematics. Each problem is usually written as a story. When you read this story you are not sure what to do first or what strategy will help you solve it.

Some maths stories are pretty straight forward: e.g. "Jack has $68, Ali has $72 and Sally has $84. How much do they have altogether?" Although you don't yet know the answer to this problem, you know exactly what to do – you just have to add up three numbers. So it's NOT a problem for you, it's a procedure. We won't include many of these stories in this book.

Instead, we'll investigate what a typical problem solving cycle looks like. We'll then use this cycle to explore a large assortment of real-life problems which you don't yet know how to solve. Our suggested scaffold shows at least one way to solve each problem. You'll be challenged to practise strategies used by effective problem solvers. You'll be challenged to make these strategies part of your own thinking.

Together we'll instill the confidence, skills and knowledge to help your brain create its own effective problem solving centre.

Which personal strategies help you solve problems?

Although most people can solve everyday problems, some people are more effective at solving problems than others. Here are some of the things that an effective problem solver would always advise you to do:

Ten year old Andrew Wiles heard of a famous university problem called *Fermat's Last Theorem* in 1963. He wanted to be the first person to solve it and thirty-one years later he did. It was in 1994, 350 years after the problem was first posed. What incredible patience!

Many problems require more than one strategy to find a solution. Have a back-up plan.

If you get stuck, discuss your problem with a friend. Two or more heads might be better than one.

Enjoy exploring something new, even if you don't find the right answer. Be curious and ask plenty of "what if ...?" questions.

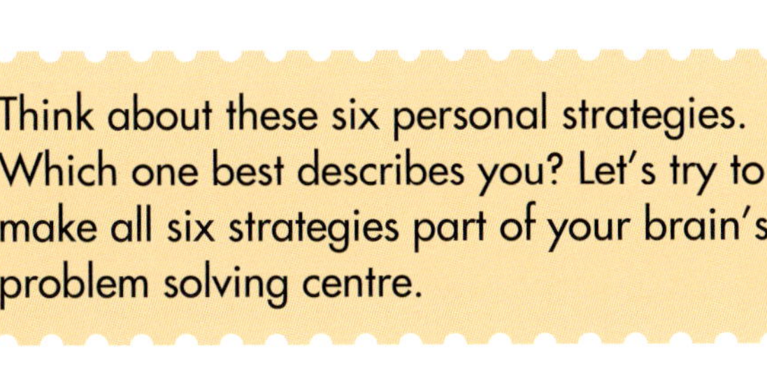

Think about these six personal strategies. Which one best describes you? Let's try to make all six strategies part of your brain's problem solving centre.

Leonardo da Vinci was a famous Italian problem solver who loved to explore new ideas. After experiments with muscles and bones in the human body, he created the first design for a humanoid robot in 1495. It moved with pulleys and cables.

What does an effective problem solving cycle look like?

If you need any reminders, just look at Useful Maths Facts on pages 135-151.

Before you start to solve a problem it's best that you already know and can easily recall your basic maths facts. If you think this describes you, then you are ready to go.

Although all problems are different, a cycle helps you structure the whole process. There are many examples out there, but I really like this one. Let's see how this cycle can work for you.

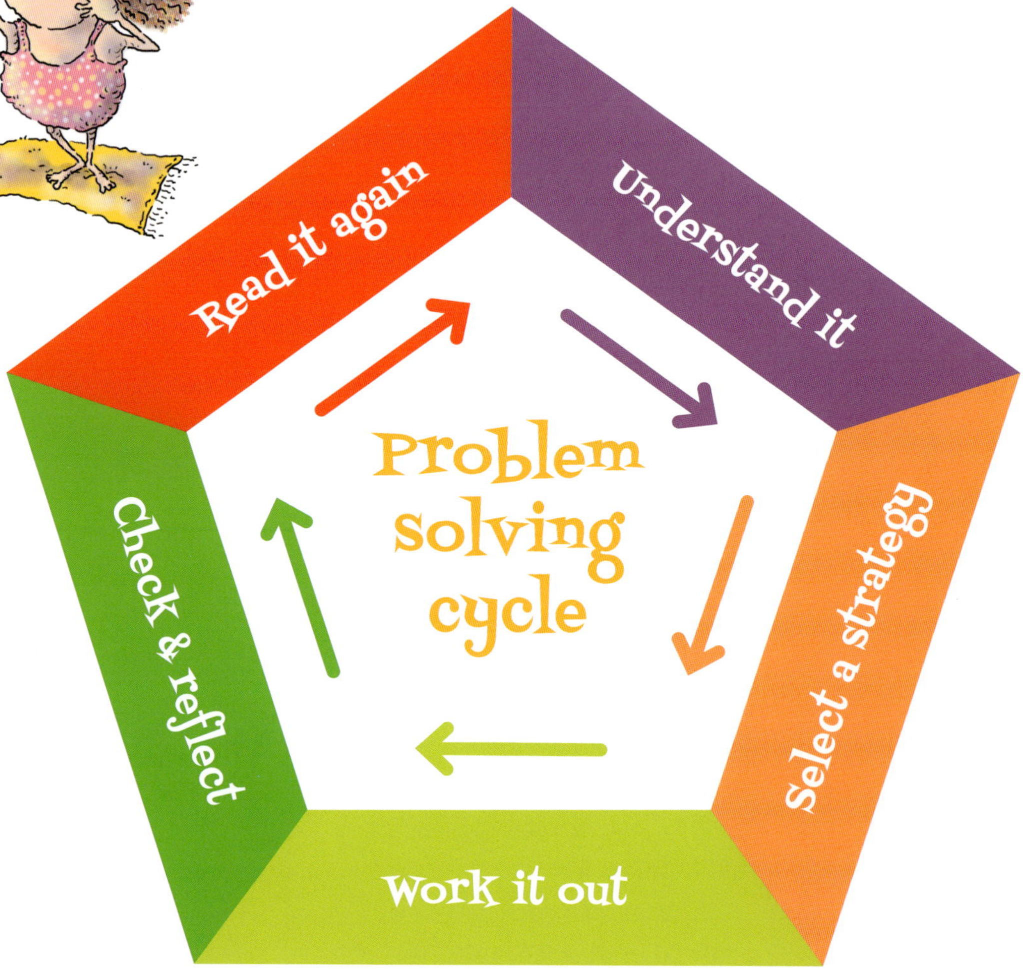

Problem solving cycle

Read it again

Understand it

Select a strategy

Work it out

Check & reflect

Read it again

It may seem obvious but always read your problem twice – once just to get a feel for it and the second time to really focus on what the problem is about.

Believe it or not, many people make a mistake right at the start of this problem solving cycle. They misread the problem.

Understand it

After you've read your problem twice, think about what it tells you. Does this problem make sense to you? Is there a word you don't understand? You may like to circle this word.

What do you already know? You might draw a line under key facts.

Is there any extra information you think is not important? If so, you can cross this out.

Now it's time to prove you understand your problem and you're clear about what you're trying to find out. Without looking back at your problem, in your own words say what you know and have to do, even if you say this silently.

Say in your own words what your problem wants you to do.

Now it's time to select an effective problem solving strategy.

Select a strategy

Once you understand what you are trying to do, these 7 problem solving strategies work well for most types of maths problems:

Visualise it

Draw a table or graph

Guess and check

These are the 7 strategies we want to make part of your brain's problem solving centre.

Which strategy will you select this time? What makes you think this one will work best for you now? Have you solved something like this before? If so, which strategy did you use then?

Take a risk, select one, jump in and see where that takes you.

Work it out

OK, so you know what your problem is about and you have selected one strategy to try first. But what mathematics do you use to solve it? Is it about Number? Measurement? Geometry? Data? Chance?

Is it something you can work out in your head or do you need pencil and paper or a calculator?

If it's a number problem, do you need to add or subtract, multiply or divide? How can you write this problem as a number sentence? Can you estimate what the answer might be?

Phew! There's lots to do here! That's why you need to know your basic maths facts before you start to solve a problem. Most people like to have plenty of scribble paper and pencils to use at this stage of the cycle.

Keep trying to work it out until you think you have a solution.

Check & reflect

Does your solution work? You now need to go back to your problem, read it again and check if your solution fits. That's why it's called a cycle. It only ends once you're convinced your answer fits the problem. Was your solution what the problem asked you to find?

If your strategy didn't work this time, restart the cycle. Try again. Reread the problem.

If your strategy did work, could there be a more effective strategy? Or could you try another strategy just to check?

If your strategy did work, how might you solve a similar problem in future? Could you still solve the problem if one thing was changed? To help you transfer your strategy to a future problem, say things like What if …? or I wonder if …

Use this 5-step cycle when you are not sure how to solve a maths problem. The steps provide a structure to help you think.

COMMON PROBLEM SOLVING STRATEGIES

This is one of the most useful strategies you can use to solve a problem. It is made up of many little strategies, all of which use the power of our brain to think in pictures as well as words.

Visualising can be quite difficult, so don't panic if you have trouble visualising things this way. The funny thing is that this strategy is often one of the most effective ways to solve a problem. It's worth persevering to improve your skills.

Builders, architects and town planners use this problem solving skill. So do car mechanics, doctors and landscape designers.

Imagine it

This **Visualise it** strategy is where you sit back, relax and let your imagination do the work. Try to make an object or event appear inside your head. If you need a purple sphere, try and see that purple sphere even though there is nothing really there. If you need to see a beetle from above, try to see that inside your head too.

The trick is that sometimes you need to make that image inside your head behave differently. Instead of staying still, you may need this image in your head to move in a different direction or rotate about a point.

Most times you imagine with your eyes open. You imagine going behind an object to count the edges, faces or vertices. You imagine what is around a corner, under a table or inside a room.

Do you know what Einstein said?

"The true sign of intelligence is not knowledge but imagination."

Calendar problems

You imagine when you read a calendar.
What are the dates before or after the month shown?

Look at this desk calendar for March 2016.

- This is a Time problem. The information is in a grid. It's organised by days of the week. Notice 1 March is a Tuesday.
- There are 2 spaces before this – a pale grey 28 and 29. What do these mean? They are the last 2 days of February and 2016 must be a Leap Year as February has 29 days.
- Look at the last day of March. It's a Thursday. Notice there are 2 more spaces after this with a pale grey 1 and 2. What do these mean? These are the first 2 days of April.

Now let's use some imagination.

Grandma and Grandpa

Grandma and Grandpa celebrated their 50th wedding anniversary on 6 April 2016. What day of the week was this?

- Imagine counting forwards from 2 April.
- Sunday will be 3 April but it's not shown on our calendar.
- Use your imagination to continue counting the days.
- Imagine another row magically appears at the bottom of this calendar.
- You now discover 6 April was a Wednesday.

And all this happens inside your head. We don't need to write it down or draw a picture. We just need to see it in our mind.

Let's imagine another calendar problem.

Charlie at the vet

Our dog Charlie had a vet appointment 8 days before Friday 4 March 2016. When did Charlie go to the vet?

- If we focus our mind on Friday 4 March on this calendar, we can see the first day before is 3 March.
- Keep counting back until you reach 8 days. This time you imagine an extra row above the line we actually see.
- If you count back 8 days you get a Thursday. But what was the actual date?
- Now you know where to stop, you can continue counting back from 28 February, the pale grey number on the far left of the top row. That's 27, 26, 25.
- So 8 days earlier must be Thursday 25 February.

Try this

The birthday

Today is the last Monday in March 2016. Your friend's birthday is 16 April. How many days away is this? What day of the week is it?

Fraction problems

You imagine when you play with fractions.

Here are some half shapes. To reflect each shape across the dotted line, the mirror line, imagine what the whole shape looks like. Try to do this without actually drawing in the other half. See the whole shape inside your mind.

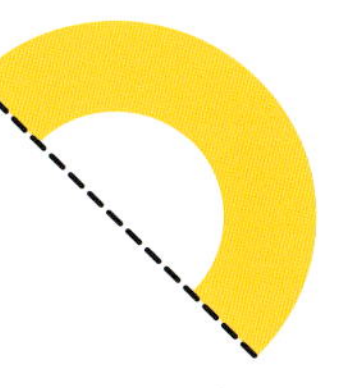
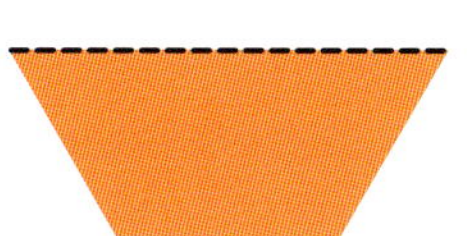

This is what the flipped shapes look like. Is this what you imagined too?

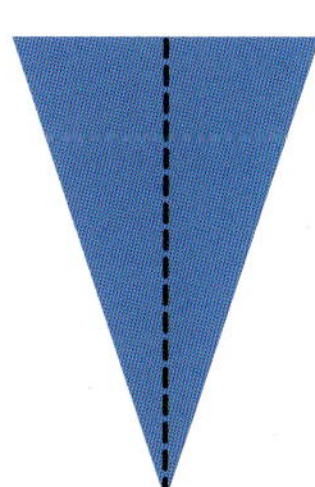

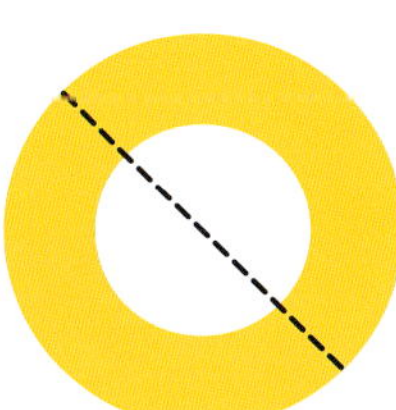
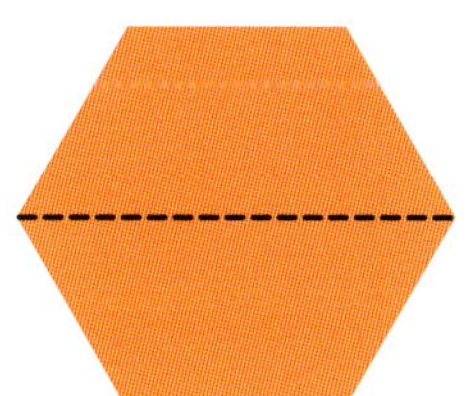

This ability to flip, slide or even turn a shape in your mind will help you to be an effective problem solver.

Flip this

Myra cuts out a red shape and holds it like this.

She flips this shape horizontally.

Describe what Myra's shape looks like now.

Read it again

Understand it

I have to describe what this shape looks like when it's flipped along the horizon line.

Select a strategy

Visualise it and imagine it happening in my head.

Work it out

To flip this shape from right to left along the horizon line, imagine placing a mirror on the left-hand side of this shape.

What flipped image will I see in the mirror?

I think I see the shape like a letter "L" but the long piece is going to the left. The short piece is standing up. It looks like a letter L that has fallen backwards.

Check & reflect

If I use a mirror the reflected red shape now looks like this. That's exactly what I imagined.

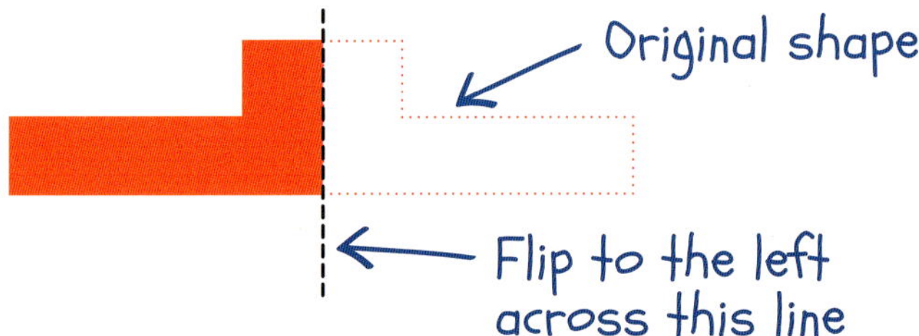

Is another solution possible?

Yes. I can also reflect this shape the other way along the horizon from left to right. This time it will look like this. Both solutions are possible.

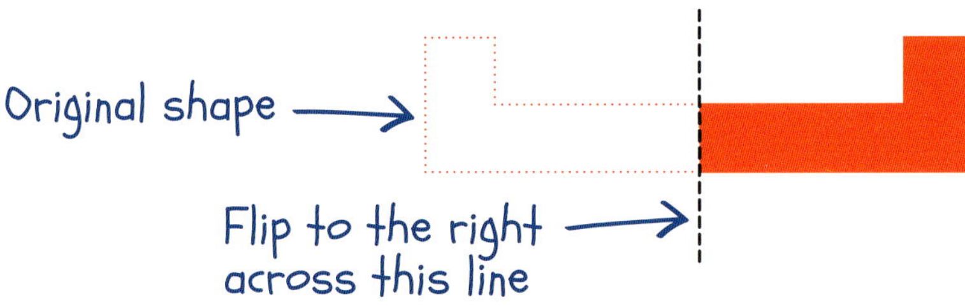

Let's try another **Visualise it** problem where you imagine the solution.

Look at the length of the smaller cube below. How many times will it fit across the length or width of the larger object? Do this just using your eyes.

Stacking cubes

Huan made a rectangular prism by stacking small cubes. He drew this picture to scale.

All the small cubes are this size:

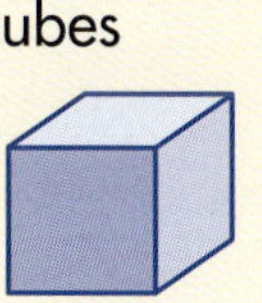

How many cubes did Huan use to build his 3D object?

Work it out

- Imagine each cube fitting into the total shape.
- It definitely looks longer than 2 cubes. I estimate 3 cubes fit along the bottom edge.

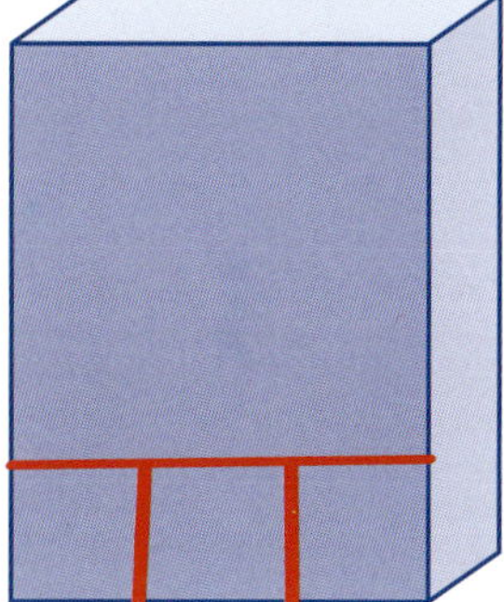

- Now imagine the rows stacked on top of each other. The base looks shorter than the height so there are more than 3 rows. I estimate 4 rows.
- That's 4 × 3 small cubes. I estimate Huan used 12 small cubes to build his rectangular prism.

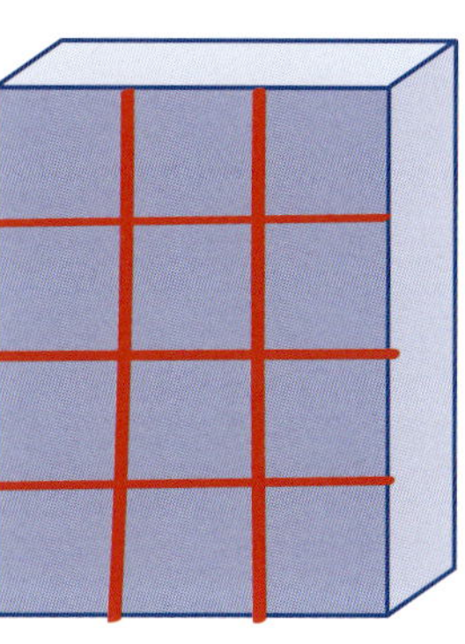

Check & reflect

Here is what the stack really looks like. **Imagine it** was an effective strategy. Huan used 12 small cubes.

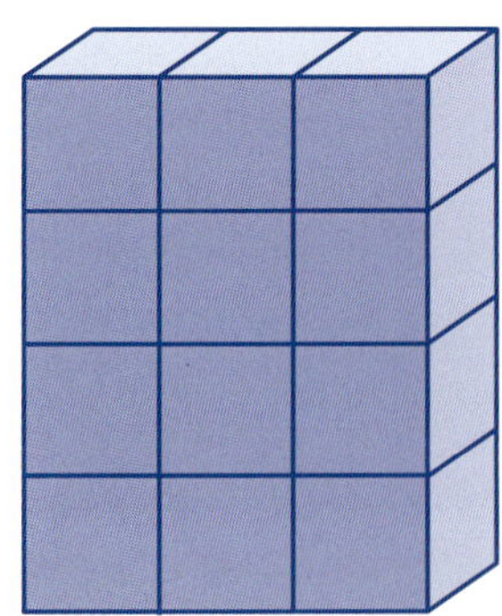

Staircase

Zoya built this small staircase.

Imagine you pick up this whole staircase and turn it in any direction.
A face is a flat surface.

How many faces does this staircase have?

Challenge: Reading a map

Each 1 cm line on this grid represents 1 km.

Start at the ★.

Imagine you travel 3 km west, then 2 km north.

Next travel 5 km east then 4 km south.

Where are you now?

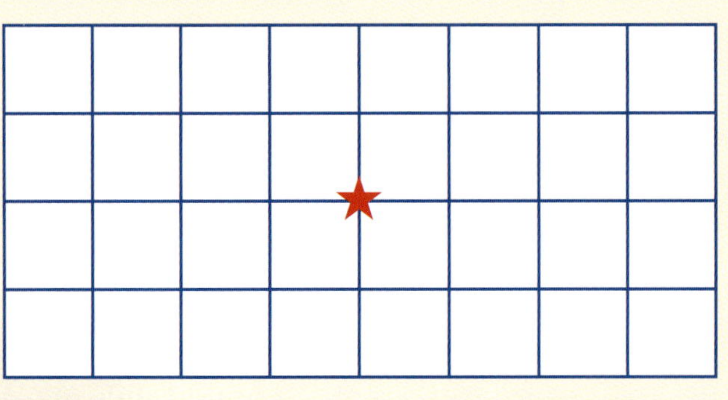

N

Make a model

Sometimes you think it's too hard to imagine. Instead, making a 3D model can help you visualise your problem. Use DUPLO or LEGO bricks, small Base 10 shorts or ones, matchsticks, plasticine, paper squares … it all depends on the problem you are trying to solve.

To solve a problem you may need to look at information in a model or make a model yourself.

Here is a DUPLO brick model.

Imagine rotating this object so you can see each side. Here is what the object looks like from 4 different views.

Is this what you imagined?

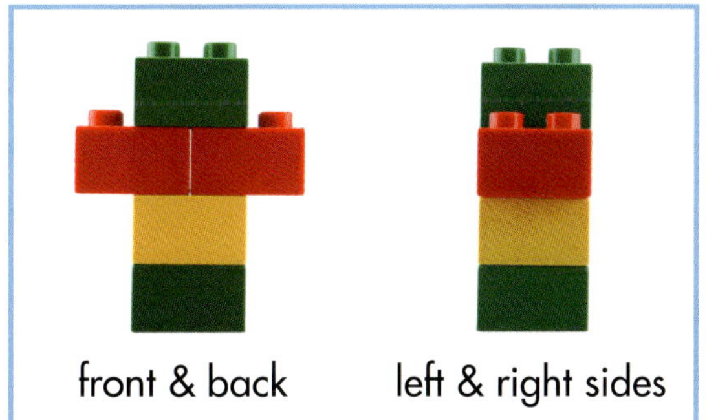

front & back left & right sides

Each view of a model can look quite different. Just hold up your model so you are looking at it directly. For example, to see the front, hold it so you can't see the top or the bottom or another side.

This is what the model looks like if you draw each view.

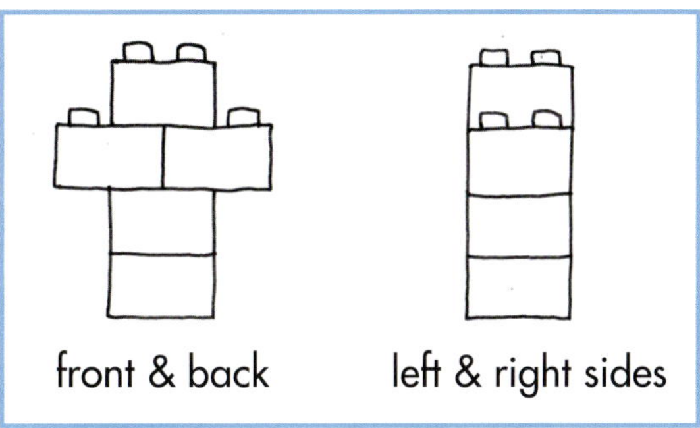

front & back left & right sides

Your final model needs to match each view whether you copy from a photograph or a drawing. Architects and builders use models and drawings to help them solve building problems.

Mystery Object

Joe built a mystery object. This is what it looks like from 4 different views.

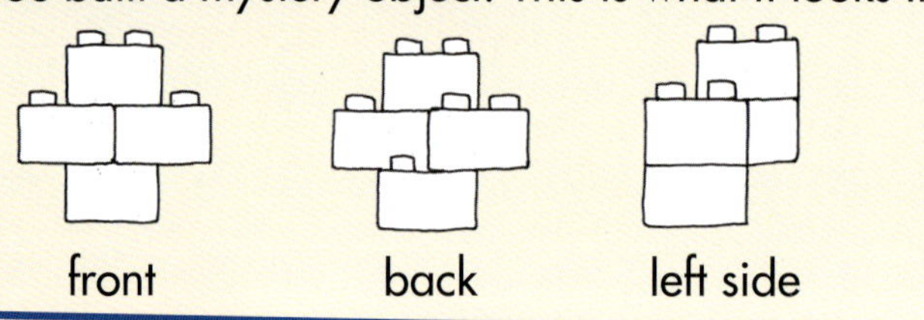

Read it again

Understand it

I need to construct a 3D object so that it matches these 4 views.

Select a strategy

I'll make my own model with DUPLO bricks to help me **Visualise it**.

Work it out

- I'll start with the front view. Each small detail has to fit exactly.
- Now I have to look at my model to see if it matches the back, left and right side views.
- I notice that this problem doesn't tell me what the top and bottom views look like. So I don't need to check these views.
- I'll keep trying until I construct a model that works for all 4 views. Phew!

Check & reflect

Finally, I did it. Here's what the actual object looks like. The colour isn't important, just the actual shape.

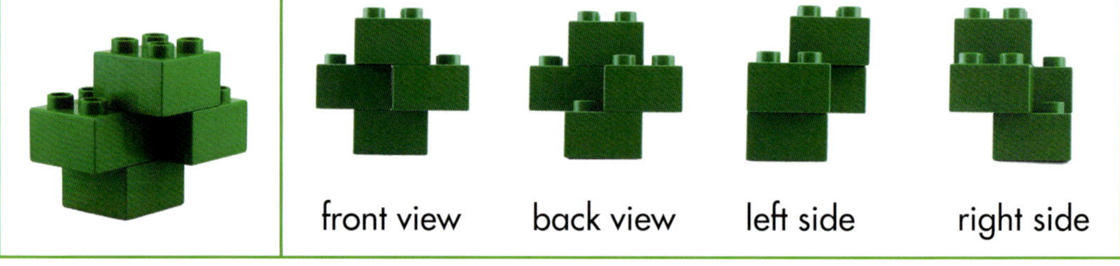

Finished model

Try this

Here is a DUPLO model seen from the front, back and each side. What does the finished model look like?

front & back view

left & right view

This is what it looks like as a drawing.

front & back view

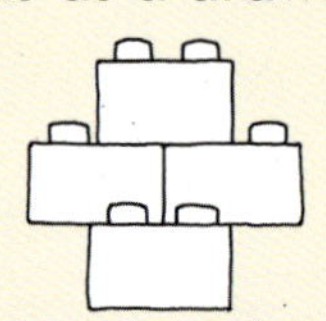

left & right view

You can **Make a model** using anything. You don't have to always use building bricks.

Grilled toast

Max is camping. He wants to toast 3 slices of bread but his grill only takes 2 slices at a time. Each side takes 1 minute to toast. How can he do this in the fastest time?

Select a strategy I'll make a model to help me visualise the problem.

Work it out I can use 3 sheets of paper to represent the toast. I'll write front and back on each slice and label them A, B and C.

1 minute — Slice A front | Slice B front

1 minute — Slice A back | Slice B back

1 minute — Slice C front

1 minute — Slice C back

That's 4 minutes altogether to toast all 3 slices front and back.

Check & reflect

When I reread the problem, it asks for the fastest way. What if there's a faster solution?

The first minute seems fine:

1 minute

But I can alter the second minute like this:

1 minute

And I can alter the third minute like this:

1 minute

Now the job is done in only 3 minutes. That's 1 minute faster. That's 25% faster than my first solution. The paper squares helped me discover a more efficient solution.

Plasticine is another useful modelling tool. Here's one way it can help you solve a problem.

Cutting logs

Bish is cutting wood for a fire. He wants to cut a huge log into 9 equal pieces so it fits in his truck. Each cut takes him 7 minutes. How long will it take to cut 9 pieces?

Work it out

I'll use plasticine to represent Bish's log and a plastic knife for the saw.

I need to work out how many cuts altogether. I estimate 9 cuts.

My estimate was out. I needed only 8 cuts.

Each cut takes 7 minutes so it takes 8 × 7 minutes to cut. That's 56 minutes.

Check & reflect

When I reread the problem, it asks for the answer as time. So 56 minutes sounds correct. That's slightly less than an hour to do the job.

Could I use another strategy to check? I can draw a diagram like this:

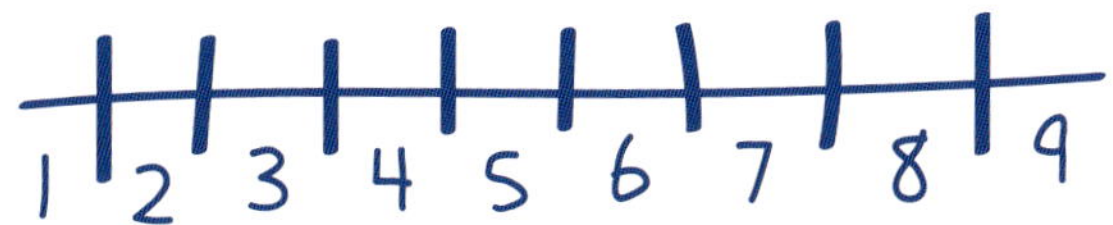

So yes, Bish makes 8 cuts to create 9 logs and each cut takes 7 minutes. I know 8 × 7 = 56. Bish takes 56 minutes to cut his log.

Making a model with sticks is another way to help you visualise a problem. Small coloured sticks are available in your local craft shop.

Remember, we're trying to build a problem-solving centre in your brain.

In a matchstick problem you follow a rule to move individual sticks to create new shapes. Don't overlap or break any stick, unless the puzzle asks you to do this. And always try to imagine first, before you model the problem with sticks.

Amy's shape

Amy made this shape with 12 sticks.

How can she move 4 sticks to create one 2D cross?

Work it out

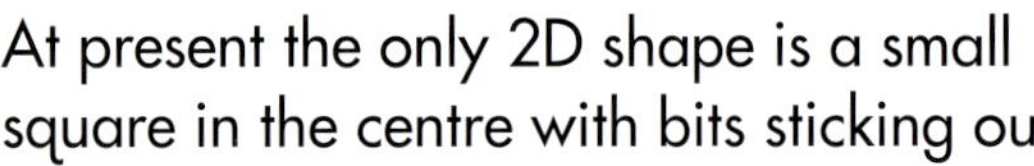

At present the only 2D shape is a small square in the centre with bits sticking out.

I have to imagine which sticks to move to make a cross. There will be no gaps, just one perimeter made from 12 sticks.

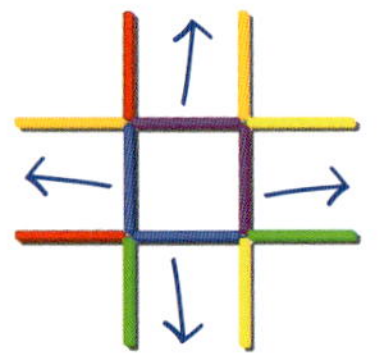

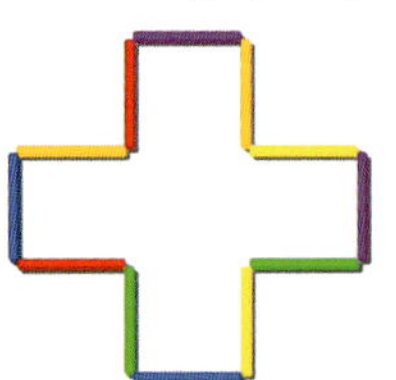

I can move the 4 inner sticks to the outside like this.

Check & reflect

I know it's correct because I've created the large cross.

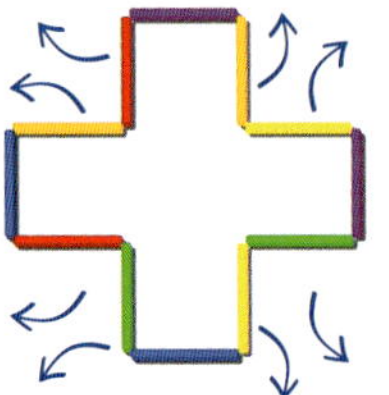

What shape will I get if I move more sticks?

If I move these 8 sticks I make a large square.

Josh's hexagon

Josh built this hexagon using 12 sticks. There are 6 triangles inside this hexagon.

Move 4 sticks to create 3 triangles.

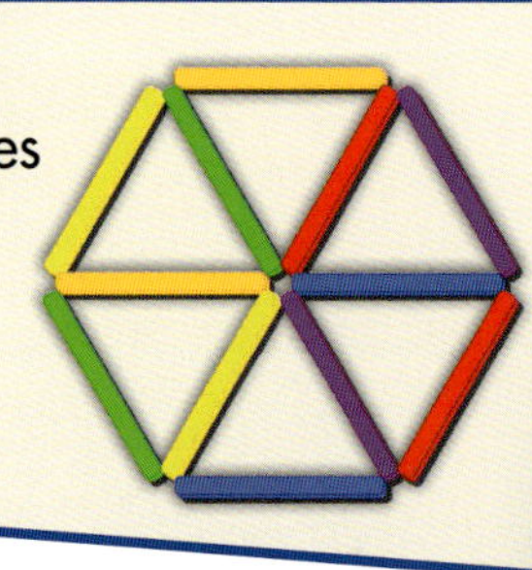

Act it out

Another way to visualise your problem is to act it out. It's like making a model except this time instead of substituting blocks, paper or plasticine you do all the actions yourself to discover your solution.

Catching the ski lift

Holly, Molly, Patz and Jatz sat together on the ski lift. Jatz sat on the right of the group. Patz didn't sit next to Jatz. Holly didn't sit next to Jatz. The girls sat together. Holly sat between a boy and a girl.

Read it again

Understand it

I need to work out the exact position where each person sat on this ski lift. I know that Jatz is on the far right. I can cross this sentence out now.

Select a strategy

The position words are confusing. I'll visualise the problem by acting it out with my friends.

Work it out

Jatz

I'll write name cards for my friends to hold so I know which one is which. I know Jatz sat on the right, that's Seat 4.

Molly Jatz

But there are still more bits of information to think about. Patz didn't sit next to Jatz. So Patz didn't sit in Seat 3. He must be in Seat 1 or 2.

And Holly didn't sit next to Jatz. So Holly didn't sit in Seat 3. That only leaves Molly. She must sit in Seat 3.

Holly Molly Jatz

The girls sat together so Holly must be in Seat 2.

That leaves Patz in Seat 1.

Check & reflect

Patz Holly Molly Jatz

I need to reread the question to see if my solution matches the clues.

✓ Yes, Jatz is on the far right.
✓ Yes, Patz is not next to Jatz.
✓ Yes, Holly is not next to Jatz.
✓ Yes, Holly is sitting between a boy and a girl.

Is this the only correct solution? I think so as Holly can't be 1st or 3rd.

Act it out is a useful strategy to help you solve a money problem, especially if it includes buying, selling, lending or paying back. Use play money to act out each transaction.

Horse trading

Grandpa bought a horse called Brandy for $600. Later he sold Brandy to my Uncle Bill for $700. Uncle Bill then sold Brandy back to Grandpa for $800. Grandpa then sold Brandy to Aunty May for $900. Did Grandpa make any money on this trading?

Read it again

Understand it

There are 4 different money amounts. I need to figure out if Grandpa gained any money, broke even or made a loss.

Select a strategy

I tried to work it out in my head first, but I was confused. I'll use play money to **Act it out**.

Work it out

- Grandpa starts with $600 and no horse.

- Brandy costs him $600.
  Now he has $0 but he has a horse.

- Uncle Jack pays $700. Now Grandpa has $700 and no horse.

- Grandpa buys Brandy back for $800. He must have borrowed that extra $100 from a friend. So he is minus $100 but he has the horse.

- Grandpa then sells Brandy for $900. He can now pay the $100 back to his friend and he still has $800, but no horse.

Check & reflect

Grandpa started with $600 and finished with $800. He made an extra $200 from horse trading. Acting it out with play money helped me keep track of how much money Grandpa had at any one time.

Draw a diagram

Always try to solve a word problem in your mind first. Remembering your basic maths facts will also be effective. But if you feel you still need help, **Draw a diagram** to help you visualise your problem. A diagram can help you think.

Here are some different ways to draw a diagram:

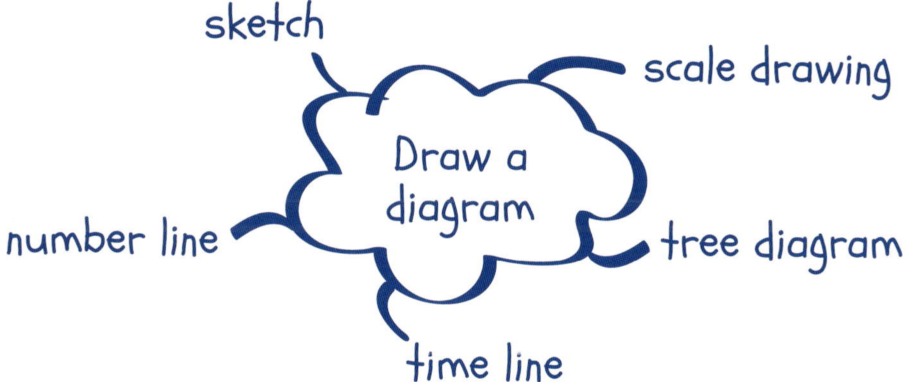

Draw a sketch

- A sketch is a picture that shows a key fact in your problem.
- A square might represent a cube (even though this is not accurate).
- A stick figure might represent a person or an animal.
- An initial might represent someone's name.

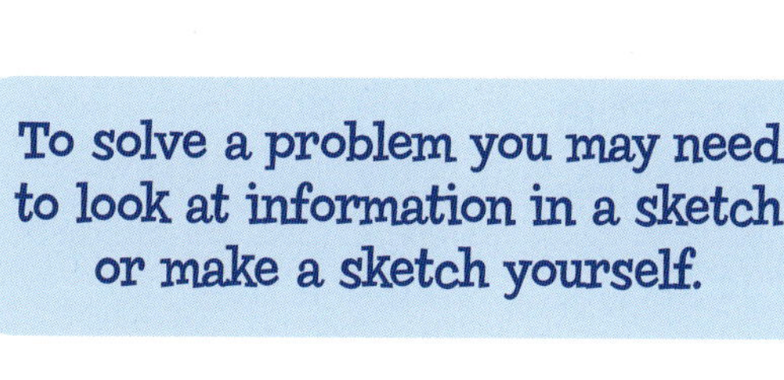

Pizza night

Seven friends share some pizzas.

Everyone eats $\frac{3}{8}$ of a pizza, plus $\frac{3}{8}$ of a pizza was left at the end of the meal.

How many pizzas did they buy?

Read it again

Understand it

This is a fraction problem. 7 people ate pizzas and I need to calculate how many pizzas there were altogether.

Select a strategy

I'll draw a sketch of the pizzas to help me solve this problem.

Work it out

When I reread this problem it says each person ate $\frac{3}{8}$ of a pizza. So I'll draw my pizzas in eighths.

I'll draw 2 pizzas as with one pizza 7 people would get only $\frac{1}{8}$ each with one piece left over.

Five people can each eat $\frac{3}{8}$ of a pizza if there are 2 pizzas. I need to draw another pizza.

My sketch shows they need 3 pizzas altogether.

Check & reflect

I can see another way to solve this.

7 people eat $\frac{3}{8}$ of a pizza and there is another $\frac{3}{8}$ left.

That makes 8 groups of 3 pieces or 24 pieces in total.

8 pieces = 1 pizza so 24 pieces = 3 pizzas.

Growing tomatoes

Sally loves growing tomatoes. She has 10 plants in 5 rows and each row has exactly 4 plants in it. What does her tomato garden look like?

Read it again

Understand it

I have to find a way to make rows of tomato plants. I know there are 5 rows.

Select a strategy

I'll draw a sketch to help me visualise the problem.

Work it out

I can draw 5 rows like this and put 2 marks to show the plants in each row.

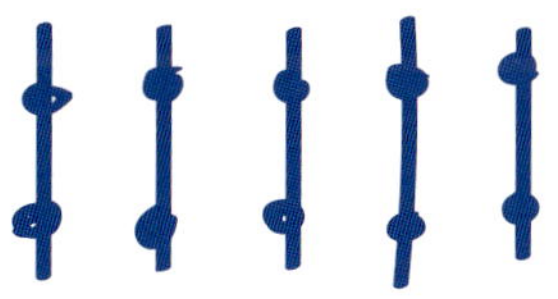

5 rows
2 plants per row
10 plants

That was too easy. It wasn't even a problem for me.

Check & reflect

When I reread the problem I notice that I missed something important. Sally has 4 plants in each row. I have only 2 plants in each row. So my solution is not correct yet. I'll try again.

Work it out

I'll try changing direction.

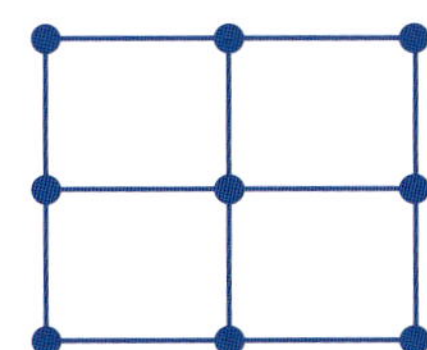

5 rows
3 plants per row
9 plants (with 1 left over)

I'll try crossing them over each other.

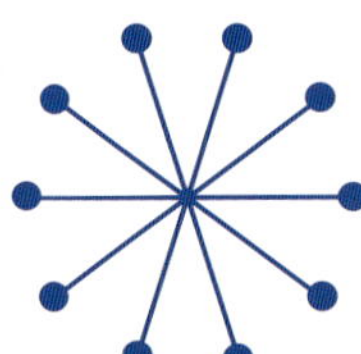

5 rows
3 plants per row
10 plants

I still don't have 4 plants in each row.

I need the rows to cross over even more so I can get more plants in a row. I'll try a star shape like this:

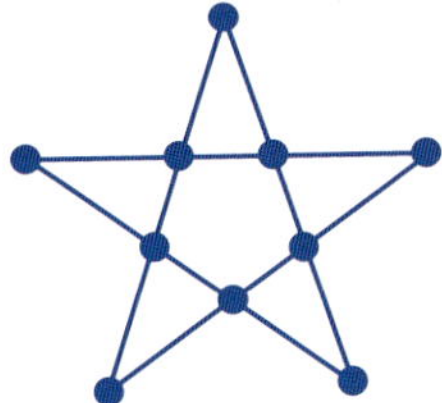

Check & reflect

So that's how Sally did it! What a creative gardener. Her design has 5 rows with 4 tomato plants in each row. She still has only 10 plants because 5 plants are counted twice.

What if Sally had 12 plants?

I can think of at least 2 different solutions.

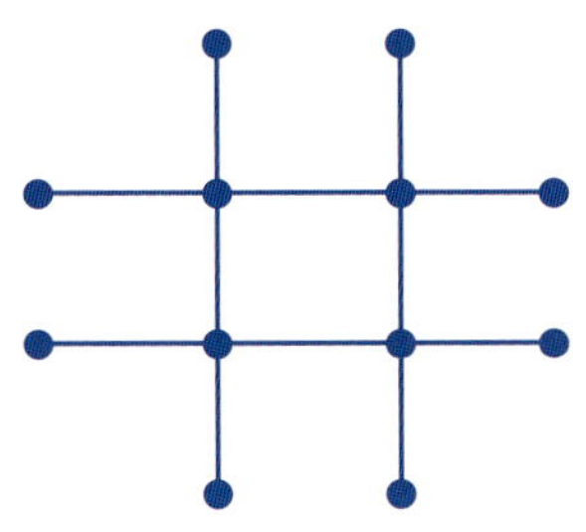

4 rows
4 plants per row
12 plants

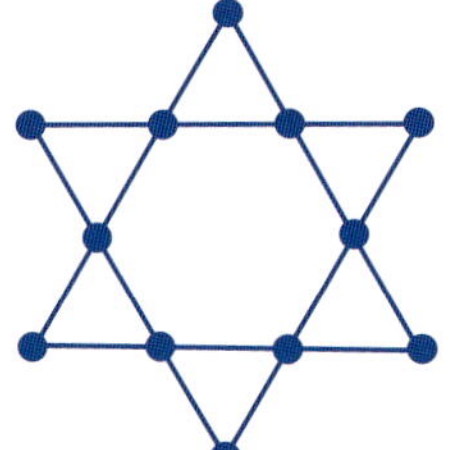

6 rows
4 plants per row
12 plants

Drawing a diagram can help with fractions too. Look at fraction shapes and try to "see" smaller shapes hiding within them. Or try to "see" the new shape when 2 or more shapes are combined. A quick sketch can help you think about your solution.

Laying turf

Josh uses units of turf to help his family create a new lawn.

This shape is 1½ units.

What does one unit look like?

Work it out

- If this shape is one and a half, that's the same as 3 halves.
- I need to find 3 identical shapes hiding within this shape.
- I can see a right angle triangle.

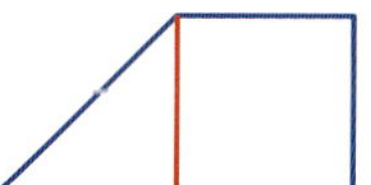

- I know I can divide the square that remains into 2 triangles too.

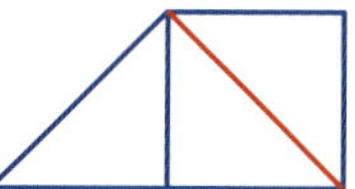

- So there are 3 triangles. These are the 3 halves.

Check & reflect

The triangle is ½ a unit. The square is 1 unit.

Is there another way to solve this problem? I could put 2 triangles together to create this shape.

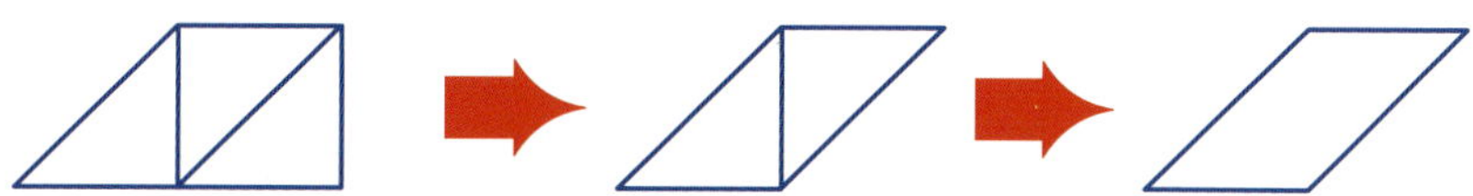

But it's more likely the turf comes in squares rather than this parallelogram.

The hidden shape in a fraction problem doesn't have to be a square.

Try to visualise these hidden or missing shapes mentally first. **Draw a sketch** is your back up plan.

Unit shapes

If this shape is made from ½ a unit, what does 1 unit look like?

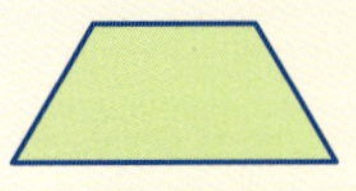

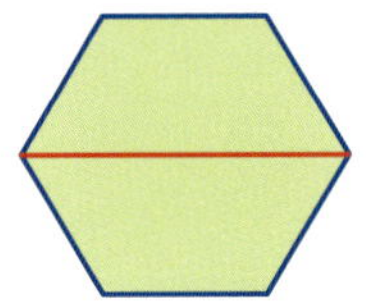

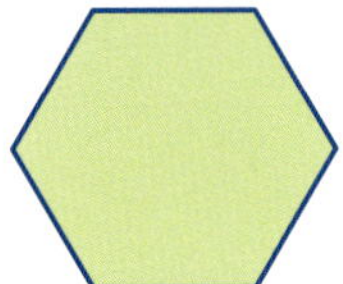

½ unit 2 halves 1 unit

In fact there are many ways this unit can become a whole unit.

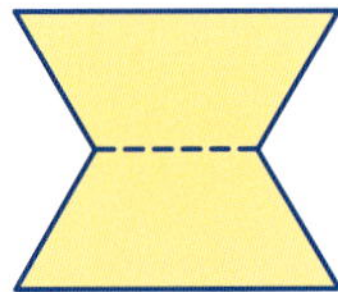

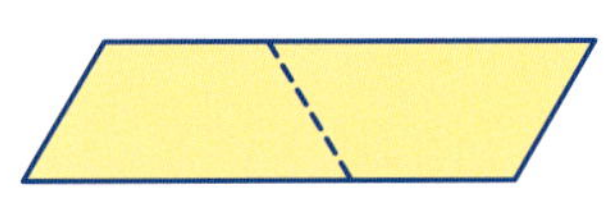

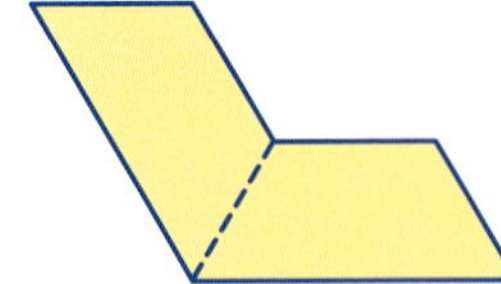

More unit shapes

If this shape is made from 2 units, what does 1 unit look like?

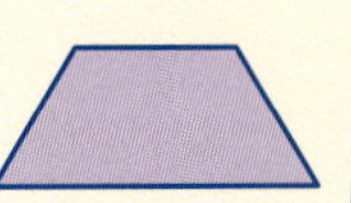

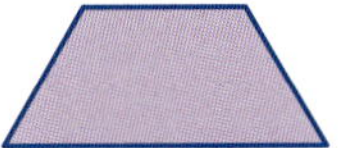

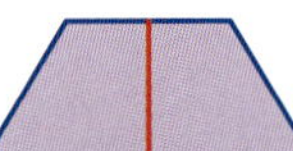

Even more unit shapes

If this shape is made from 3 units, what does 1 unit look like?

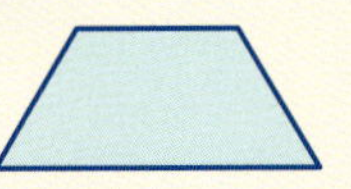

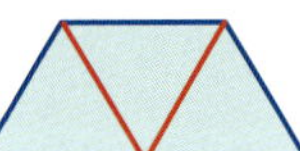

Designers, architects, town planners, landscape designers, clothes designers all use **Draw a sketch** to solve problems.

Laying grass

Josh can lay 3 grass squares in half a minute. How many squares will he lay in two minutes?

Work it out

If you can't use your mental skills to solve this, imagine it in your head then sketch what you see. There is more than one way to sketch a solution.

This is what he lays in half a minute:

Doubling this is what he lays in 1 minute.

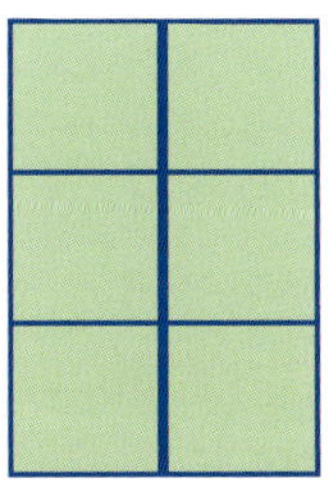

Or it could look like this.

So Josh lays 6 grass squares in 1 minute. And double that in 2 minutes.

Check & reflect

Josh lays 2 × 6 = 12 grass squares in 2 minutes. If Josh kept working like this he could lay 24 grass squares in 4 minutes but after that he'd probably need a break.

Unit shapes

If this shape is made from 2 units, what do 3 units look like?

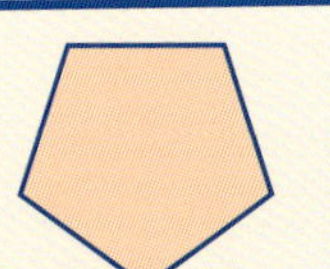

A sketch with lines and arrows can help you solve problems that involve family relationships.

You might sketch your family like this:

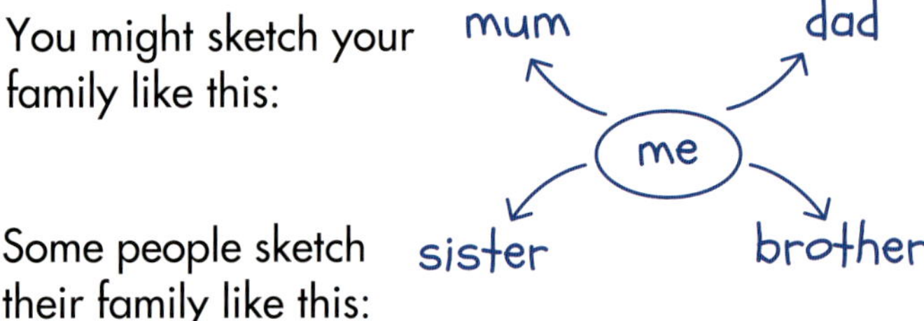

Some people sketch their family like this:

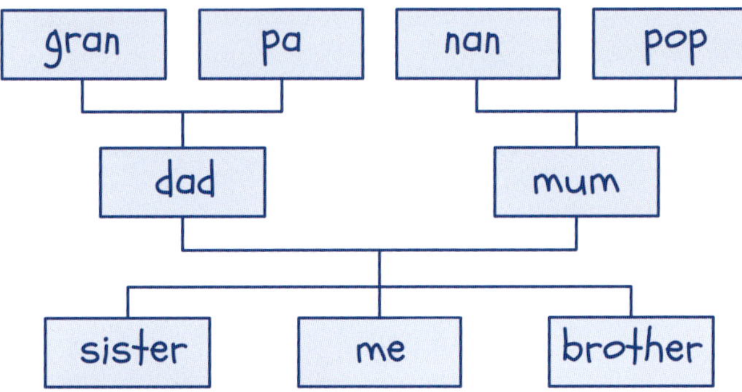

Family ties

Who is your uncle's father's only grandchild?

Work it out

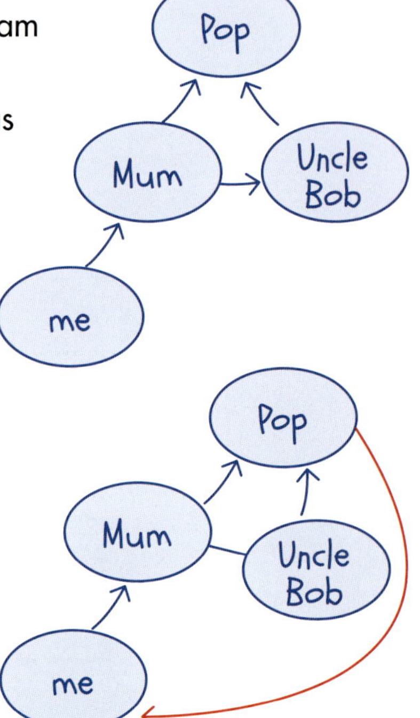

- I tried to solve this in my head but it's spinning. I'll draw a diagram to help me sort it out.
- It's not about my real family as my Pop has 7 grandchildren.
- When I reread the question it talks about my uncle's father. My uncle is my mum's brother. Their father is my Grandfather. I'll draw what that looks like.
- But now when I reread the question it says that Pop has only one grandchild.

Check & reflect

Drawing a diagram helped me sort it out. In this problem there is only one grandchild: me.

Draw a number line

A number line helps you jump forwards and backwards with numbers. It may look a bit messy doing this but use it just to work something out. To solve a problem you may need to read a number line or draw one yourself.

Jumpy kangaroos

Three kangaroos jump along a beach. Kangaroo A jumps half as many times as Kangaroo B. Kangaroo B jumps 12 times. Kangaroo C jumps 3 times as many jumps as Kangaroo A. How many times does Kangaroo C jump?

Work it out

This is a number puzzle. I can draw a number line to help me visualise my solution. I know Kangaroo B made 12 jumps.

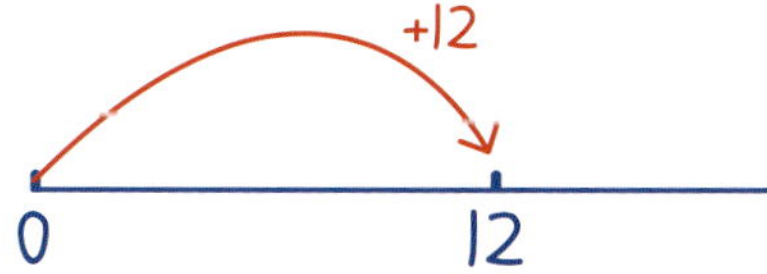

If Kangaroo A jumped half as many times, that's half of 12. That's 6 jumps.

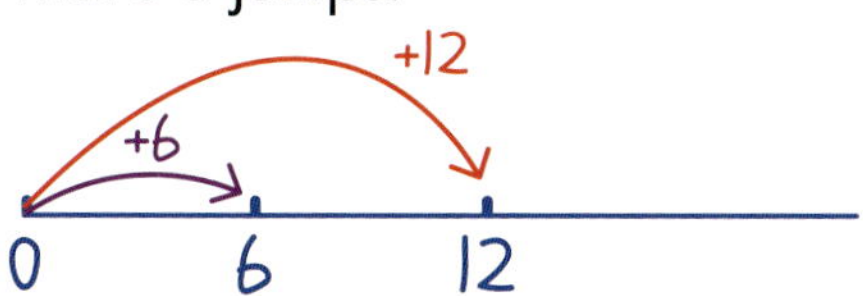

Kangaroo C jumps 3 times as many jumps as Kangaroo A. That's 6, 12, 18 or $3 \times 6 = 18$.

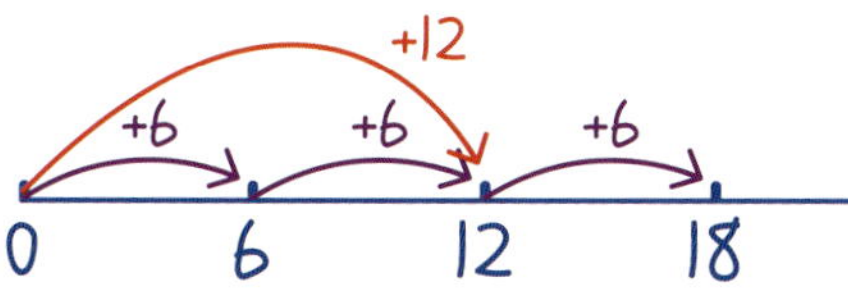

Check & reflect

Kangaroo C makes 18 jumps. When I reread this problem my solution fits all the clues.

ABC jumps

Kangaroo A made 8 jumps and Kangaroo C jumped twice as far as Kangaroo A. Kangaroo B jumped half way between Kangaroo A and Kangaroo C. How far did Kangaroo B jump?

Draw a time line

A time line is like a number line except it's always about time. Time can be seconds, minutes, hours, days or years. Yes, you got it – it can be about any time period at all. To solve a problem you may need to read a time line or draw one yourself.

2000 BCE | 1000 BCE | 0 | 1000 CE | 2000 CE

Years

It can even be about days of the week or months of the year. You can draw it like this too:

Mon	Tues	Wed	Thurs	Fri	Sat	Sun

Days of the week

Omar's puzzle

Omar likes to talk weirdly. He asked his friend this question – "If yesterday's tomorrow is Thursday, what day is the day after tomorrow's yesterday?"

Work it out

- This is a logic puzzle. It looks impossible for me to solve mentally. I'll draw a timeline to make sense of this information.
- It's just a puzzle so I can ignore what today really is.

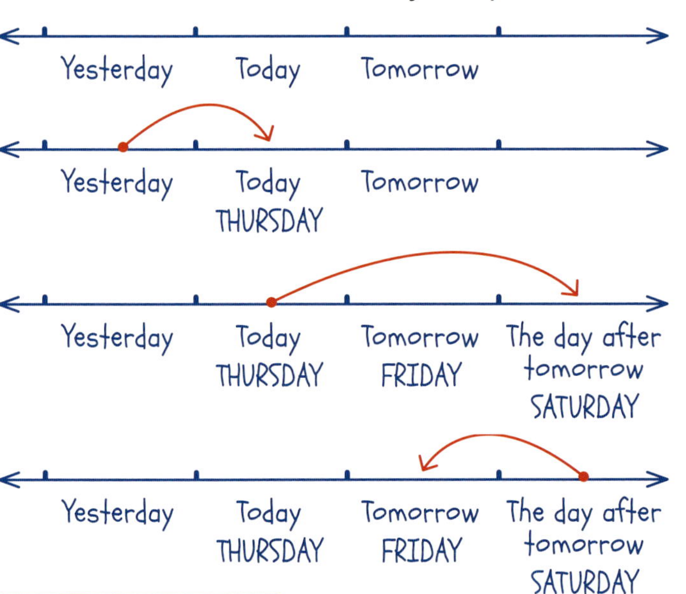

- I drew the arrows in both directions as the time is past, present and future.
- Now I can draw in each time as I read each section.
- "Yesterday's tomorrow" is today. "Today" is Thursday.
- This shows "the day after tomorrow". If today is Thursday that's Saturday.
- This shows Saturday's "yesterday".

Check & reflect

So the answer to Omar's crazy question is Friday. The number line was an amazing way to help me visualise this information effectively.

Birthday

Omar asked another friend this question – "Your birthday is in May. My birthday is 2 months before 3 months after your birthday. When is my birthday?"

Draw a scale drawing

Use cm² grid paper to draw something to scale. Look for the information that tells you what the scale represents. For example, 1 cm might be 1 m, 10 m, 100 m, 1000 m, it all depends on the problem. To solve a problem you may need to read a scale drawing or draw one yourself.

If you don't have grid paper, imagine a grid as you sketch on blank paper.

Billy's walk

Billy the blue tongue lizard loves to walk around his territory twice a day. How far does he go each day?

Scale ⊢⊣ 5 m

Work it out

- This scale drawing tells me lots of information. Even though no measurements are shown, each unit on this grid represents 5 m.
- First I need to work out the perimeter, the total distance around this area. It doesn't matter where I start to count, but I'll start in the top left corner.
- There are 20 units and each unit is 5 metres long.
- The total distance is 5 × 20 = 100 m.

Did you reread the question?

Check & reflect

Billy walks 100 metres every day.

When I check again, I notice something I missed. Billy walks around his area twice each day. So my answer should be double 100 m. Billy actually walks 200 m every day.

Not all perimeter measurements need to be shown in a scale drawing. This diagram shows only some measurements.

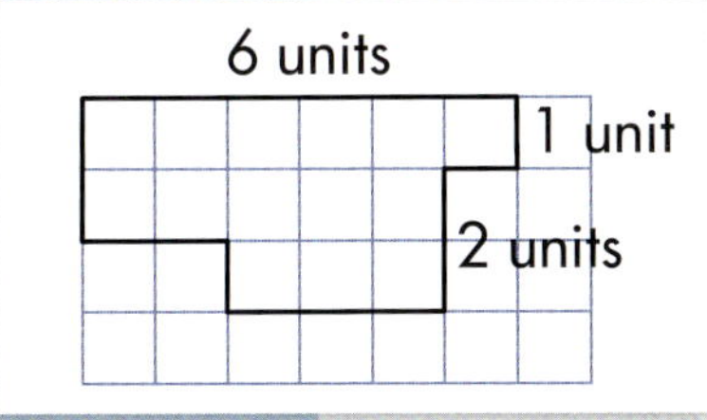

Work out the missing perimeter measurements using logical thinking.

In fact, if the drawing is to scale, you don't even need grid lines to help you at all. Just visualise it.

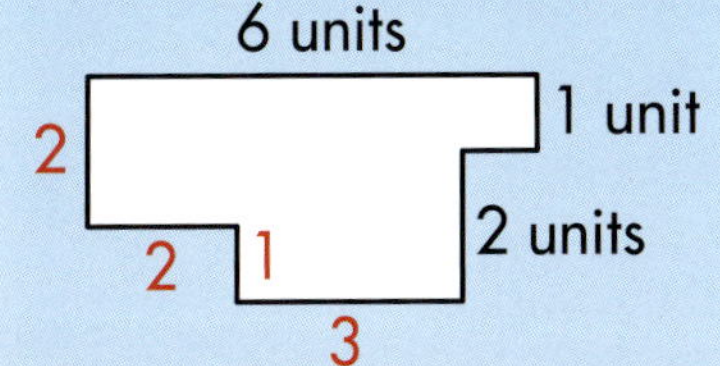

Farmer Holly

Farmer Holly wants to fence off a rectangular area to hold some sheep. She has 24 units of fencing material. What is the largest area she can enclose?

Work it out

I need to find the largest area that has a perimeter of 24 units. I'll use grid paper to help me draw to scale. Each unit on this grid represents a unit of fencing.

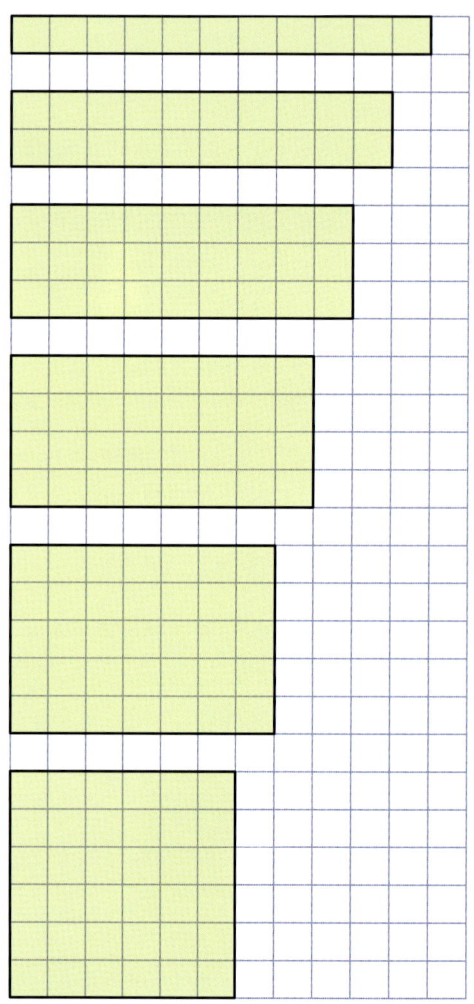

Area = 1 × 11 = 11 square units

Area = 2 × 10 = 20 square units

Area = 3 × 9 = 27 square units

Area = 4 × 8 = 32 square units

Area = 5 × 7 = 35 square units

Area = 6 × 6 = 36 square units

Check & reflect

I notice a pattern in these diagrams. The area gets larger as the shape gets closer to a square. The largest rectangular area I can create with 24 units is 36 square units. This is the best shape for Holly to build.

Try this

18 units

What's the largest area Farmer Holly can enclose if she only has 18 units of fencing material?

Draw a tree diagram

A tree diagram is a set of lines that look like the skeleton of a tree. The lines expand out like branches. The tree diagram can stand up or lie on its side. It can even be upside down.

A tree diagram helps you visualise problems where you need to list combinations of 2 or more items. The tips of the smallest branches show you the total number of combinations.

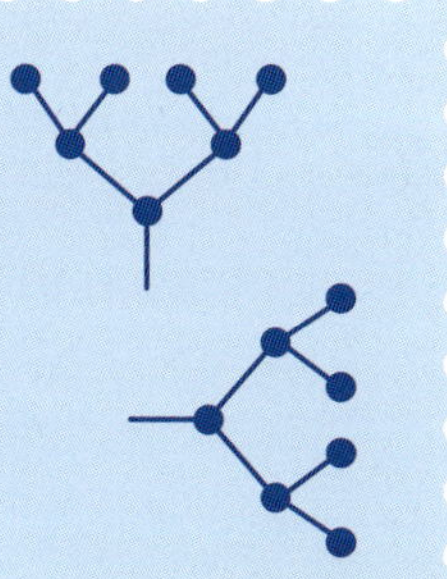

New car

Chen's family wants to buy a new car. They love the colours red and white. They love sedans, station wagons and 4-wheel drives. How many different car choices do they have?

Work it out

- The 1st thing to do is list either all the colours or all the different car types. It doesn't matter which one you start with.

Leave space between each item so you can list the next set of items without getting squashed.

red — sedan
red — station wagon
red — 4 wheel drive
white — sedan
white — station wagon
white — 4 wheel drive

- List the 3 car types beside each colour. This list can be a word, a photo, a drawing or even a symbol. Join a line from the colour to each car type.
- Each colour has 3 different car possibilities. Altogether there are $2 \times 3 = 6$ possible colour and car combinations for this family to select.

They selected the white station wagon. I wonder which one you would choose?

Check & reflect

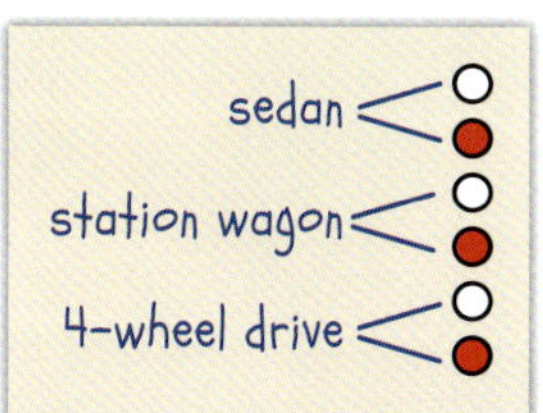

If you start with the car types first, this is what the tree diagram looks like.

This time the colours are shown as actual coloured dots. It still shows 6 different possibilities.

A tree diagram helps you work out complex combinations too.

Ice-creams

Japan's top 4 ice-cream flavours are vanilla, chocolate, green tea and strawberry. Ken only wants 3 scoops. How many different 3-scoop combinations can he select?

Work it out

- This time I'll list the 4 different flavours across the page.

Vanilla

Green tea

Strawberry

- I'll use coloured dots for the 2nd scoop.

2rd scoop:

- I'll use coloured dots again for the 3rd scoop.

3rd scoop:

Vanilla

- The 3rd scoop branches of this tree diagram show me the total number of combinations.

Check & reflect

There are 16 different possibilities for each flavour, so that's 4 × 16 different combinations.
I know 4 × 10 = 40. I know 4 × 6 = 24.
So 40 + 24 = 64.
Ken has 64 different combinations to select from.

I wonder what we could discover about this many ice-cream scoop combinations?

Tree diagrams also work effectively in reverse. Start from the ends of the small tree branches and work down towards the trunk. Remember it doesn't matter in which direction your tree is facing.

Soccer competition

Irene loves to play soccer. Next Saturday her team is in a knock-out competition with 7 other teams. Each team that loses is out of the competition. How many games will be played next Saturday?

Work it out

There are 8 teams. Each team plays 1 other team, so that's 4 pairs to start with. The winners of the first round will play another until there is only one team left. I can show what happens with a tree diagram.

The first two teams are shown like this: Team A Team B

The whole knock-out competition like this:

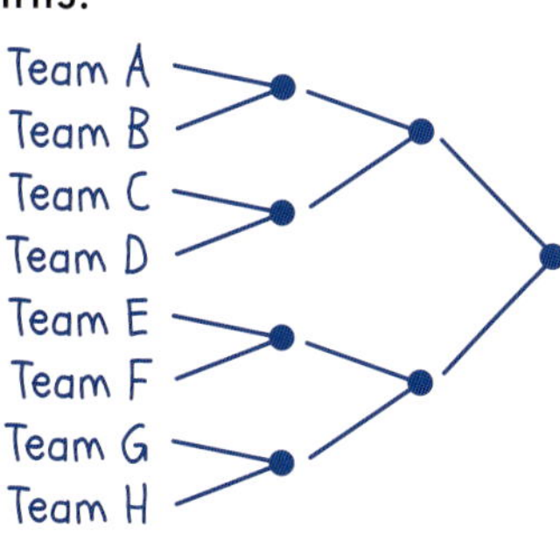

All I need to do is count up how many games were played. The dots show me the winners of a game, so I can just count up all the dots. There are 7 dots so that's 7 games. That's 1 fewer than the number of teams.

Check & reflect

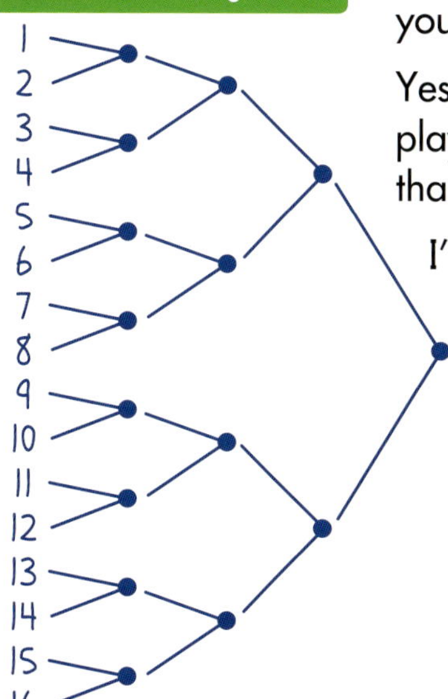

I wonder how many knock-out competition teams you need for this to work? I'll try halving 8.

Yes, this works for 4 teams. They need to play 3 games and 3 games is 1 fewer than the number of teams.

1 2 3 4

I'll try doubling 8.

Yes, this works for 16 teams. They need to play 15 games and 15 games is 1 fewer than the number of teams.

Zaha Hadid

Who said buildings have to be rectangular?

Zaha Hadid was one of the most famous architects in the world. An architect is someone who designs buildings and supervises their construction. Imagine all the mathematical problems involved in this process.

Zaha was born in Iraq in 1950 and died in 2016. As a child she was always asking questions and making her own decisions. After visiting the beautiful Cathedral of Cordoba in Spain as an 11-year-old, she decided to become an architect.

Her parents wanted Zaha to be an astronaut but her obsession was architecture. She started by redesigning the family guestroom and her own bedroom. "Architecture is no longer a man's world. This idea that women can't think three dimensionally is ridiculous."

Perhaps inspired by the beautiful arches of Cordoba, Zaha focussed on visualising solutions to architectural problems using curves, instead of straight lines. She said "... the world is not a rectangle", and "there are 360 degrees, so why stick to just one?"

Working with a large team of people using computers to help explore and create multiple perspectives and geometric shapes, Zaha created amazing curved structures. She was the first woman to win the Pritzker Architecture Prize (2004) and the Royal Institute of Architects Gold Medal (2016).

SPOTLIGHT on a famous Problem Solver

Zaha's Sheikh Zayed Bridge (2010) in Abu Dhabi looks like a wave flowing across the river. She used concrete arches to support a 4-lane highway. The bridge is 64 m tall, 61 m wide and 842 m long.

Zaha's beautiful Heydar Aliyev Centre (2012) in Azerbaijan has no sharp angles. The building is 74 m high and covers an area of 5.75 hectares. It blurs the division between the interior walls and floor and the external building and its landscape.

Zaha was inspired by the geometry of moving water to create the curved shape of the London Olympics Aquatic Centre (2012). It is 45 m tall, covers an area of 15 950 square metres and holds 2500 people.

Zaha's spectacular Mathematics Gallery at the Science Museum, London (2016) is imagined as a wind tunnel. It connects ideas about curves with science, maths and art.

What can you do to solve maths problems like Zaha?

- ✓ use spatial visualisation as a strategy
- ✓ work as a team to brainstorm your ideas
- ✓ think about curves not just straight lines.

Draw a table or graph

Our word "table" comes from an old Latin word for a board or a plank. People used a table to record long lists of numbers. We still refer to our list of multiplication and division facts as "learning our tables".

A table is also a diagram that helps you sort information logically. A table helps you see patterns, identify gaps or see relationships between data. A table usually has at least 2 columns and at least 2 rows.

You can draw your table by hand or use a computer program. Before you draw a table, how many columns and rows do you need? You can always add or remove these later if you have too many or too few. And remember to label the columns or rows to remind you what your problem is about.

Draw a table

The race

Bella and 3 friends swam a 200 m race. Bella's time was 4 minutes and 20 seconds. Lee's time was 3 minutes and 55 seconds. Saba's time was 5 minutes and 45 seconds. Lucy's time was 4 minutes and 40 seconds. What was the fastest swimmer's total time in seconds?

Read it again

Understand it

There are 4 swimmers. The table shows how long it took them to swim 200 m. I have to find who swam 200 m in the fastest time. I have to convert this to seconds.

Select a strategy

First I'll put the data into a table to help me think about all the numbers.

Work it out

- I need 3 columns and 5 rows in my table.

	Minutes	Seconds
Lee	3	55
Bella	4	20
Lucy	4	40
Saba	5	45

- I'll arrange the times in order from shortest to longest.
- Now I have to work out who swam the fastest. The fastest swimmer swam in the shortest time. So Lee swam the fastest.
- How many seconds was that?
- Lee swam 200 m in 3 minutes and 55 seconds. There are 60 seconds in 1 minute.
  3 × 60 is 60, 120, 180.
- Then add 55 seconds by counting up.
  180 plus 20 is 200 plus 35 makes 235.

Check & reflect

Lee swam 200 m in 235 seconds.
The slowest swimmer was Saba.
Lucy swam 20 seconds slower than Bella.
Bella swam 25 seconds slower than Lee.

Ian Thorpe (Australia) swam 200 m in 1:45.51 minutes at the 2000 Sydney Olympics.

Federica Pellegrini (Italy) swam 200 m in 1:52.98 minutes at the 2009 World Championships.

Proportional reasoning problems can often be solved using a table.

Making a flag

The Indian flag is designed proportionally. For every 2 units of height it has 3 units of width. Praveen makes a flag that is 40 cm high. How long should he make it?

This is also called a "ratio table".

Read it again

Understand it

I need to work out how to make a flag so it is in the right proportions.

Select a strategy

I could take a guess but if I'm wrong it can take ages to work out. I'll make a table to help me think logically.

Work it out

- When I read the question again, it says it is 2 units long and 3 units high. I'll start with that.

Height	Width
2	3

- I'll try larger proportions. I can double this to make it larger. Doubling still keeps the proportions the same.

Height	Width
2	3
4	6

- I notice that 40 is 10 × 4. All I need to do is multiply each number by 10.
- This tells me for every 40 units of height you need 60 units of width.

Height	Width
2	3
4	6
40	60

Check & reflect

Praveen should make his flag 40 cm high and 60 cm wide.

What if Praveen used other lengths? I can continue this table to work out lots of different size Indian flags.

Here are some more proportions.

Height	2	4	6	8	20	40	80	200	400	600	800
Width	3	6	9	12	30	60	120	300	600	900	1200

How heavy is it?

A 20 m rope has a mass of 3 kg.
How heavy is 80 m of the same type of rope?

Understand it

I have to work out the mass of a rope. It will be much heavier than 3 kg.

Select a strategy

I have to think in proportions. I'll draw a table to help me. I need one column to record the length of the rope and one column to record the mass.

Work it out

- I'll record what I know about the 20 m rope first.

Length of rope in metres	Mass of rope in kilograms
20	3

- I can now double the measurements and they will stay in proportion.

Length of rope in metres	Mass of rope in kilograms
20	3
40	6

- If I double these measurements again that will tell me my answer.

Length of rope in metres	Mass of rope in kilograms
20	3
40	6
80	12

What pattern can you see in this number table?

Check & reflect

Looking at the table I can see that an 80 m rope will have a mass of 12 kg.

I notice a pattern – the original numbers are multiplied by 4.

4 × 20 = 80 and 4 × 3 =12.

Another way to solve a problem like this is to multiply by the same amount.

This keeps the proportions the same.

I can multiply by any number to make the rope larger.

	Length of rope in metres	Mass of rope in kilograms
Original rope	20	3
6 × original rope	120	18
7 × original rope	140	21
100 × original rope	200	30

I can divide by any number to make the rope smaller.

	Length of rope in metres	Mass of rope in kilograms
Original rope	20	3
÷ 2	10	1.5
÷ 4	5	0.75
÷ 10	2	0.3

By dividing the measurements I worked out that a 2 m skipping rope probably has a mass of 0.3 kg or 300 g.

You can make a table with as many columns and rows as you like. It all depends on the problem you are trying to solve.

Black alpacas

Chloe's farm has 127 alpacas.
One in every 5 alpacas are black.
About how many black alpacas does she own?

Work it out

- I have to figure out how many black alpacas are on Chloe's farm.
- I know each group of 5 has 1 black alpaca and 4 alpacas that are not black.
- I can keep drawing more groups but I'd have to draw a lot to get to 127 alpacas.

- This ratio table will help me organise the data.

Black alpaca	Not black alpaca	Total
1	4	5

- If I multiply these by the same number the proportion will stay the same.
- I didn't get 127 alpacas but I can see that I can add some of these numbers to get pretty close.

20 + **4** + **1** = 25

Black alpaca	Not black alpaca	Total
1	**4**	**5**
2	8	10
4	**16**	**20**
20	**80**	**100**

Check & reflect

Chloe has about 25 black alpacas in her herd. To check I can add up the matching **80** + **16** + **4** in the "not black" column. That's 100.

25 + 100 = 125. The 2 extra alpacas could be any colour.

A different strategy is to break it into smaller parts. In each group of 5 alpacas one alpaca will be black. I know there are 127 animals. I now need to work out how many multiples of 5 there are in 127. I can write this as a number sentence:

$127 \div 5 = \square$

$5 \times \square = 127$

I can do that in my head as I know there are 20 groups of 5 in 100 and another 5 groups in 25. So that's 25 groups of 5 with 2 left over. Chloe has approximately 25 black alpacas on her farm.

Scones

Hedda uses these ingredients to make 12 scones:

- $1\frac{1}{2}$ cups of flour
- $\frac{1}{2}$ cup of milk
- $\frac{1}{4}$ cup of sultanas
- $\frac{1}{2}$ cup of lemonade
- Pinch of salt

What ingredients will she need to make 36 scones?

Work it out

- This is another proportional reasoning problem. I'll draw up a ratio table to keep everything organised.
- This is what Hedda needs to make a dozen scones.

Number of scones	Cups of flour	Cups of milk	Cups of sultanas	Cups of lemonade	Pinches of salt
12	$1\frac{1}{2}$	$\frac{1}{2}$	$\frac{1}{4}$	$\frac{1}{2}$	1

- Double these numbers to show the ingredients for 2 dozen scones.

Number of scones	Cups of flour	Cups of milk	Cups of sultanas	Cups of lemonade	Pinches of salt
12	$1\frac{1}{2}$	$\frac{1}{2}$	$\frac{1}{4}$	$\frac{1}{2}$	1
24	3	1	$\frac{1}{2}$	1	2

- Add these 2 layers to get the ingredients for 3 dozen scones.

Number of scones	Cups of flour	Cups of milk	Cups of sultanas	Cups of lemonade	Pinches of salt
12	1½	½	¼	½	1
24	3	1	$\frac{1}{2}$	1	2
36	$4\frac{1}{2}$	$1\frac{1}{2}$	$\frac{3}{4}$	$1\frac{1}{2}$	3

Check & reflect

The table shows me the ingredients for 36 scones. Hedda needs $4\frac{1}{2}$ cups flour, $1\frac{1}{2}$ cups milk, $\frac{3}{4}$ cup sultanas, $1\frac{1}{2}$ cups lemonade and 3 pinches of salt.

What if I keep going with this table? I can find the ingredients to make a smaller number or a larger number of scones.

Number of scones	Cups of flour	Cups of milk	Cups of sultanas	Cups of lemonade	Pinches of salt
6	$\frac{3}{4}$	$\frac{1}{4}$	$\frac{1}{8}$	$\frac{1}{4}$	$\frac{1}{2}$
12	$1\frac{1}{2}$	$\frac{1}{2}$	$\frac{1}{4}$	$\frac{1}{2}$	1
24	3	1	$\frac{1}{2}$	1	2
36	$4\frac{1}{2}$	$1\frac{1}{2}$	$\frac{3}{4}$	$1\frac{1}{2}$	3
48	6	2	1	2	4
60	$7\frac{1}{2}$	$2\frac{1}{2}$	$1\frac{1}{4}$	$2\frac{1}{2}$	5
72	9	3	$1\frac{1}{2}$	3	6

I don't think anyone will make fewer than 6 scones.

And 72 scones may not fit in the oven so you might need to do it in two batches of 36 scones instead.

Challenge

Five shearers take 1 hour to shear 100 sheep.

How long will it take 2 shearers to shear 100 sheep?

Mathematicians, statisticians, accountants, shop keepers, secretaries, bakers, chefs and government officials all use **Draw a table** as a problem solving strategy.

Read a table and make a graph

Tables aren't used just for proportional reasoning problems.

Survey data is usually collected in the form of a table. A two-way table lets you compare information from different sources.

Many people find it easier to read and analyse data when it is presented as a graph. A graph is a picture of the information in a table.

But how do you effectively read the information in a graph? What do the numbers along the vertical axis mean? Are they marked in groups of 2, 5, 10, 20? What do the heights of the columns mean?

To solve a problem you may need to read a graph or make one yourself.

Favourite birds

Joe collected data from Year 4, 5 and 6 about their favourite birds. This table shows Joe's data:

Our favourite birds

	Budgerigars	Magpies	Kookaburras	Lorikeets
Year 4	12	4	6	9
Year 5	10	8	7	6
Year 6	4	7	10	7
TOTAL	26	19	23	22

Joe created this side by side column graph from his data. Notice the vertical axis is marked in groups of 2.

Our favourite birds

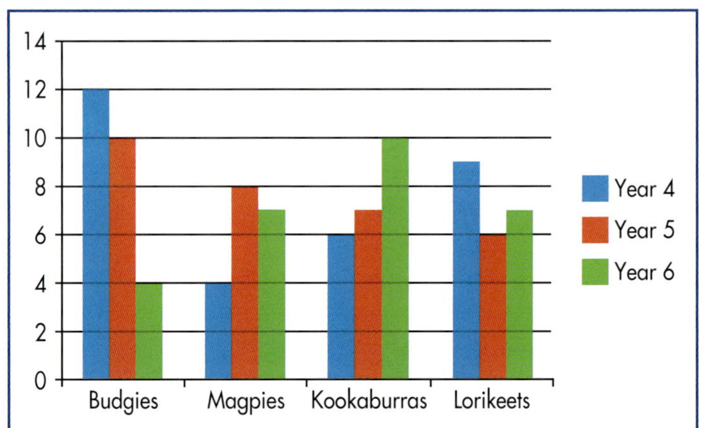

Joe was disappointed as you can't instantly see which bird was the most popular. You can only see the most popular bird in each year group.

Joe then made a combined column graph. Notice the vertical axis is marked in groups of 5.

Our favourite birds

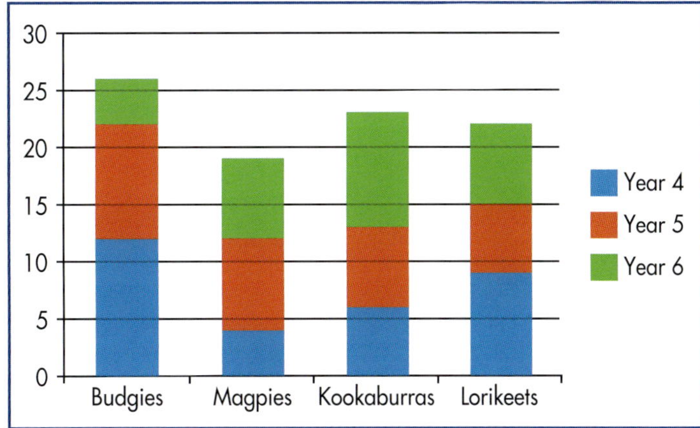

The 3 bits of data for each bird are now presented as one column. Joe can instantly see that budgies are the favourites and magpies the least favourite. By comparing the heights, you can also see that kookaburras are the second favourite bird and lorikeets are the third favourite, or second least favourite.

Joe also made a pie graph showing the total number of likes for each bird.

Our favourite birds

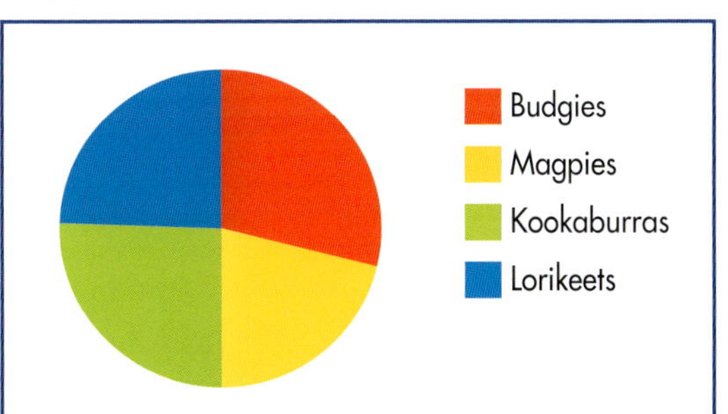

Notice that there are no numbers on this graph. Instead you use proportional reasoning to compare the coloured sectors.

- The red sector, or fraction of the circle, is slightly larger than the green sector. Budgies are the favourite bird.
- The yellow sector is slightly smaller than the blue sector. Lorikeets are more popular than magpies.
- The yellow sector is the smallest so magpies are the least popular bird.

Joe liked this way to display the data in his table best of all.

Which data display do you think is the most effective?

Dance styles

Sam collected data from her classmates about favourite dance styles.

These 2 pie graphs show the boys' and girls' preferences.

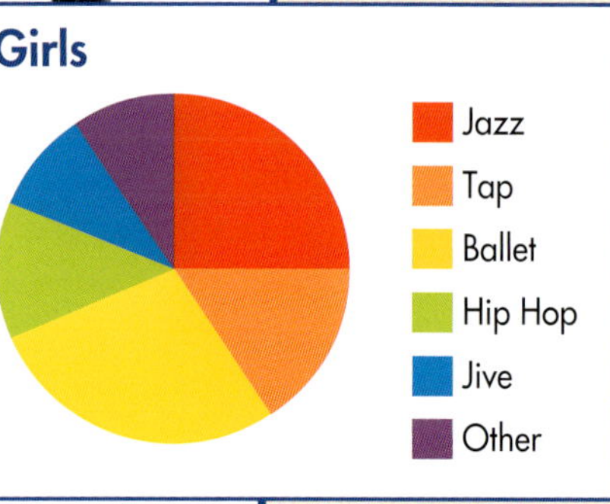

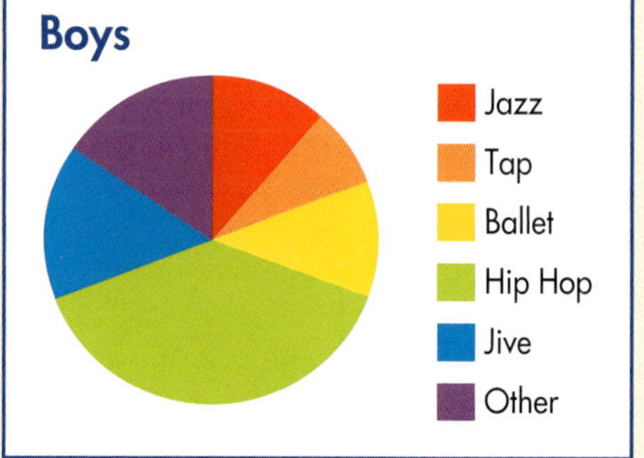

Make 3 statistical statements about these two graphs.

Work it out

- This is an open problem. The challenge is to find something to say about what I see in these two graphs. I can say whatever I like but I should use statistical words like "more than", "the most popular" and "a larger proportion of".
- I think I should compare the boys with the girls and not just talk about one pie graph.

1. It looks like the yellow sector is the largest on the girls' pie graph. So ballet is their favourite dance style. But this sector is quite small on the boys' graph. I'd say that almost double the number of girls like ballet compared to boys.
2. A large proportion of boys like hip hop the best. This sector looks about 3 times the size of the sector for girls liking hip hop. So about 3 times as many boys like hip hop compared to girls.
3. About double the number of girls like jazz compared to boys.

Check & reflect This is Sam's data table:

	Jazz	Tap	Ballet	Hip Hop	Jive	Other
Boys	3	2	3	10	4	4
Girls	8	5	9	4	3	3
TOTAL	11	7	12	14	7	7

My statements were fairly correct. When you read a pie graph you are only looking at the size of the sector, not the exact numbers, so it gives you a pretty good visual idea.

Reading a pie graph or a bar graph

Even though data may not be given in numbers, use **Visualise it** to estimate the size of sectors in a pie graph or the size of a section in a bar graph.

Use proportional reasoning to divide a circle or rectangular bar into same size parts. The better you are at imagining these proportions, the better you will be at solving pie and bar graph problems.

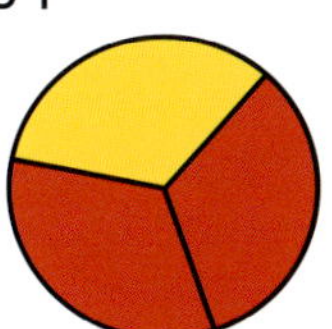

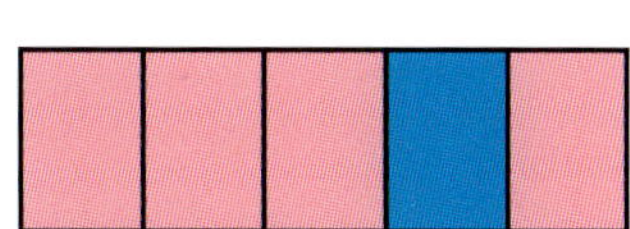

This pie graph shows $\frac{1}{3}$ and $\frac{2}{3}$.

This bar graph shows $\frac{1}{5}$ and $\frac{4}{5}$.

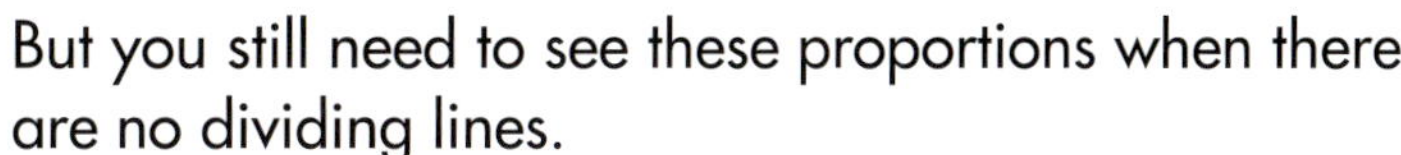

But you still need to see these proportions when there are no dividing lines.

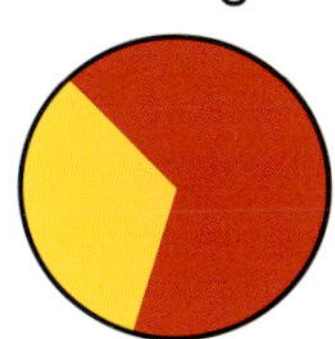

See more examples like this in Useful Maths Facts on p. 141.

Read a picture graph

Picture graphs look quite confusing at first. What you see is not what you get. In a picture graph a symbol is used to represent a quantity of objects or events.

When you were younger, a graph like this meant something else. If you saw one object it represented one object. Now you are older, once you are told the code or scale, each object represents more than 1 object.

Jan's Daily Biscuit Graph

Monday	Tuesday	Wednesday

Scale: One biscuit represents 100 biscuits

In this picture graph, each biscuit represents 100 biscuits.

 = 100

A picture graph lets you visually see large numbers on a graph. If each biscuit represented 1, the graph would go right off the page, off the table and possibly out the door.

- On Monday Jan sold 3 × 100 biscuits.
- On Tuesday she sold 5 × 100 biscuits.
- On Wednesday she sold 7 × 100 biscuits.

To find out how many biscuits were sold in 3 days, add up 300 + 500 + 700.

That's 1500 biscuits.

What if each biscuit in this picture graph represents 500 biscuits?

 = 500

Now the graph shows Jan sold 3 × 500 biscuits on Monday. That's 1500 biscuits.

What if each biscuit in this picture graph represents 1000 biscuits?

 = 1000

Now the graph shows Jan sold 3 × 1000 biscuits on Monday. That's 3000 biscuits.

Dolphin spotting

A large pod of dolphins lives in the Hawks Nest area. This picture graph shows sightings over one year. There were 5000 dolphins spotted over summer. How many dolphins were seen in Winter?

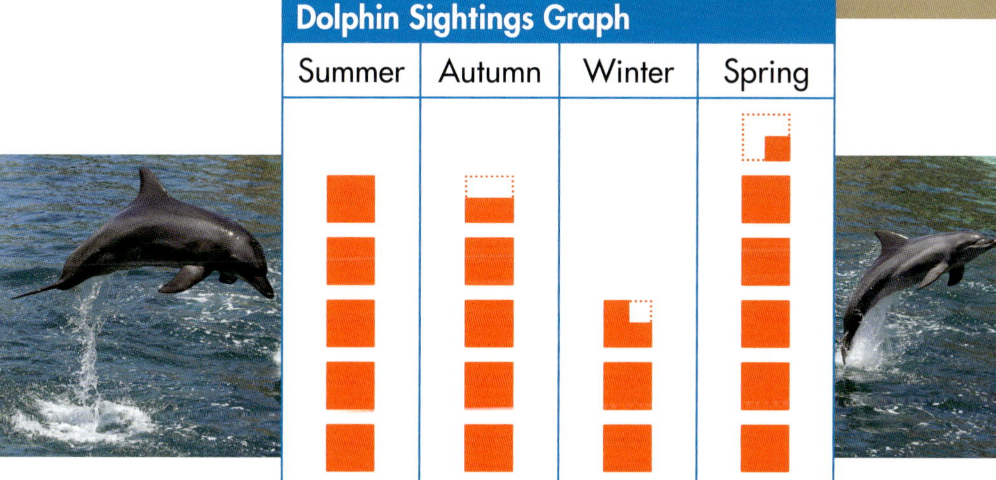

Work it out

- There is no scale on this graph.
- I know 5000 dolphins were seen in summer. There are 5 squares in the summer column of this picture graph. Each square must represent 1000.
- There are 2 full squares and ¾ of a square in the Winter column. So there are 2000 dolphins plus that ¾ of a square.
- 1 square = 1000 so ¼ must be ¼ of 1000. That's 250 and ¾ must be 1000 – 250 = 750.

Check & reflect

I calculated 2000 + 750 dolphins spotted in Winter. That's 2750 dolphins, about half as many as in Spring. Most sightings were in Spring. Winter had the fewest sightings.

Try this

Spring Boat Races

Lucy created this picture graph to show the number of boats racing at her yacht club in spring.

Write at least 3 different maths facts about this graph.

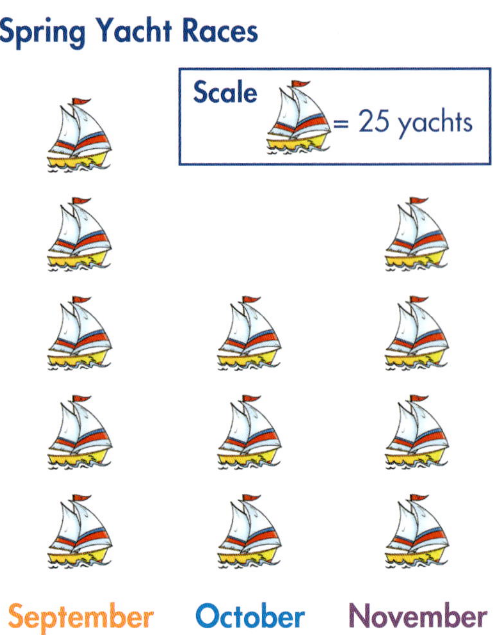

Challenge

This pie graph shows the proportion of 5 different fruits sold worldwide in 2013.

Write at least 3 different maths facts based on this graph.

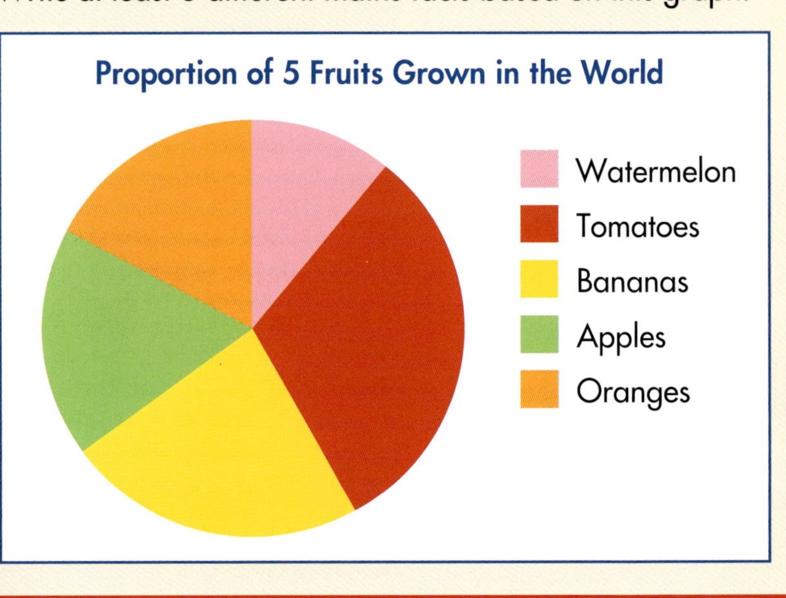

Read or make a line graph

Every point in the line graph means something.

A line graph shows you events that change over time. Draw in points on the graph based on your data then connect the points with a line. This is called "plotting a line graph". Use graph paper to make your life easier.

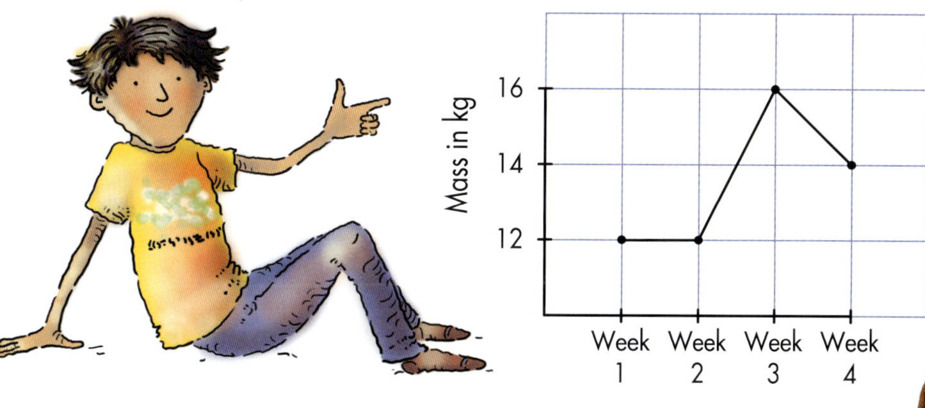

This line graph shows the mass of Sean's new dog Molly over 4 weeks.

Notice Molly's mass starts at 12 kg. After one more week it is still 12 kg. By Week 3 Molly's mass has increased to 16 kg. Sean has been overfeeding Molly! By week 4 Molly's mass is decreasing. It is now 14 kg.

A line graph is also an effective way to display changes in temperature.

Darwin's temperature

Look at this table. It shows the temperature in Darwin over 24 hours for one day in Winter.

Time	12:00 midnight	3:00 am	6:00 am	9:00 am	12:00 midday	3:00 pm	6:00 pm	9:00 pm	12:00 midnight
Temperature	19°C	17°C	16°C	20°C	26°C	28°C	25°C	20°C	18°C

Use 1 cm graph paper to create a line graph from this information. Write at least two comments about your graph.

Work it out

- On 1 cm^2 grid paper, I'll make the horizontal axis **Time**. My scale is 1 cm = 3 hours.
- I'll make the vertical axis show **Temperature**. My scale is 1 cm = 2°C.
- Now I can plot each temperature from the table.

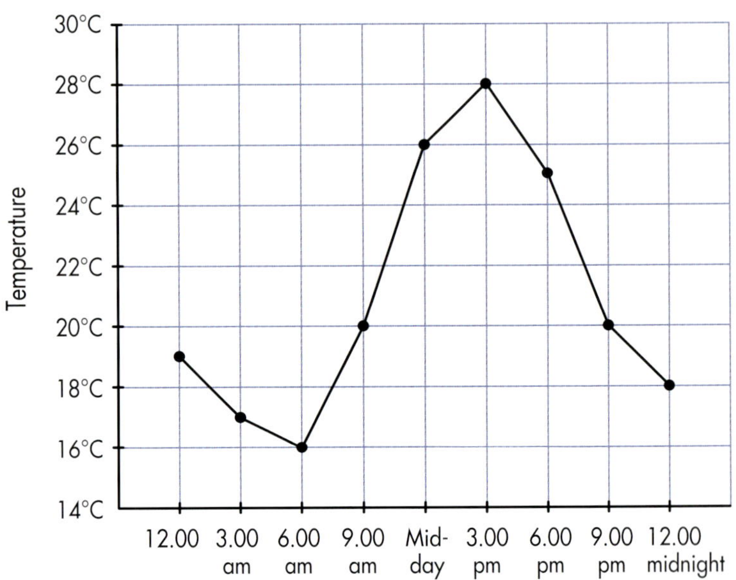

There are plenty of things to notice in this line graph:

- The lowest temperature was at 6:00 am and the highest was at 3:00 pm.
- The temperature rose 6°C from 9:00 to 12:00 midday.
- 24 hours later it was 1°C colder at midnight.
- The temperature dropped 5°C from 6:00 pm to 9:00 pm.

Check & reflect

I could keep a record of Darwin temperatures over a week. I can then compare data over a larger period of time. Or graph Darwin's temperatures for one day in Summer, Autumn, Winter and Spring and see what that shows you about temperature changes. Or I could research the hottest and coldest parts of the world and make another line graph.

On 13 September 1922, El Aziza in Libya recorded 58°C, the highest temperature humans can live in. In 2005, the uninhabited part of the Lut Desert in Iran recorded a temperature of 70.7°C.

No human can survive that!

The bike ride

On Saturday Alex and her family went for a bike ride. This graph shows how far from home they travelled.

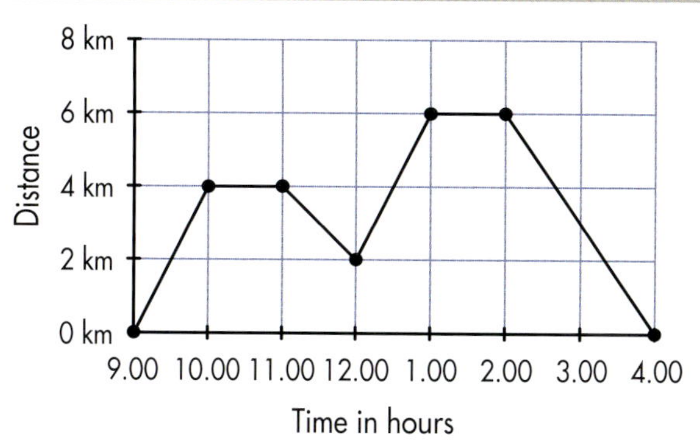

What do you think this graph means? Some people see two hills and say that the family rode their bikes up and down two hills. That is NOT what this graph tells you.

- Look at the horizontal axis. This shows you time passing hour by hour.
- Look at the vertical axis. This shows you how far away from home Alex and her family rode.

What do you notice about the graph from 10:00 to 11:00? What does this straight line on the graph mean?

- It shows that the family didn't travel further away or closer to home.
- They probably stopped for morning tea and a chat in a park or at a friend's house.
- They are 4 km away from their home.

The same thing happens from 1:00 to 2:00. What does this straight line on the graph mean?

- They probably stopped to have lunch.
- They are 6 km away from home.

What happened at 12:00 midday? What do you think this dip in the line graph means?

- It shows that between 11:00 and 12:00 the family travelled closer to home.
- They are now only 2 km away from home.

Why does this line graph go right down to the horizontal axis at 4:00 pm?

- This shows that from 2:00 to 4:00 the family travelled back home.
- At 2:00 they were 6 km away.
- At 4:00 they were 0 km away.

Srinivasa Ramanujan

Who said you can't use your own strategies?

Srinivasa Ramanujan was one of the world's greatest mathematicians, who created 1000s of new ideas using very unusual methods. Imagine all the mathematical problems involved in this process.

Ramanujan was born in India in 1887 and died in 1920. He came from a poor family, was very shy and suffered from bad health. His early school life was not enjoyable but he loved playing the "goats and tigers" strategy game with his mum. He excelled at mathematics with the best exam scores in his district. He was obsessed by maths and didn't want to study anything else.

Ramanujan was a fast thinker and completed maths exams in half the time. At 13 he memorised any maths book he was given. He challenged teachers with endless questions about fractions and prime numbers. He spent all his time scribbling equations on scraps of paper and on his slate board, memorising formulas and small details. He used his own unexpected strategies to solve problems and could even say the digits of pi to many places.

When Ramanujan was 15, he discovered an old book with 5000 maths ideas. Without help, Ramanujan worked out what each idea meant, one by one. Imagine how long it took him to explore 5000 ideas.

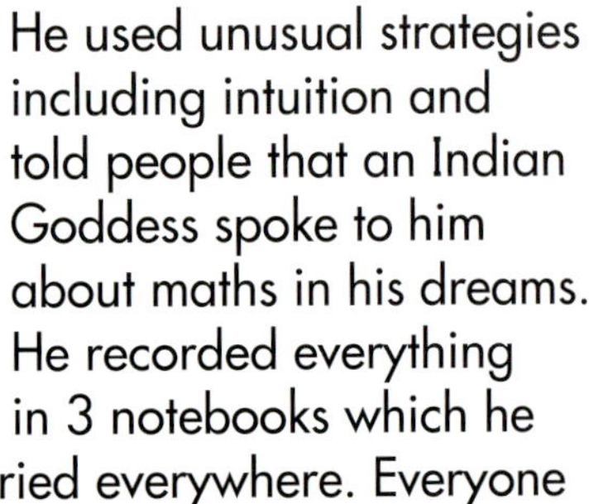

He used unusual strategies including intuition and told people that an Indian Goddess spoke to him about maths in his dreams. He recorded everything in 3 notebooks which he carried everywhere. Everyone knew Ramanujan was a genius.

SPOTLIGHT
on a famous Problem Solver

Ramanujan collaborated with a famous mathematician, Professor Hardy, in England. This was one of the greatest partnerships in the history of mathematics.

Their best discovery was a formula for how to partition numbers. How many ways can a whole number be divided into smaller whole number parts? e.g. 3 is 1 + 1 + 1, 1 + 2, 2 + 1, 3 + 0 or 0 + 3. An automatic teller machine today, divides and arranges your money using Ramanujan's partition theory.

It was very hard for Ramanujan to live in England as he missed his family in India, ate different food and didn't mix well. After five years there, he became very sick and returned to India.

Ramanujan was the youngest person to be a Fellow of the Royal Society UK. He was also the first Indian to be elected as a fellow of Trinity College, Cambridge.

Imagine being so famous that you have your own postage stamp. India issued a stamp in 2011 to celebrate Ramanujan's mathematical achievements.

In 2012, India declared that every year 22 December was National Mathematics Day. That's Ramanujan's birthday.

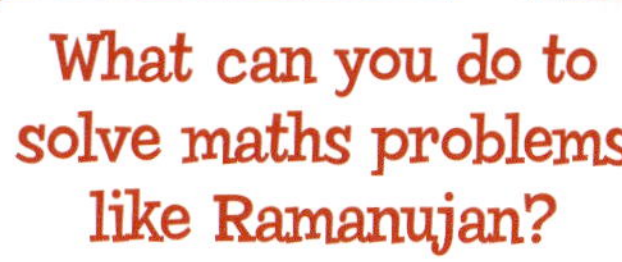

- ✓ Learn your maths facts and formulas off by heart.
- ✓ Focus on one problem at a time until you really understand how to apply it in a new situation.
- ✓ Work with a partner to solve difficult problems together.

?? Guess and check

Something is a problem when you don't know the answer and it's not obvious what to do first. **Guess and check** is a strategy to use when this happens. Take a chance and try one idea to solve your problem. If your first attempt doesn't work, try again with a different idea. Keep trying until you find an idea that works.

In a number problem, try one number and see if it works. If it doesn't work, think about this answer before trying another number. Your second guess shouldn't be random. Try to make it a closer fit.

Another name for this strategy is **Trial and error.**

Farmer Jarrad's paddocks

Farmer Jarrad loves squares.
He always builds square paddocks for his cows.
The total area of his latest paddock is 841 m^2.
How long is each side?

The answer to this problem is not obvious.

The side must be larger than 10 because 10 × 10 = 100.
The side must be less than 100 because 100 × 100 = 10 000.

Jump in and try a number somewhere between 10 and 100.
Use a calculator to help you if necessary.

50 × 50 = 2500 so it's less than 50.

25 × 25 = 625 so it's larger than 25.

30 × 30 = 900 so it's less than 30.

Try 29 as you know 9 × 9 ends in a 1 because 9 × 9 = 81.

Yes it's **29 × 29 = 841**.

Jarrod's square paddock has sides 29 m long.

Problems don't always have just one solution.
An open problem is one where the problem can be solved in many ways.
Guess and check is a useful strategy for many open problems.

Crocodile mass

Three crocodiles together have a mass of 2 tonnes.
The mass of one of the crocodiles is 788 kg.
What is the individual mass of the other 2 crocodiles?

Break this down into smaller facts first.

- You know the total mass is 2000 kg.
- You know one crocodile has a mass of 788 kg.
- You know the other two crocodiles have a mass of 2000 – 788.

  That's 1212 kg.

Now your problem is:
"Find two numbers that add to 1212."

There is not one expected answer. There are many possible answers.

As long as you find two numbers that add to 1212 your solution is mathematically correct. If necessary, use a calculator to help you discover the number pairs.

555 + 657 **438 + 774** **259 + 953**

But … most crocodiles have a mass of up to 1000 kg, so try to find answers where one number is not larger than 1000.

Lolong, a saltwater crocodile from the Philippines, was the largest in the world.

He died in 2013. He was 6.17 m long with a mass of 1075 kg.

Year 4 students

Vicky collected survey data about 158 students in Grade 5. She discovered there are 16 more girls than boys. How many boys are in Grade 5?

Read it again

Understand it

The total number of students is 158. I need to work out how many boys are in Grade 5. There are 16 more girls than boys.

Select a strategy

I'll take a guess and see what happens.

Work it out

I need 16 more girls.

What if there are 100 girls? That leaves 58 boys. That's far too few.

What if there are 80 girls? Then there are **20 + 58** boys. That's 78 boys, so there's only 2 more girls.

I'll try 90 girls. That's **10 + 58** boys or 68 boys. That's 22 more than the boys.

If you get stuck, discuss your problem with a friend. Two or more heads might be better than one.

Keep trying

How annoying I still haven't worked it out. I've asked my friend to help me.

85 + 73 = 158 … the difference is **85 – 73 = 12**. We're getting closer.

86 + 72 = 158 … the difference is **86 – 72 = 14**. We're almost there.

87 + 71 = 158 … the difference is **87 – 71 = 16**. Yes, we found it!

Check & reflect

There are 87 girls and 71 boys in Vicky's Grade 5.

Guess and check is not very efficient.

There must be a better strategy to use.

This time I'll take away the extra 16 girls.

158 – 16 = 142

This must be the girls and boys together.

I divide this by 2 to get equal numbers of boys and girls.

142 ÷ 2 = 71

So there are 71 boys and 71 + 16 girls. That's 87 girls.

Break it into smaller parts was a much faster strategy.

Ticket sales

Duffy and Bev sold 440 tickets to a concert.
Bev sold 66 more tickets than Duffy.
How many tickets did Duffy sell?

Wheels

Ten bicycles and cars are in a yard. The bikes all have 2 wheels. The cars all have 4 wheels. There are 26 wheels altogether. How many bikes are in the yard?

Understand it

There are 10 vehicles and 26 wheels.
I have to work out the number of bikes from the clues.
There must be at least 1 bike. There must be at least 1 car.

Select a strategy

I'll try **Guess and Check**.

Work it out

I guess 5 bikes and 5 cars.

The bikes have 5 × 2 wheels – that's 10.
The cars have 5 × 4 wheels – that's 20. 10 + 20 = 30.
That's 4 too many wheels. So 5 bikes is not right yet.

Try again

I guess 4 bikes and 6 cars. **4 × 2 = 8** bike wheels.
6 × 4 = 24 car wheels.

6 + 24 = 32. Still 6 wheels too many.

Try again

I guess 6 bikes and 4 cars. **6 × 2 = 12** bike wheels.
4 × 4 = 16 car wheels.

12 + 16 = 28 wheels. That's getting closer to 26 wheels.

Try again

I guess 7 bikes and 3 cars. **7 × 2 = 14** bike wheels.
3 × 4 = 12 car wheels.

14 + 12 = 26 wheels. That's what I want.

Remember, you need patience to solve some problems. That took 4 guesses.

Check & reflect

There are 7 bikes in the yard.
There are 3 cars.

There are 10 vehicles and 26 wheels altogether.

That matches what I was trying to find out.

Guess and check was pretty messy. Is there a more effective strategy?

If all the vehicles are bikes, that's **10 × 2 = 20** wheels.

I need another 6 wheels. Cars have 2 more wheels than bikes. Those missing 6 wheels must belong to 3 cars. Imagine 3 cars with 2 front wheels up in the air. There are 3 cars and 7 bikes.

Visualise it.

This strategy works the other way round too.

If all the vehicles are cars, that's **10 × 4 = 40** wheels. That's 14 wheels too many. Bikes have 2 fewer wheels than cars. Those extra 14 wheels must belong to 7 bikes I imagined were cars. There must be 7 bikes and 3 cars.

How many Zercks?

Spaceman Matt lands on Planet Z. Creatures there have either 3 or 5 legs. Zeds have 3 legs and Zercks have 5 legs. A group of 11 creatures surround him. He quickly counts 11 heads and 43 legs. How many Zercks are there?

Constructing shapes

Max uses 42 sticks to construct 9 shapes.
Each side is made from 1 stick.
He makes triangles and hexagons.
How many of each shape does Max make?

Guess and check helps you solve 2D shape problems too.

Work it out

- This is like the previous problem about Wheels.
- I'll try the **Guess and check** strategy first.
- I know Max has 42 sticks. I know he makes 9 shapes.
- Triangles use 3 sticks. Hexagons use 6 sticks.
- He could make 4 triangles and 5 hexagons.
- That's 4×3 and 5×6 sticks. **12 + 30 = 42**.

Wow! I guessed correctly the first time!

Check & reflect

Max used 12 sticks to make 4 triangles and 30 sticks to make 5 hexagons. That's 9 shapes altogether.

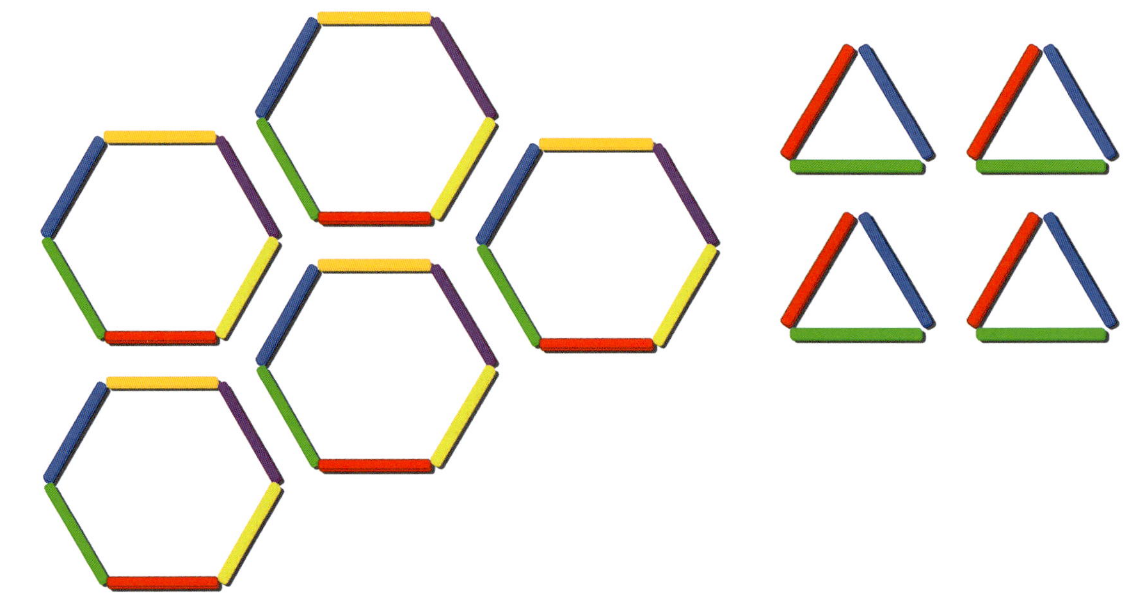

That was a lucky guess. Visualise it to check your answer.

Imagine Max makes all triangles.
He'd use **9 × 3 = 27** sticks.
That's 15 sticks less than 42 sticks.

Hexagons use 3 more sticks than each triangle.

15 ÷ 3 = 5

These missing 15 sticks must belong to 5 hexagons instead of 5 triangles.

There are 5 hexagons and 4 triangles.

This strategy works the other way too.

Imagine Max makes all hexagons.
He'd use **9 × 6 = 54** sticks.
That's 12 too many sticks.

Triangles use 3 fewer sticks than hexagons.

12 ÷ 3 = 4

These extra sticks must belong to 4 triangles instead of 4 hexagons.

There are 4 triangles and 5 hexagons.

Another strategy is to draw a ratio table.

	Number of shapes				
Max's shapes	2	3	4	5	6
Triangles (3 sides)	6	9	**12**	15	18
Hexagons (6 sides)	12	18	24	**30**	36

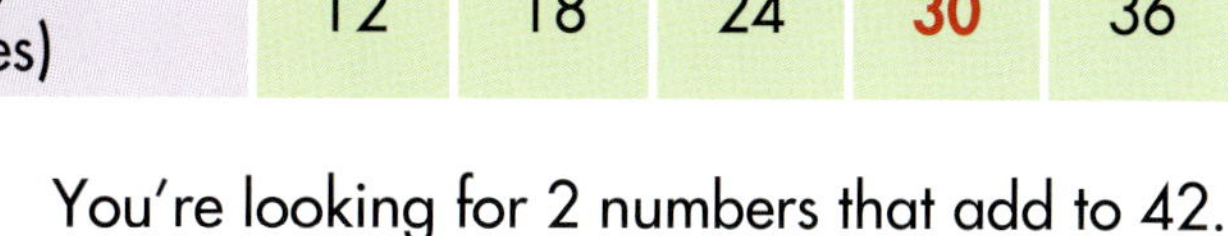

You're looking for 2 numbers that add to 42.

12 + 30 = 42

There must be 4 triangles and 5 hexagons.

Use **Guess and check** to solve a variety of stick puzzles.
Use **Visualise it** strategies too to help you see the answer.

12 sticks

Try this

Move 4 sticks to create 5 equal size triangles.

Try to see the sticks moving inside your head before moving them with your hands.

Make it true

Try this

Take away 2 sticks so that this number sentence is correct.

Challenge

Move only 2 sticks to make the highest possible number from these 24 sticks.

Guess and check is a useful strategy when you don't know where to start.

Clockface addition

Chun draws a straight line across a clockface. The sum of the numbers on one side is the same sum as the numbers on the other side of this line. How does she do it?

Read it again

Understand it

The numbers 1 – 12 are in a circle. Find where to draw a line so that each side adds to the same number. I don't know what that number is.

Select a strategy

I don't know where to start so I'll try **Guess and Check**.

Work it out

What happens if I draw a line here?

The numbers add up to 21 and 57, so that's not right yet.

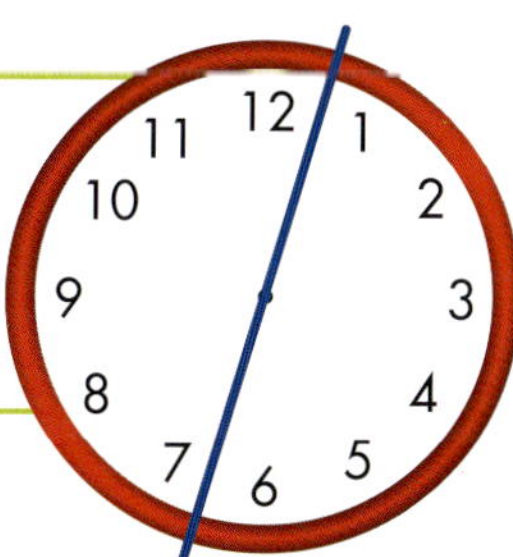

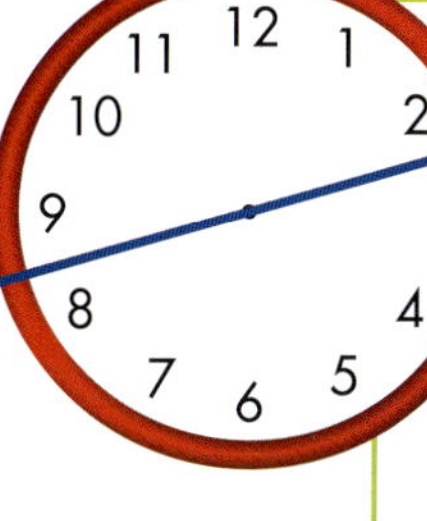

What if I draw a line here?

The numbers add up to 33 and 45, so that's still not right, but the numbers are closer.

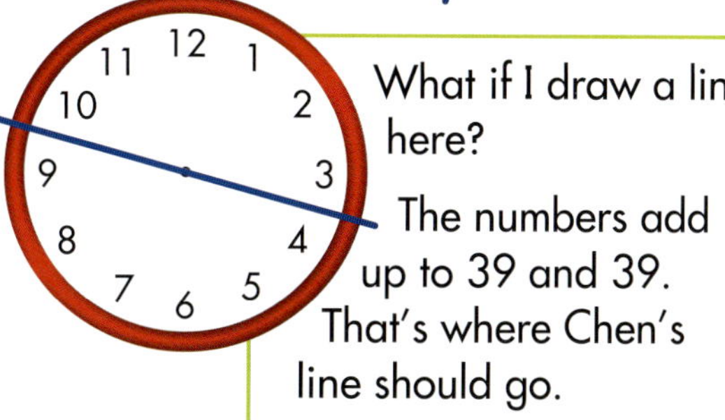

What if I draw a line here?

The numbers add up to 39 and 39. That's where Chen's line should go.

Check & reflect

It took 3 attempts to find the right position.

I notice 3 pairs of number on each side and each pair adds to 13.

3 × 13 = 39

What if I divide this into quarters do the numbers in each quarter have the same sum? (No, they don't)

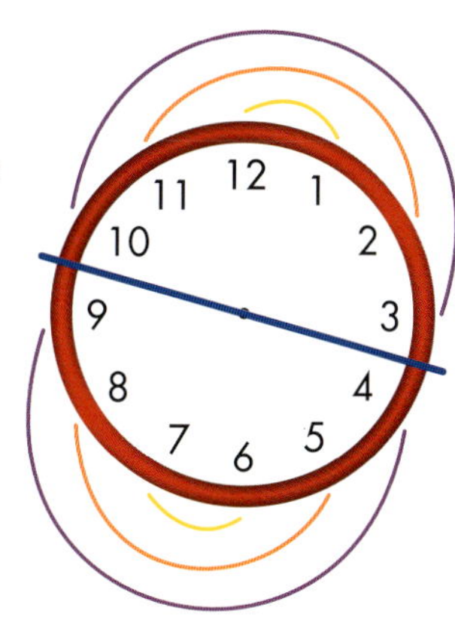

Be curious and ask plenty of "what if ...?" questions.

Guess and check is an effective strategy for most number puzzles.

Number triangle

Jaden loves triangles.

He found a way to put the digits 0, 1, 2, 3, 4 and 5 onto this diagram so that each side adds to 7.

Can you do it too?

0 1 2 3 4 5

I loved to create number puzzles. You can read more about me on pages 110–111.

Work it out

- I created my own digit cards with paper and scissors.
- I kept trying numbers in each position until I found a combination that works.
- It took 5 attempts.

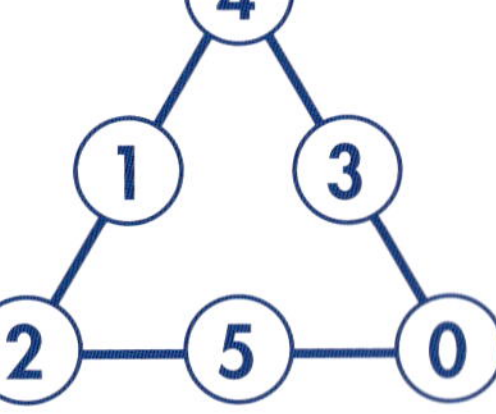

Check & reflect

I wonder if there are other combinations that add to 7? I tried but I don't think there are any others that work.

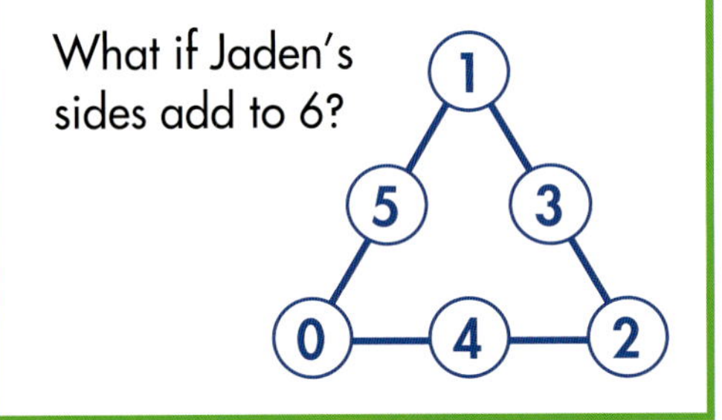

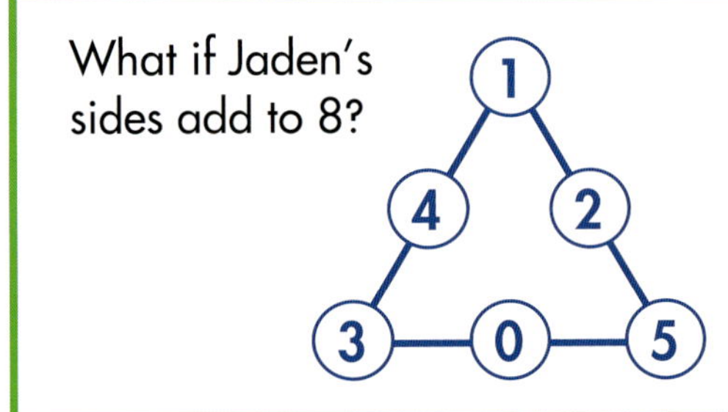

Add to 9

Jaden found a way to put the digits 0, 1, 2, 3, 4 and 5 onto this grid so that each side adds to 9.
Can you do it too?

Guess and check is a perfect strategy to help you solve a maze problem.

Which path?

The red paths in this maze make the shape of a house.
Charlie starts at the spot marked ●.
He discovers a way to walk along every path only once.

If he doesn't walk along any path he's been on before, how does he do it?

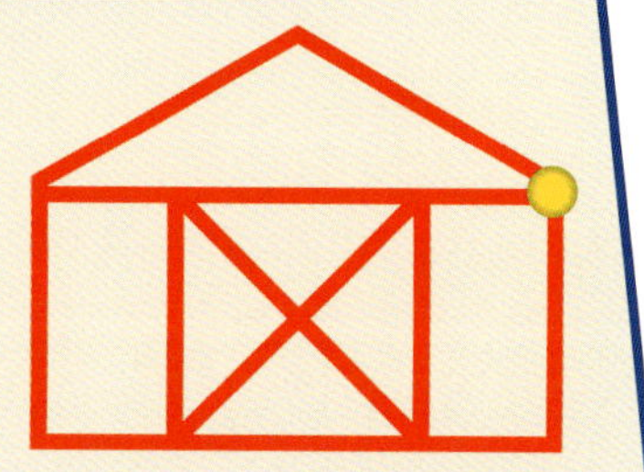

Work it out

I traced a path with my finger but I haven't solved it yet. I realised I can trace some paths without crossing over. I'll break it up into smaller parts.

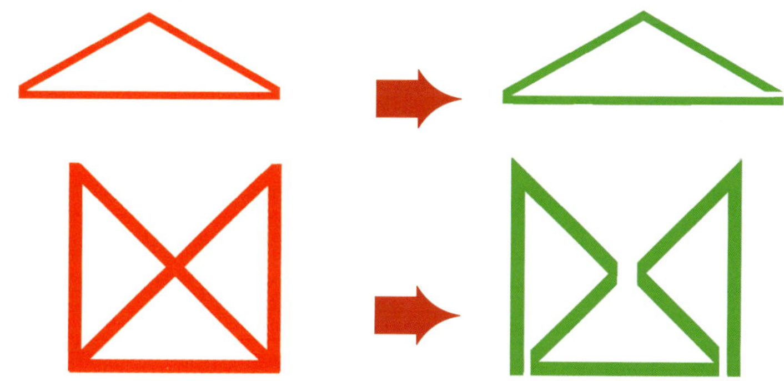

Now I'll put all that together.

This is how Charlie walked along the whole maze.

Check & reflect

With more practice I'll get better at looking at shapes and breaking them down into smaller shapes to help me solve maze problems.

Draw this triangle

Draw this triangle without retracing any line and without taking your pencil off the paper.

Sofia Kovalevskaya

Who said girls can't do maths?

Sofia Kovalevskaya was the first woman in Europe to be a Mathematics Professor at a University. Imagine all the problems she had to face to make this happen.

Sofia was born in Russia in 1850, 100 years before Zaha Hadid. Sofia died in 1891. She was very shy and nervous as a child and her dad thought she didn't need to learn any mathematics because she was a girl. Her nickname was "Tiny Sparrow" and if she didn't eat her soup she had to stand in a corner.

To save money, when Sofia was 11 her father used old maths notes as wallpaper in her bedroom. Sofia read and explored these notes as she went to sleep. She learnt many equations and formulas by heart. She impressed her grandfather, an uncle and a neighbour with her enthusiasm for solving mathematical problems.

As a 14-year-old, Sofia taught herself more maths from a book in the library. Luckily the author was a neighbour and convinced her dad to let her go to school as she had solved all the problems in his book. Mathematics was now her passion.

In the1800s, Russian women could not go to college or university or have an important job. Sofia had to overcome huge obstacles to become the first European woman to get a doctorate in mathematics and the first woman to become a university professor.

SPOTLIGHT on a famous Problem Solver

She wrote 10 different papers about her solutions to maths problems, including in 1888 when she wrote about how a 3D solid rotates around a point. She won a 5000 franc prize for this new idea. Sofia also wrote about the rings of Saturn. She said they were shaped more like eggs than ellipses.

Imagine having parts of outer space named after you.

★ The 45 km diameter 1859 Kovalevskaya asteroid is named after Sofia.

★ The Kovalevskaya crater on the far side of the moon is named after Sofia.

ПОЧТА СССР 1951г.
40 коп.
С.В.КОВАЛЕВСКАЯ-
ВЫДАЮЩИЙСЯ
РУССКИЙ МАТЕМАТИК

Sofia's portrait also appeared on a Russian postage stamp in 1951.

What can you do to solve maths problems like Sofia?

✓ Think about who inspires you to love mathematics.

✓ Identify the parts of maths that you love best.

✓ Share your best solutions with your friends.

Break it into smaller parts

Solve a simpler problem is another name for this strategy.

Break it into smaller parts is a useful strategy where a problem has two or more small bits of information you can use to work out the whole solution.

It is also useful if there are large or complex parts to your problem. Look for a simpler problem to solve. Find a new problem that uses only a small amount or smaller numbers.

Which numbers?

Eric and Mia pick up a random card each from a pack of number cards 1–30. Eric notices the difference between their two numbers is 11. Mia notices the product of their two numbers is 60.

Which numbers do they pick?

This problem involves subtraction and multiplication. There are quite a few number facts to think about. Take each fact one at a time.

There are many possible combinations that have a difference of 11.

To narrow it down, list all the number combinations from 1–30 that give a product of 60.

Draw a table to keep everything organised.

	Factors of 60				
	2	3	**4**	5	6
	30	20	**15**	12	10
Difference	28	18	11	7	4

Now you have a simpler problem to solve.

Which of these combinations have a difference of 11?

Yes, 4 and 15 must be the two cards that Eric and Mia select.

Sometimes it looks like there is a simple solution staring at you. About 50% of adults get this next problem wrong. They try **Guess and check** and jump in saying it must be $100 and $10.

They have read the problem but not fully comprehended it. This simple solution adds up to $110 but $100 – $10 = $90. It's not right yet as the guinea pig would then cost only $90 more. Let's see how you go.

Emily's pets

Emily buys a guinea pig and a mouse for $110. The guinea pig costs $100 more than the mouse. How much does each animal cost?

Understand it

There are 2 animals. Together they cost $110. The guinea pig costs $100 more than the mouse.

Select a strategy

I'll try **Break it into smaller parts**.

Work it out

- I can work this out mentally. I know the guinea pig costs $100 more, so subtract that cost from $110.

  $110 – $100 = $10

- The 2 animals share this extra $10 equally so I'll find a half.
- The mouse costs $5 and the guinea pig costs $5, plus the extra $100.

Check & reflect

Emily pays $5 for her mouse and $105 for her guinea pig.

Together that's **$105 + $5 = $110**, the correct amount.

Break it into smaller parts is an effective strategy.
Can I apply this thinking to another problem like this?

How heavy?

PK cat and her kitten together have a mass of 4.5 kg.
PK is 3 kg heavier than her kitten.

What is their individual mass?

Work it out

- PK is 3 kg heavier so subtract that from the total mass. **4.5 kg – 3 kg = 1.5 kg**.
- The 2 cats share this extra mass equally, so I'll find a half.

  Half of 1.5 g is the same as half of 1 kg and half of 0.5 kg. That's 0.5 kg and 0.25 kg.
- The kitten has a mass of 0.75 kg.
- PK has a mass of 0.75 kg plus the extra 3 kg.

Check & reflect

PK's mass is 3.75 kg. Her kitten's mass is 0.75 kg.
Together that's **3.75 + 0.75 kg**.

If I do this in my head that's 3.75 + 0.25 makes 4 kg.
And the other 0.5 kg makes 4.5 kg. That's the correct amount.

Try this

Water use

Ali and Imran use 265 L of water in a day. Ali uses 80 more litres than Imran. How much do they each use?

I don't have any magical ability … Before I work out any details, I work on the strategy. Once you have a strategy, a very complicated problem can split up into a lot of mini-problems.

Terry Tao (Professor of Mathematics, UCLA and winner of Fields Medal and Breakthough Prize in Mathematics)

Challenge

Mum makes 36 muffins. They are either berry or banana. There are 8 more banana muffins than berry muffins.

How many of each does Mum make?

Problems can be quite simple when you break them into smaller parts.

Rescue dogs

The rescue shelter has 10 dogs for sale. If 8 are adults, what fraction are pups?

Work it out

This is a proportion problem.

- I know 10 – 8 = 2 so there are 2 pups.
- 2 out of 10 dogs are pups. $\frac{2}{10}$ are pups.
- This is the same fraction as 1 out of 5. That's $\frac{1}{5}$.

Check & reflect

- One fifth of the dogs are pups. That's 1 in every 5 dogs.
- Another strategy is to say $\frac{8}{10}$ is the same as $\frac{4}{5}$.
- $\frac{4}{5}$ dogs are adults and the other $\frac{1}{5}$ must be pups.

What if I extend this solution to larger numbers?

- If there were 20 dogs, 4 would be pups.
- If there were 40 dogs, 8 would be pups.
- If there were 100 dogs, 20 would be pups.

To calculate the total number of dogs, I notice that you multiply the number of pups by 5 each time. Now I can work out many possibilities where the proportion is 1 in every 5.

- If 7 are pups, there are 5 × 7 = 35 dogs.
- If 12 are pups, there are 5 × 12 = 60 dogs.
- If 37 are pups, there are 5 × 37 = 185 dogs.
- If 759 are pups, there are 5 × 759 dogs.

  I'd need my calculator to work that one out.

Remember, be curious and ask plenty of "what if ...?" questions.

Electricity bill

Last year Jaya's electricity bill was $400.
This year her bill is $480.

What fraction increase is this?

Work it out

- This is another fraction problem.
  I can break it into smaller parts.
- Jaya paid $80 more. What fraction of $400 is $80?
  That's like ? × 80 = 400.
- I know 5 × 8 = 40 so 5 × 80 = 400.
- $80 is one fifth of $400.

Check & reflect

Jaya paid one fifth more for her electricity.

If I use a visual strategy to check, I can draw this as a diagram.

Find the sum

Blaise Pascal loved to play with numbers.

Can you find a fast way to add up all the counting numbers from 1–10?

1, 2, 3, 4, 5, 6, 7, 8, 9, 10

When the numbers in a problem are really large, look for a simpler problem to solve.

Work it out

- The slow way is to add every number in order.

  1 + 2 + 3 + 4 + 5 + 6 + 7 + 8 + 9 +10

- If I look at the start and finish I notice that pairs of numbers add to 10.

1 2 3 4 5 6 7 8 9 10

That's easy to calculate now.

(4 × 10) + 15 = 55

Check & reflect

The sum of the numbers 1 – 10 is 55.

- The fast way was to see a pattern.
- If I look again I can see an even easier way to calculate.

1 2 3 4 5 6 7 8 9 10

That's **5 × 11 = 55**

What if I had to add the numbers from 1 – 100?

Carl Friedrich Gauss loved to play with numbers too.

Carl was only 8 years old when he realised there was a fast way to add all the numbers from 1 – 100.

He saw fifty pairs of numbers that add to 101.

1 2 3 4 5 ... 50 51 ... 96 97 98 99 100

That's **50 × 101 = 5050**

Count to 1 million

Emma loves to count. How long will it take her to count to a million if she counts 1 number every second and counts for 8 hours non-stop each day?

Work it out

My estimate is 10 days. The numbers are so large I'll solve a simpler problem first.

- How far will she count in 60 seconds? **60**
- How far will she count in 60 minutes?
  60 × 60 = 3600 in 1 hour
- How far will she count in 8 hours?
  I'll use a calculator to work it out.
  8 × 3600 = 28 800 in 8 hours.
  Emma can count to 28 800 in 1 day.
- How many days to count to a million?
  How many groups of 28 800 in 1 million?
  Using my calculator, **1 000 000 ÷ 28 800 = 34.72**.
  I can round that up to 35.

Check & reflect

My estimate was way out.
It will take Emma about **35 days** to count to 1 million.
She'd be crazy!

I wonder how long it would take to count to a billion?

- A billion is 1000 × 1 million.
  That's 1000 × 35 days or 35 000 days.
- There are about 365 days in one year.
  My estimate is about 100 years as 350 is close to 365.
- **35 000 ÷ 365 = 95.89**
  That's about 96 years.

It's possible, but extremely unlikely, that anyone would ever do this.

Solve a simpler problem works for 3D or 2D problems too.

Heptadecagons

Carl Friedrich Gauss loved heptadecagons. That's a polygon with 17 sides. He even wanted one drawn on his gravestone.

How many different diagonals can you draw from just one corner of this shape? A diagonal is a straight line joining 2 opposite corners.

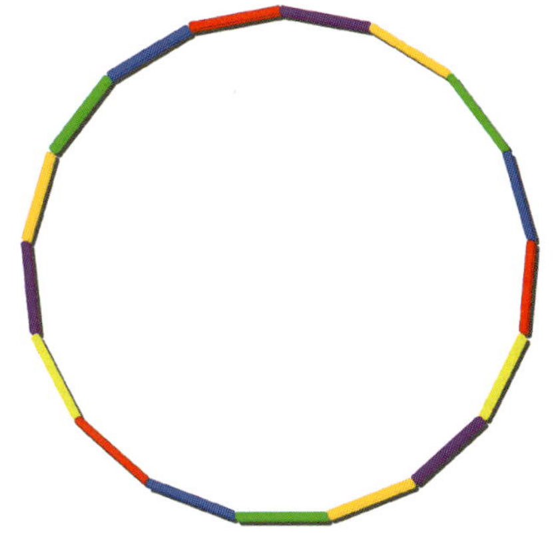

Work it out

I don't need to find all the diagonals, just all the diagonals I can draw from 1 corner. My guess is 16, but to discover my solution I'll start with the simplest polygon I can draw.

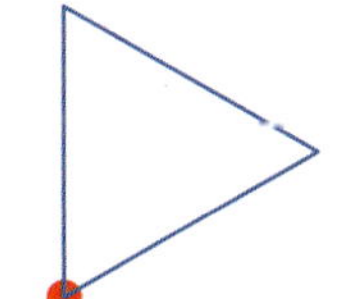

A triangle has no diagonal. There are not enough sides yet.

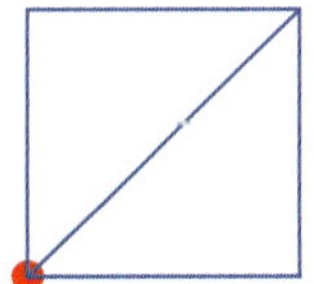

I can draw 1 diagonal on this square.

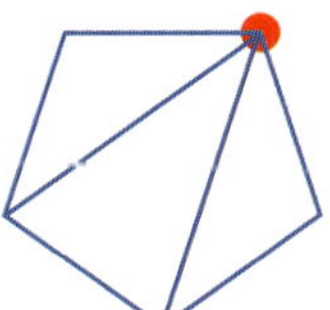

I can draw 2 diagonals on this pentagon.

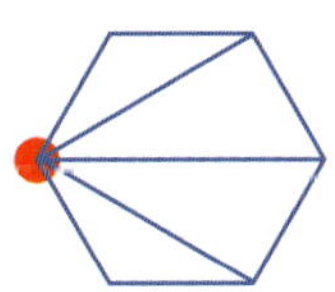

I can draw 3 diagonals on this hexagon.

A pattern is emerging. I'll record and continue my discoveries in a table.

Number of sides	3	4	5	6	7	8	9	10
Number of diagonals from 1 corner	0	1	2	3	4	5	6	7

The difference is always 3 as 3 – 0 = 3, 4 – 1 = 3, 5 – 2 = 3 and 6 – 3 = 3. I'll draw 3 more to check.

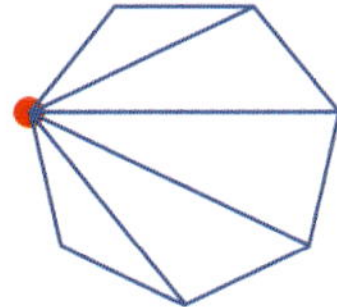

I can draw 4 diagonals on this septagon.

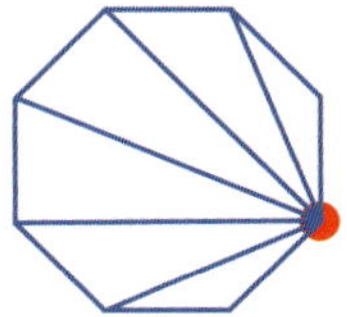

I can draw 5 diagonals on this octagon.

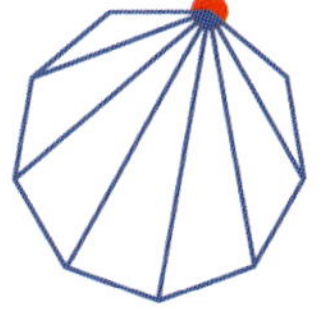

I can draw 6 diagonals on this nonagon.

If this pattern is extended to 17 sides, I should be able to draw **17 – 3 = 14** diagonals. My estimate doesn't match this but at least I had a go.

Check & reflect

I had to draw a large heptadecagon so I can see the diagonals. It follows the pattern. It does have 14 diagonals.

Carl Friedrich Gauss would be very happy with this diagram. Here is what the finished problem looks like.

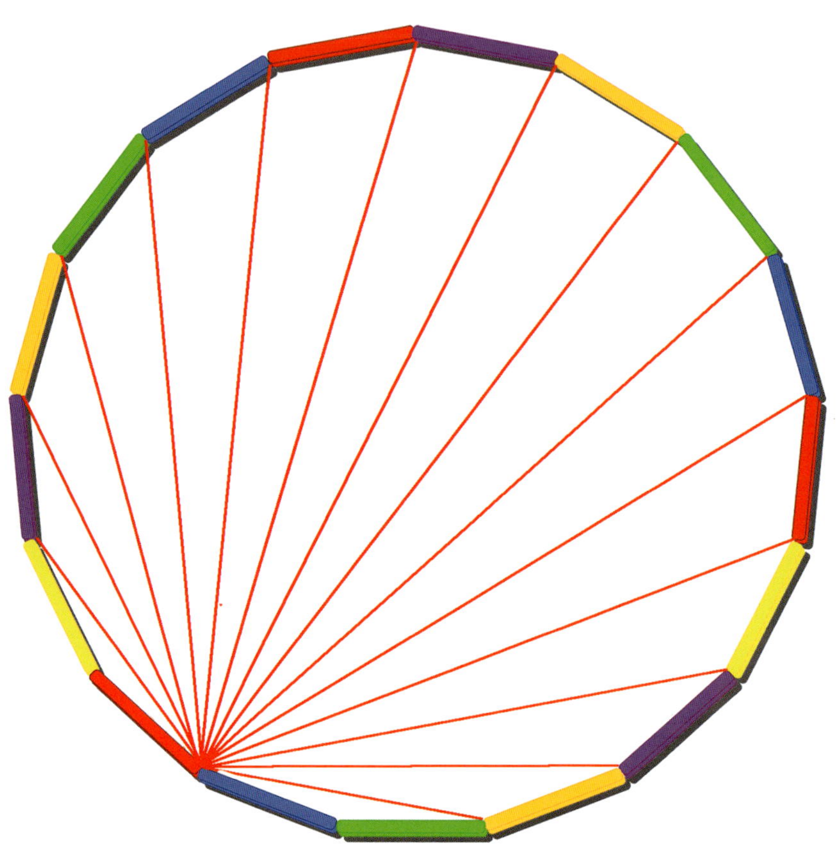

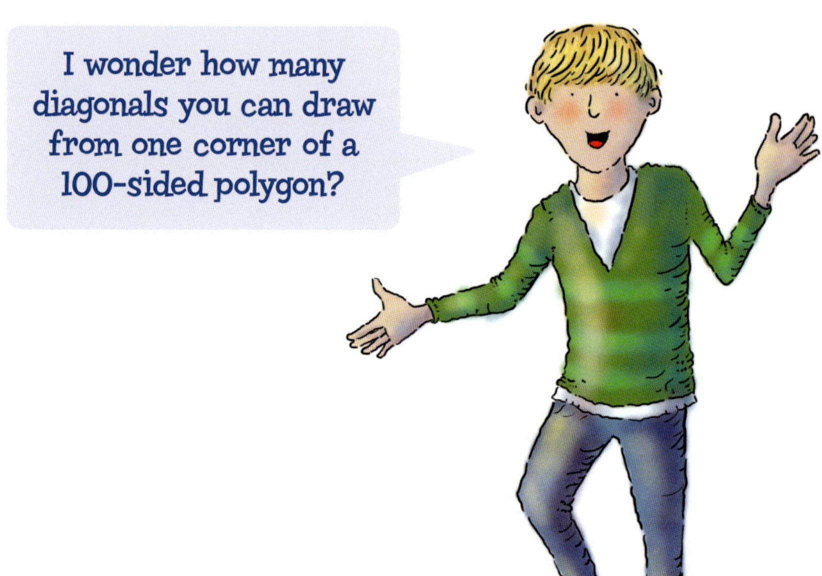

How many handshakes?

When Jack's debating club wins the Grand Final, all 10 members shake hands with each other. How many handshakes is that altogether?

Work it out

I can **Solve a simpler problem** by thinking about 2 people, then 3 then 4 and seeing if I can **Look for a pattern**.

2 people  That's 1 handshake.

3 people  That's 3 handshakes or 2 more than for 2 people.

4 people 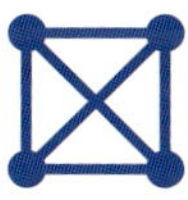 That's 6 handshakes or 3 more than for 3 people.

It looks like you add 4 more than 6 for 5 people. That will be 10 handshakes. I'll try drawing it to check.

It looks like the pattern for 5 people is:
1 + 2 + 3 + 4

So the pattern for 10 people should be:
1 + 2 + 3 + 4 + 5 + 6 + 7 + 8 + 9

Number of people	2	3	4	5	6	7	8	9	10
Number of handshakes	1	3	6	10	15	21	28	36	45

+2 +3 +4 +5 +6 +7 +8 +9

I can see a simpler way to add these numbers:

1 + 2 + 3 + 4 + 5 + 6 + 7 + 8 + 9

That's **(4 x 10) + 5 = 45**

Check & reflect

The ten people in Jack's club would shake hands 45 times if everyone shook hands once.

Blaise Pascal

Who said you can't have fun with numbers?

Blaise Pascal is thought to be the first person to invent and build a mechanical calculator. Imagine all the mathematical problems involved in this process.

Blaise was born in France in 1623 and died in 1662. His dad taught him at home but banned maths books as he thought they would tempt Blaise away from learning Greek and Latin. Blaise secretly became obsessed with geometry and invented his own names for geometric shapes.

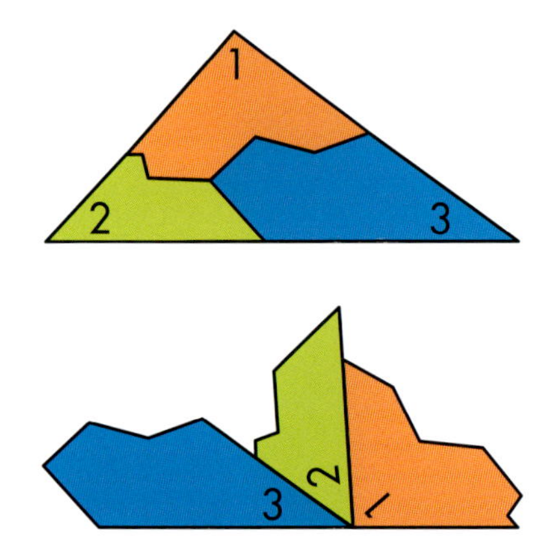

When Blaise was 12, he discovered 3 angles in a triangle always add up to 180°. His dad then let him read the most famous book about geometry, Euclid's *Elements*, packed with data about ancient Greek shapes and numbers.

When Blaise was 16, he discovered the Mystic Hexagram. If you draw any hexagon in a circle, with the corners touching the circumference, the 3 pairs of opposite sides meet at points that lie on a straight line. This is called the Pascal line and it even works if you draw your hexagon in an oval shape.

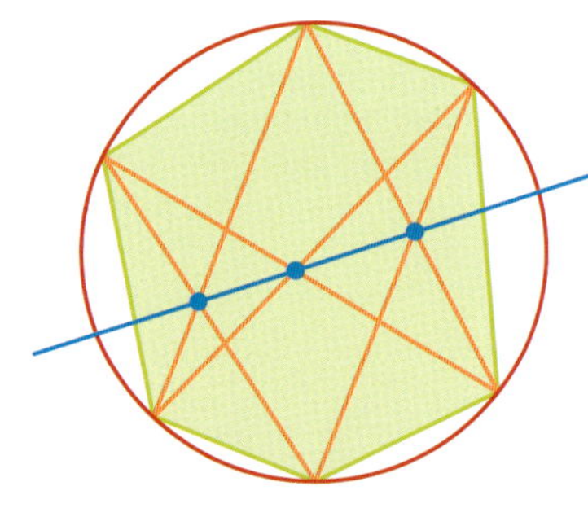

SPOTLIGHT on a famous Problem Solver

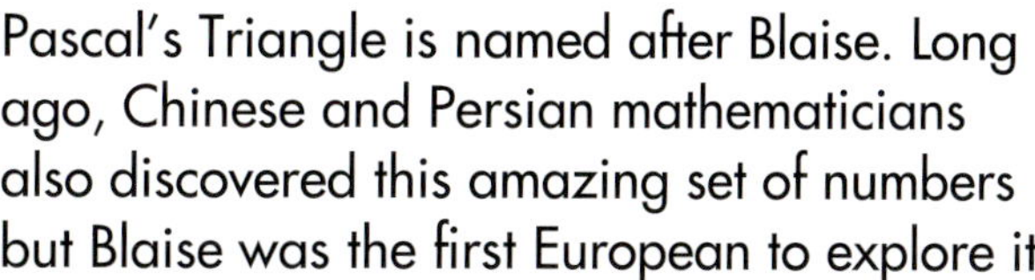

Pascal's Triangle is named after Blaise. Long ago, Chinese and Persian mathematicians also discovered this amazing set of numbers but Blaise was the first European to explore it.

Pascal is a computer programming language.

His dad was a tax collector and gave Blaise long columns of numbers to add. To escape the boredom Blaise invented a machine to do the job instead. His first invention, the Arithmetic Machine, could only add to 5-digits. Blaise then used trial and error to invent the Pascaline, which used gears to process large numbers. He made 50 prototypes before he was happy. This evolved into the microprocessors we use in our computers today. And we still use his gear system in our car odometers and home electricity or water meters.

The SI unit of pressure, pascal (Pa), is named after Blaise. His experiments showed that a column of mercury in a barometer was shorter if you went high up a mountain. So air pressure was less.

In France, his home town University is also named after him.

What can you do to solve maths problems like Blaise?

- ✓ Persevere until your problem is solved.
- ✓ Look for patterns in shapes and numbers.
- ✓ Enjoy exploring something new, even if you don't find the right answer.

Work backwards

Not all maths problems start at the beginning. Some problems tell you the finish of the story and you have to work out how the story started. **Work backwards** is an effective strategy to help you solve this sort of problem.

Mum's trip

Mum left home and arrived at the airport 2 hours later at 3:45 pm.

What time did she leave home?

In this problem you know when she arrived at her destination.

You do not know when she started her trip.

The number sentence looks like this:

□ + 2 hours = 3:45 pm

The information at the start of this number sentence is missing.

If you **Work backwards** you will undo these actions.

3:45 pm – 2 hours = □

Just take 2 hours off 3:45.

Mum left home at 1:45 pm.

Work backwards to undo this action.

Sometimes you need to do more than one action. The **Work backwards** strategy helps you keep these actions in order.

In the pool

Children are playing in a pool.
18 more jump in, then 5 get out.
There are now 25 children in the pool.
How many were in the pool at the start?

The number sentence looks like this:

☐ + 18 – 5 = 25

Work backwards to undo these actions.

25 + 5 – 18 = ☐

30 – 18 = ☐

12 = ☐

So 12 children were playing in the pool at the start of this story.

You can draw this story as a time line too. Remember a time line is about events or actions in a time sequence. It is not the same as a number line.

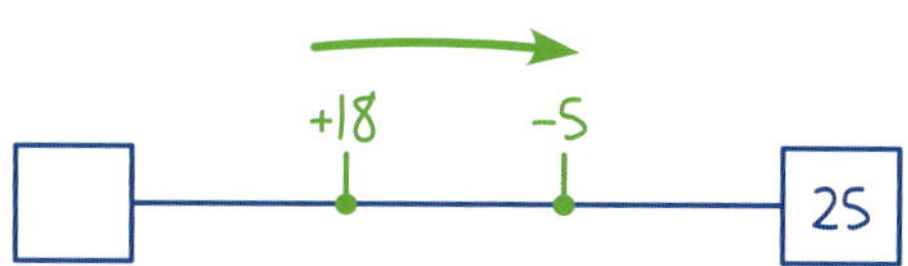

If you **Work backwards** it looks like this:

Heavy parcels

Three heavy parcels have a mass of 120 kg.
The scale reads 93 kg when the red parcel is taken off.
The scale reads 38 kg when the blue parcel is taken off.
Just the yellow parcel is left on the scale.
What is the mass of each parcel?

Read it again

Understand it

There are 3 numbers but these are not all the mass of a parcel.

120 kg is the combined mass of all 3 parcels.

How heavy is each parcel?

Select a strategy

I know the mass of the yellow parcel at the end of this story so I'll try the **Work backwards** strategy.

Work it out

- The yellow parcel has a mass of **38 kg**.
- The blue parcel has a mass of **93 – 38 kg**
  I can count on from 38 to 93.
  2 + 50 + 3 = 55 kg
  The mass of the blue parcel is 55 kg.
- The red parcel has a mass of **120 – 93 = 27 kg**

Check & reflect

38 + 55 + 27 = 120 so my calculations are correct.

Max's money

Over last year, Max did lots of odd jobs and earnt $225. Grandma gave him some money, Aunty Lee gave him $76 and dad gave him $88. How much did Grandma give him?

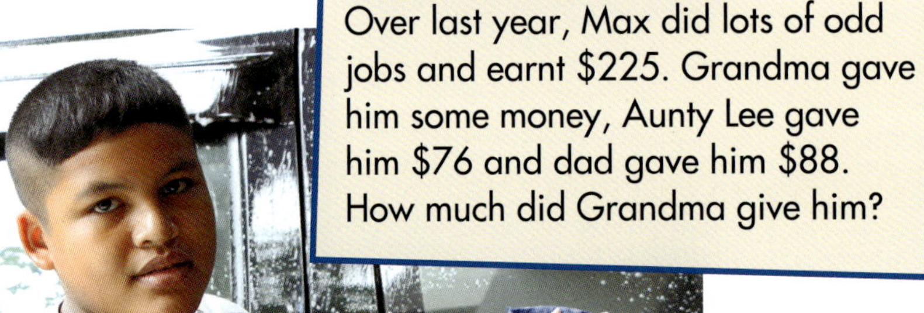

Work backwards can be combined with other strategies.
To solve this next problem use the **Draw a table** strategy too.

Apollo 11

The Apollo 11 mission lasted 195 hours, 18 minutes and 35 seconds.
Splashdown was at 16:50:35 pm on 24 July 1969.

When did this mission blast off?

Understand it

I know how long the Apollo 11 mission took. I know when it finished. I have to calculate when it started.

Select a strategy

Because I know the end of this story, I'll use the **Work backwards** strategy.

Work it out

- There are 24 hours in a day. I need to calculate how many days in 195 hours. 195 ÷ 24 = 8.125. That's 8 days and a few hours.
- 0.125 is one eighth, so 0.125 hours is $\frac{1}{8}$ of 24 hours or 3 hours.
- I can draw a table to help me keep all the data in order.

	Days	Hours	Minutes	Seconds
	24 July	16	50	35
Total mission time	8	3	18	35

Now subtract the times (days, hours, minutes and seconds) to discover the solution.

	Days	Hours	Minutes	Seconds
	24 July	16	50	35
Total mission time	8	3	18	35
	16 July	13	32	00

Check & reflect

I looked it up on the internet and confirmed my solution. The Apollo 11 mission blasted off from the Kennedy Space Centre, Florida, at 13:32:00 on 16 July 1969.

Shopping

Steve buys a $4 book with a 50% discount.
He pays only $2. He saves $2.

His friend Ness buys something with a 10% discount.
She saves $2 too.

Why did Ness save as much as Steve yet she only has a 10% discount?

Work it out

- This doesn't make sense. How can they both save $2 yet their discounts are not the same? I'll use **Work backwards** to sort out all the information.
- I'll draw a table too.

	Original cost	Discount	Saving	What they paid
Steve	$4	50%	$2	$2
Ness	?	10%	$2	?

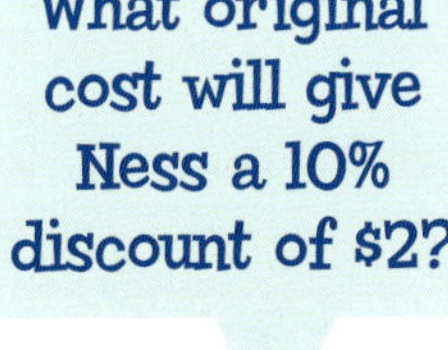

- Steve buys something that costs $4 but with a 50% discount he saves $2. Steve pays $4 – $2 = $2.
- What about Ness? I still don't get it. I'll ask my friend Lucy to help me.
- OK, thanks Lucy, now I've got it. $2 = 10% so the full amount is 10 × $2. That's $20.
- Ness buys something that costs $20. But with a 10% discount she saves $2. Ness pays $20 – $2 = $18.

	Original cost	Discount	Saving	What they paid
Steve	$4	50%	$2	$2
Ness	$20	10%	$2	$18

Check & reflect

Ness spends $18 to save $2. Steve spends $4 to save $2. Even though they both save the same amount Steve has the better deal. If Steve bought something for $20 with a 50% discount he would pay only $10.

If you get stuck, try discussing your problem with a friend. Two or more heads might be better than one.

Quite a few maths problems involve the ages of family members or a group of friends. Instead of making it simple, a problem might twist and turn and try to confuse you. **Work backwards** can help you unravel the data.

How old?

Claire is 22 years younger than Neroli. Gordon is three times as old as Claire. Neroli is 34. How old is Gordon?

Don't panic, just calmly think about what you know.

Break this problem into smaller parts to help you think clearly.

Work it out

I'll work backwards to find Gordon's age.

- Neroli is 34.
- Claire is 22 years younger than Neroli.
- Claire must be 34 – 22 = 12.
  So Claire is 12 years old.
- Gordon is three times as old as Claire.
  That's 3 × 12 = 36.
  Gordon is 36 years old.

Neroli and Gordon might be Claire's parents.

Many problems require more than one strategy to find a solution.

You don't have to stick to just one strategy each time.

If you spot a time sequence problem where you know what happens at the end of the story but not the beginning, try the **Work backwards** strategy.

Which way?

Simon is following instructions in a direction game. His friend Dawn starts the game.

After she tells him to make a quarter turn left, he finishes facing south-east.

What direction did Simon face at the start of this game?

Work it out

I need to undo the directions to see the start of this problem.

- I know a quarter turn means a quarter of a circle. That's a 90° angle.
- On a timeline the problem looks like this.

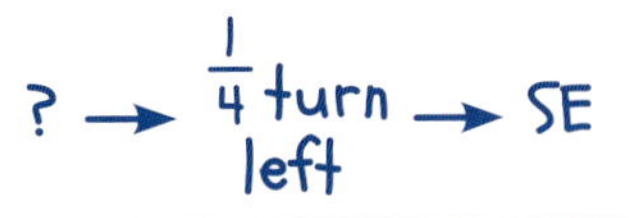

- To undo these actions I need to do the opposite.

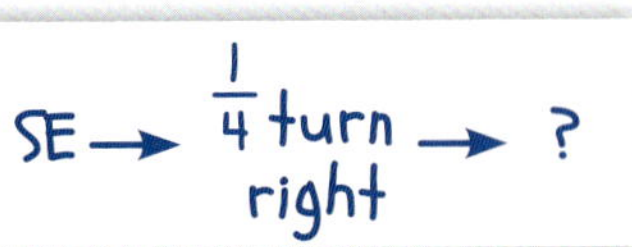

- In a circle the 8 compass points look like this:

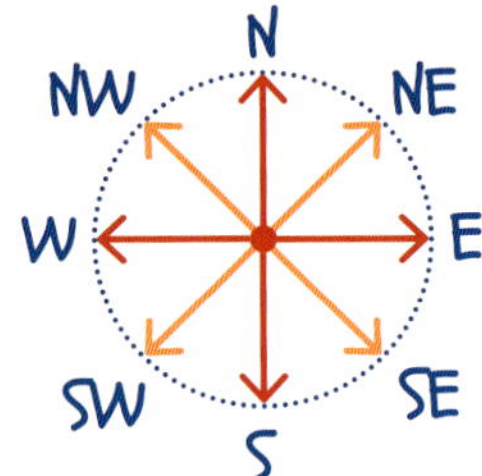

- This compass map shows me Simon started facing SW.

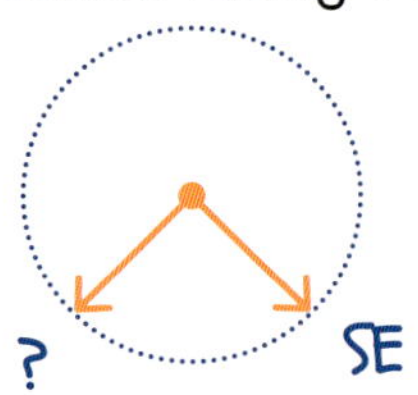

Check & reflect

I need further practice at mentally moving forwards or backwards around a compass map.

Mental direction skills are used in map reading. A map always shows North at the top, but you might be facing a completely different direction. Visualise where you face at the start. Visualise where turning left or right will take you.

Measuring lizards

Four girls measured the length of their pet lizards.

- Mia's lizard is 50 mm longer than Jaya's.
- Emma's lizard is double the length of Mia's lizard.
- Lucy's lizard is shorter than Emma's by 125 mm.
- Jaya's lizard is 205 mm long.

How long is Lucy's lizard?

Work it out

I have 4 clues.
I'll use **Work backwards** to discover the answer.

- Jaya's lizard is 205 mm so Mia's lizard must be **205 + 50 = 255**
- That means Emma's lizard must be **2 × 255**. That's **double 250 plus double 5** or **500 + 10**. Emma's lizard must be 510 mm long.
- Lucy's lizard is 125 mm shorter than Emma's lizard. That's **510 – 125**. I can do this in my head. 100 less than 510 is 410. 10 less is 400 and 15 less than that is 385.

  Lucy's lizard must be 385 mm long.

Check & reflect

That took 3 steps to solve. I'll record all the measurements and then reread the question to make sure all my calculations match the clues.

Jaya's lizard	205 mm	✓
Mia's lizard	255 mm	✓
Emma's lizard	510 mm	✓
Lucy's lizard	385 mm	✓

Yes, the clues all match my results.

You also used the **Break it into smaller parts** strategy.

The **Work backwards** strategy can be used for map-reading problems. Visualise each action. Think about what happens in real life.

The visit

Mary wants to visit her friend Kim.

On leaving her house, she turns right and walks about 30 m.

She then turns right again, walks almost 100 m then turns right to go inside Kim's house. Kim's house has a green roof and is marked with a red cross at C6.

What are the co-ordinates for Mary's house?

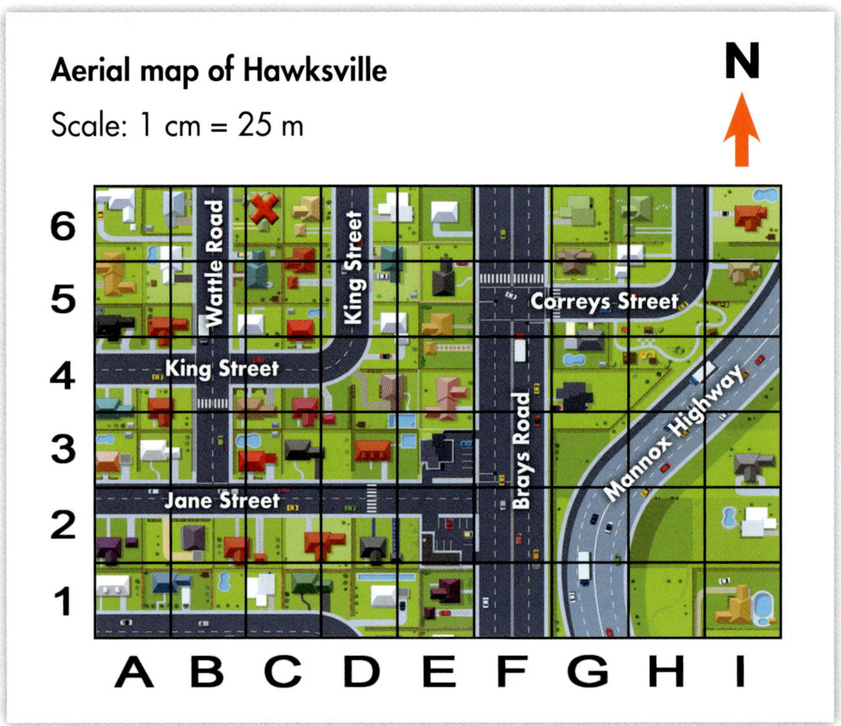

Work it out

This is like a mystery. I need to think like a detective.
I know where Mary finished her walk but not where she started.

- Kim's house is at C6.
- I can draw a timeline to show the actions like this.

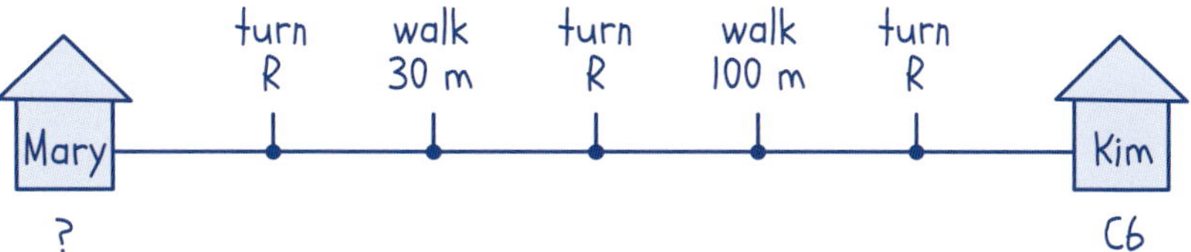

- When Mary walks back home she will undo each action.
- I can show these new actions on my timeline.

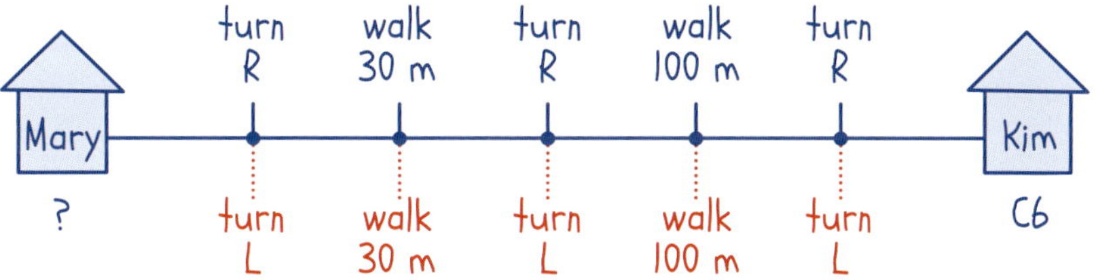

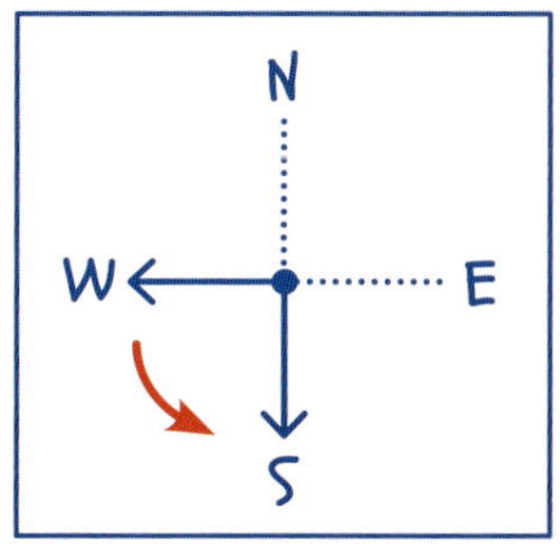

- When Mary leaves Kim's house she is facing west.
- To turn left she turns a quarter circle.
Once she turns left she now faces south.

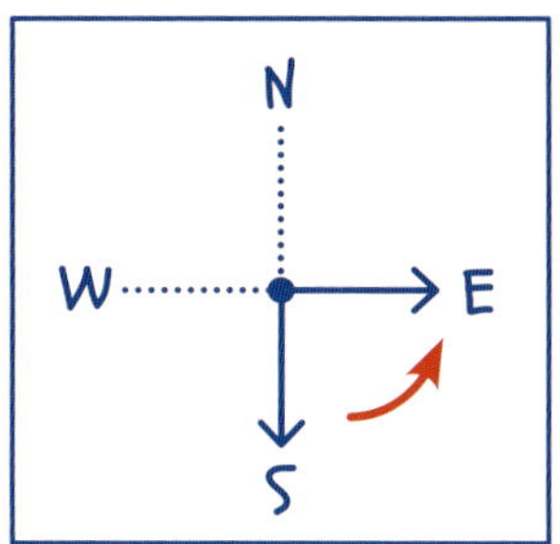

- When Mary reverses the directions like this she arrives at the corner of Wattle Road and Jane Street. She now has to turn left but which way is it?
- Remember Mary is facing south. So if she turns left she is now facing east.
- Mary's house is at C3. It has a black roof.

Check & reflect

If I reread the problem this solution fits. Phew!
Reversing each direction is the most difficult thing for me.

Practise visualising the direction you will face when you turn left or right or go straight ahead from different compass positions.

Ada Lovelace

Who said you can't fly?

Ada Lovelace created the first algorithm to be used by a machine. She is often called the mother of computer programming. A computer programmer is someone who writes a set of instructions that tells a computer what to do and when to do it. Imagine all the mathematical problems involved in this process.

Ada was born in England in 1815 and died in 1852. She was a very sick child but her mum (who was called the "Princess of Parallelograms" by Ada's dad) thought it would help if she learnt mathematics, so Ada had private tutors as girls didn't go to college or university in those days.

Ada believed intuition and imagination helped her solve maths problems.

At 12, after a long illness where she couldn't walk properly, Ada decided she wanted to fly. She examined birds to see the proportion between the wings and the body. She investigated equipment like paper, silk, feathers and a compass to help guide her when she flew. She wrote Flyology, a book about her discoveries, with plans for a steam-powered horse that lifted a person into the air. We never heard if her invention worked or not.

When only 17, Ada met Charles Babbage, the inventor of the first mechanical computer. He was so impressed by Ada's abilities he invited her to work with him. He called Ada the "Enchantress of Number". Unfortunately the computer was too costly to make but Charles persevered and invented the Analytical Engine in 1834. Ada translated data about this machine into other languages. She added an important set of her own notes explaining how the machine worked.

SPOTLIGHT
on a famous Problem Solver

Ada thought a computing machine could be more than just a number cruncher. She wanted to create a model of how our brain thinks, a machine that might write music or draw a picture. When she saw the mechanical looms using pattern punch cards in a textile factory, she transferred this idea to the Analytical Engine. People think Ada wrote the first computer program using these punch cards.

Ada was always creating a new problem to solve. In 1851, she made a model to predict the outcome in a bet. Unfortunately her model didn't work and she lost lots of money.

Today a US Department of Defence computer program is named Ada.

Ada Lovelace Day is celebrated around the world in mid October, to help promote women in science, technology, engineering and maths.

The UK Crossrail Project completed 42 km of tunnels under London in 2015. One of their giant tunnel boring machines was named Ada.

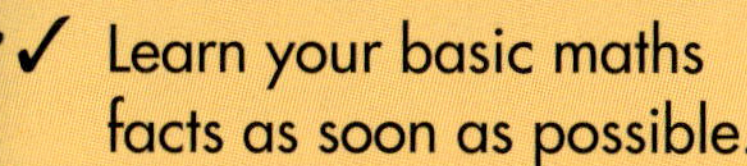

- ✓ Learn your basic maths facts as soon as possible.
- ✓ Create your own interesting maths problems.
- ✓ Write and draw diagrams to show how you solve your problems.

Look for a pattern

A pattern is a design or number that can be predicted. It is not random. There is a rule that tells you what to do or say next. Your challenge is to find the pattern rule. There are colour, shape and number patterns. Even the weather has a pattern we think we can predict. **Look for a pattern** is a useful strategy for solving problems.

70, 63, 56, 49, 42, 35, 28, 21, 14, 7, 0

This number pattern is all about 7. It's the multiples of 7 when you count backwards.

The rule is: **Subtract 7**

- If your friend calls out 42, you call back 35 (because that's 42 – 7).
- If you call out 63 your friend calls back 56 (because that's 63 – 7).

Every number in a number pattern obeys a rule. The problem is you don't always spot the rule straight away.

What are the missing numbers?

☐ 72 64 56 ☐ 40 32 24 ☐ 8 0

Can you spot the rule quickly?

Yes, this is all the multiples of 8 from 80 back to 0.

The rule is: **Subtract 8**

The missing multiples are 80, 48 and 16.

- If your friend calls out 56, you call back 48 (because that's 56 – 8).
- If you call out 24, your friend calls back 16 (because that's 24 – 8).

A number pattern can start anywhere.

15, 30, 60, 120, 240, 480, 960 ...

In this pattern the numbers double each time.

The rule is: **Multiply by 2**

- If your friend calls out 120, you'd call back 240 (because that's 2 × 120).
- If you call out 960, your friend calls back 1920 (because that's 2 × 960).

Searching for a pattern rule is like being a detective. Your eyes need to look at the original number and what it becomes.

Can you spot the rule quickly?

Number	1	2	3	4	5	6	7	8	9	10
Mystery Rule	6	7	8	9	10	11	12	13	14	15

Yes, this time the pattern rule is: **Add 5**

So if your friend calls out 78, you call back 83 (because that's 78 + 5).

If your friend calls out 809, you call back 814 (because that's 809 + 5).

Some number patterns use a combination of actions. These patterns are more difficult to discover.

Can you spot this new rule quickly?

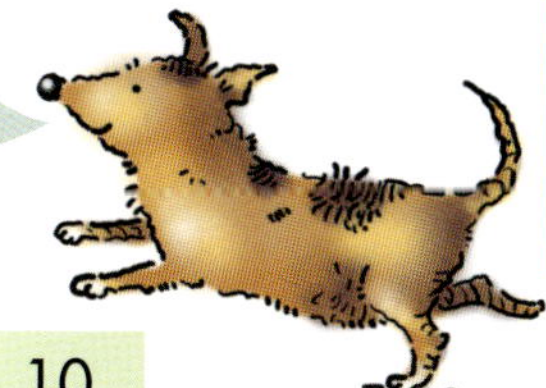

Number	1	2	3	4	5	6	7	8	9	10
Mystery Rule	11	21	31	41	51	61	71	81	91	101

The rule is: **Multiply by 10 then add 1.**

So if your friend calls out 5, you'd call back 51 (because that's 10 × 5 plus 1).

If your friend calls out 72, you'd call back 721 (because that's 10 × 72 plus 1).

Mystery rule

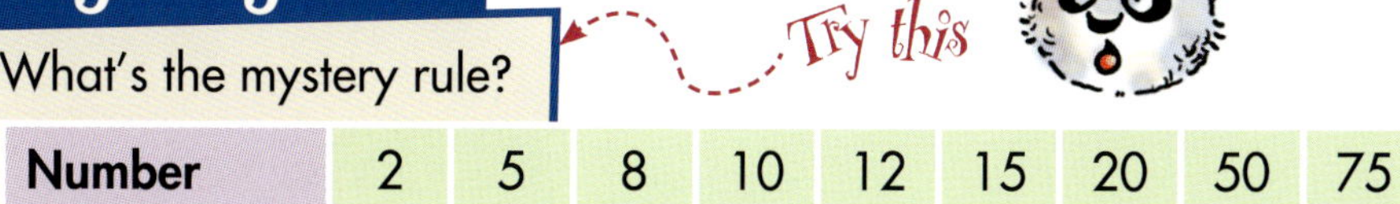

What's the mystery rule?

Number	2	5	8	10	12	15	20	50	75	100
Mystery Rule	17	20	23	25	27	30	35	65	90	115

Challenge

What's the mystery rule?

Number	1	2	3	4	5	6	7	8	9	10
Mystery Rule	4	9	14	19	24	29	34	39	44	49

Numbers and shapes can work together to create a pattern.

These are triangular numbers.

Cans are often stacked like this in a supermarket or hardware display.

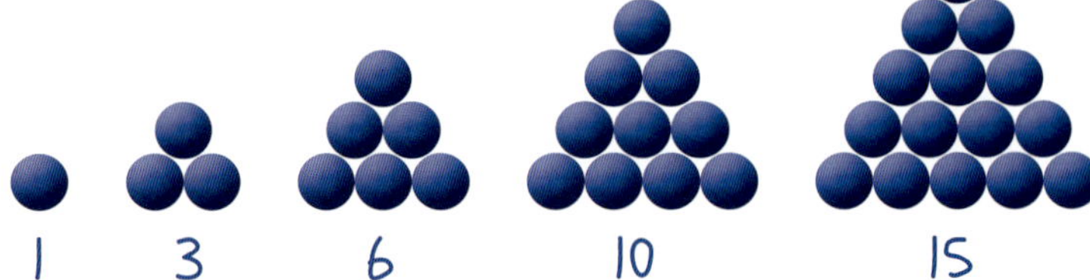

What patterns can you find hiding here?
Let's try subtraction.

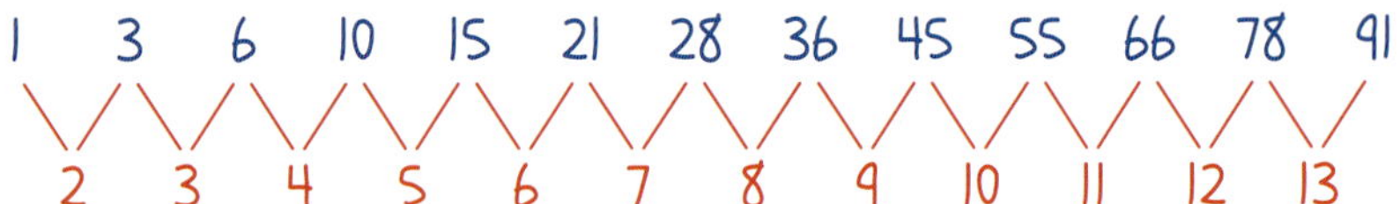

When you find the difference between consecutive pairs of triangular numbers you get counting numbers in order.

Let's try addition. What happens if you add every two consecutive triangular numbers?

1 + 3 = 4

6 + 10 = 16

15 + 21 = 36

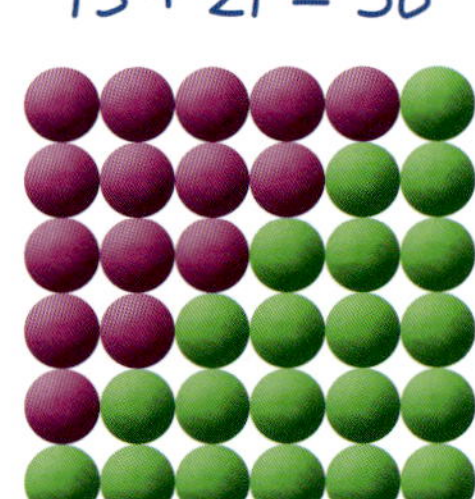

If you add every two consecutive triangular numbers you get a square number.

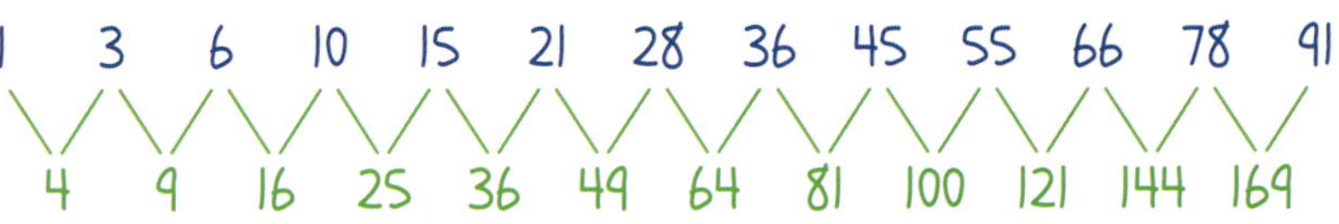

What happens if you find the difference between consecutive pairs of square numbers?

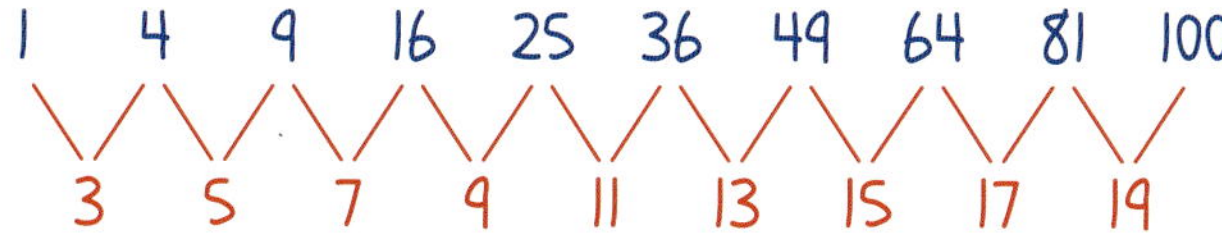

When you find the difference between consecutive pairs of square numbers, you get odd numbers in order.

What happens if you add consecutive pairs of square numbers?

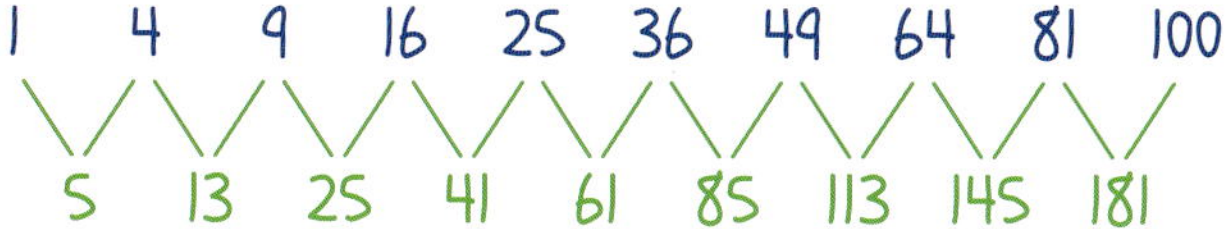

This doesn't seem to be a pattern.
I don't think this leads anywhere!

Not everything you do will create a pattern. That's why patterns are so magical when they do appear.

100s patterns

How many patterns can you discover hiding in a 100s chart?

1	2	3	4	5	6	7	8	9	10
11	12	13	14	15	16	17	18	19	20
21	22	23	24	25	26	27	28	29	30
31	32	33	34	35	36	37	38	39	40
41	42	43	44	45	46	47	48	49	50
51	52	53	54	55	56	57	58	59	60
61	62	63	64	65	66	67	68	69	70
71	72	73	74	75	76	77	78	79	80
81	82	83	84	85	86	87	88	89	90
91	92	93	94	95	96	97	98	99	100

Calculator pattern

Here is the start of a number pattern.

Continue and record the next parts of this pattern.

If you discover the rule, predict the 10th and 100th part of this pattern.

1: $0 \times 9 + 1 = 01$

2: $1 \times 9 + 2 = 11$

3: $2 \times 9 + 3 = 21$

4: $3 \times 9 + 4 = 31$

Read it again

Understand it

First I need to write more parts for this pattern.
Then I have to discover the rule.

Select a strategy

Obviously I need the **Look for a pattern** strategy.

Work it out

- I can see the next two parts of this pattern are:
  5: $4 \times 9 + 5 = 41$
  6: $5 \times 9 + 6 = 51$
- I worked it out. I can see the pattern.
  For the 6th part it was $(6 - 1) \times 9 + 6 = 51$.
  Multiply 9 by the number before then add the number.
- So the 10th part will be $(10 - 1) \times 9 + 10$.
  That's $81 + 10 = 91$.
- And the 100th part will be $(100 - 1) \times 9 + 100$.
  I used my calculator to find my solution: $891 + 100 = 991$.

Check & reflect

Number patterns are pretty amazing.

What's the 1000th part of this pattern?
$(1000 - 1) \times 9 + 1000$.
That's $8991 + 1000 = 9991$.

I just discovered an even faster way to work out the answer. Can you spot it too?

If you look at the answer to the 1000th part, it is 1 less than the part number and then 1 in the ones place.

1000 – 1 = 999.
The answer to the 1000th part is **9991**.

I don't ever need my calculator to do this anymore.

The 597th part of this pattern will be **5961**.

The 12 346th part of this pattern will be **123 451**.

I know how to record this pattern and write the matching answer.

Impress your family with a number challenge.

Record this number sentence on paper.

12 345 × 9 + 12 346 = ?

Ask someone to work it out with a calculator while you work it out in your head.

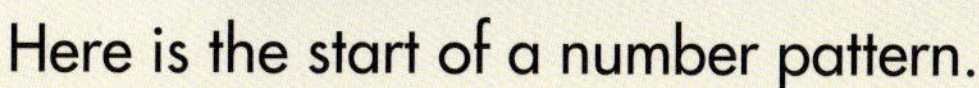

Continue the pattern

Here is the start of a number pattern.

Use your calculator to record and continue it.

If you discover the rule, predict the 9th part of this pattern.

1 × 9 + 2 = 11

12 × 9 + 3 = 111

123 × 9 + 4 = 1111

1234 × 9 + 5 = 11111

Blaise Pascal loved to play with numbers and explore what they can do. Pascal's Triangle is probably the most famous triangle in the world.

Numbers are placed on the triangle according to the rule: **Add the 2 numbers above.**

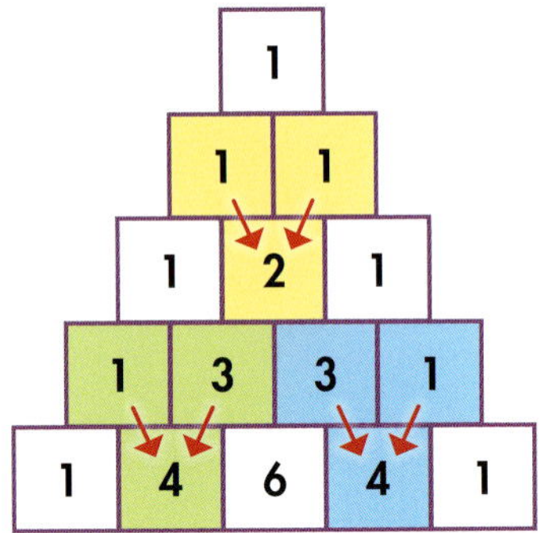

- Start by writing 1.
- Add the numbers above to create the numbers in the 2nd row.
  0 + 1 = 1 and **1 + 0 = 1**
- Add the numbers above to create the 3rd row.
  0 + 1 = 1, **1 + 1 = 2** and **1 + 0 = 1**
- Keep doing this for as many rows as you like.

The shape is like an equilateral triangle but the numbers can be written inside a circle, a square, a hexagon or even just on their own.

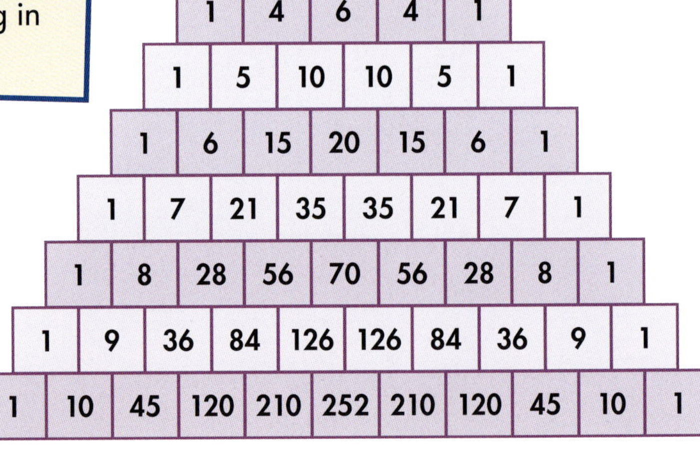

Pascal's patterns

Try this

How many patterns can you discover hiding in Pascal's Triangle?

Challenge

22	12	18	87
88	17	9	25
10	24	89	16
19	86	23	11

Srinivasa Ramanujan loved to play with numbers too. This looks like a Magic Square but it isn't like any other Magic Square. The top row is the date of his birthday, 22 December 1887. This square hides some amazing sums. Can you discover at least two addition patterns hiding here?

Look for a pattern works well with 2D and 3D space problems too. Remember, a pattern is something you can predict. It is not random.

What happens next?

In this pattern the 3D object rotates a quarter turn in a clockwise direction.

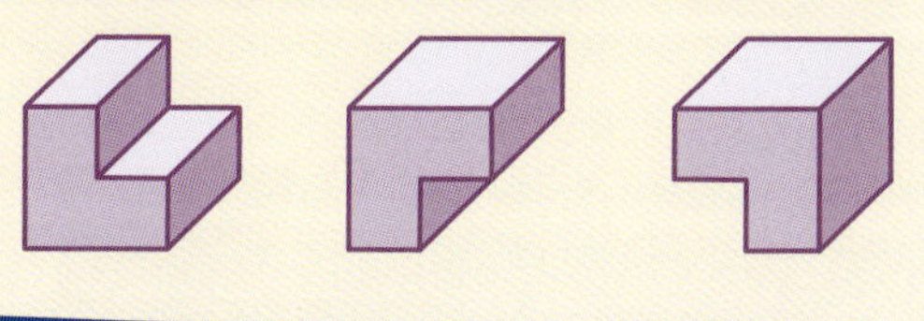

The next shape in this pattern looks like this:

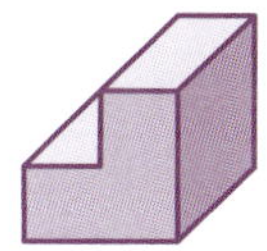

What happens next?

In this pattern the shape is a square divided into a white and a coloured triangle. The coloured triangle rotates a quarter turn in an anticlockwise direction.

The next shape in this pattern looks like this:

If you continue this pattern you will just repeat the first 4 shapes as the 5th shape is in the same position as the 1st shape.

Remember: your ability to visualise is a vital mathematical skill.

Look for a pattern can be a tricky strategy. Your eyes need to look at each small part in a complex shape. **Break it into smaller parts** is another useful strategy.

Many 2D patterns involve a turn. Turns can be clockwise or anticlockwise. They can be a quarter or a half turn. Watch what happens at a corner. Or follow a small part and notice the direction it moves.

What happens next?

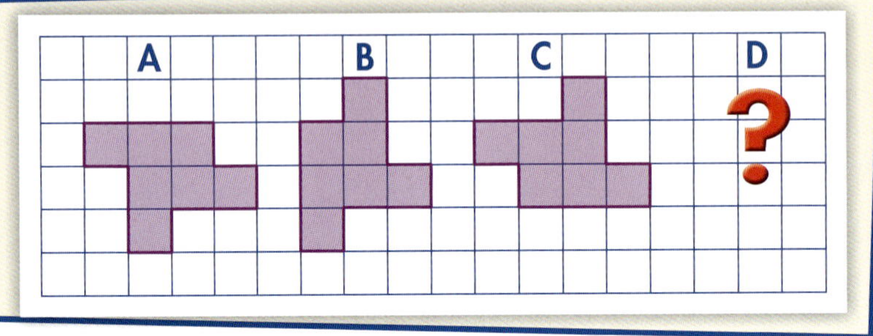

Work it out

- In this pattern the shape has bits that stick out.
- I'll visualise this shape turning in my head.
- It looks like it is turning anticlockwise.
- That bottom right corner on the 3rd shape will rotate up to the top right.
- If I turn the page anticlockwise I can see what that 3rd shape now looks like. I can copy it like this:

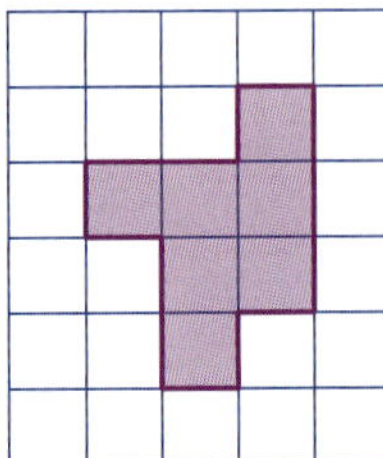

Check & reflect

Phew! Rotation patterns are not easy to follow. You need to check each small part to make sure your solution is correct.

Try this

Ness's shape

Ness folded some paper in half.
She cuts this shape.

What will it look like when Ness unfolds it?

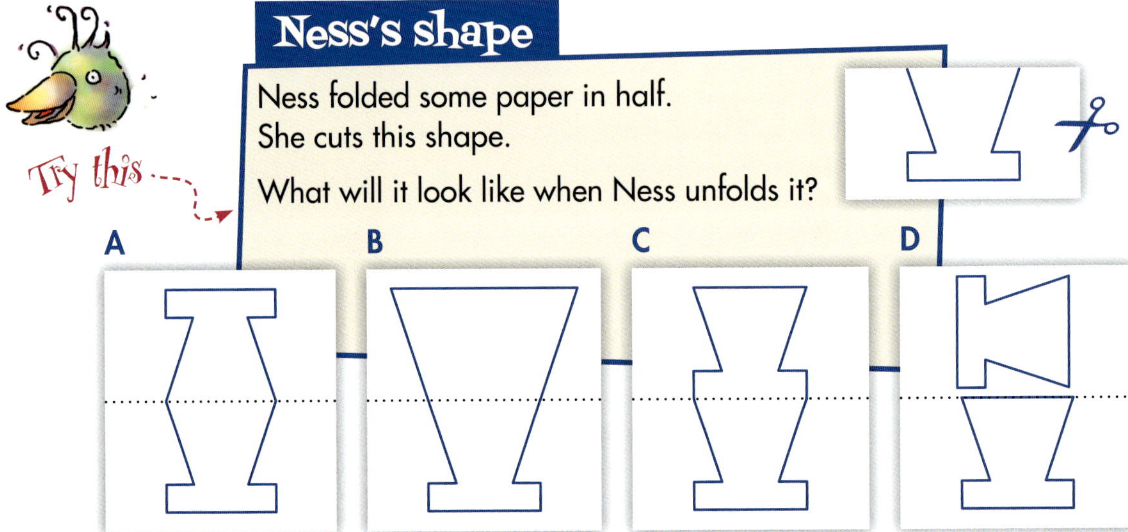

In an open problem, there are two or more possible solutions.

Here are 16 tiles. The top of each tile has a half triangle or it is completely black or white.

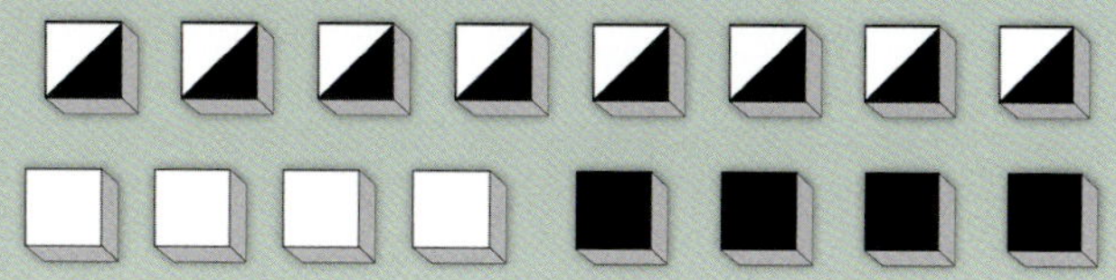

Symmetrical

Rearrange these 16 tiles in a square to create a symmetrical pattern that matches itself twice when rotated 180 degrees.

Work it out

- This is an open problem.
- There are many possible solutions.
- As long as I create something with symmetry my solution is acceptable.
- Here are some of the patterns I made with the 16 tiles.

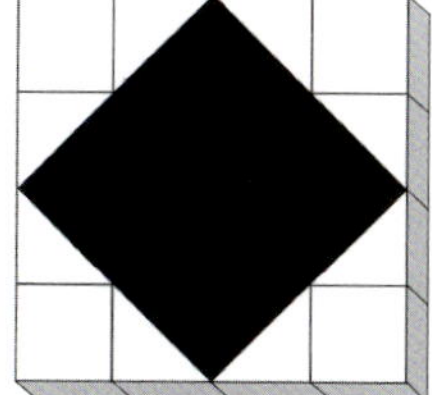

Check & reflect

I enjoy making these patterns. You try plenty of different positions until you find one you like. Here are two more I made. The zigzag one is symmetrical in the outline but the colours are opposite.

Challenge

Use these 16 tiles to create a pattern that has rotational symmetry.

Can you create one that has no line symmetry as well?

Henry Dudeney

Who said you can't invent your own maths problems?

Henry Dudeney was one of the world's most famous puzzlists. A puzzlist is someone who enjoys creating or solving puzzles. Imagine all the mathematical problems involved in this process.

Henry was born in England in 1857 and died in 1930. As a young boy he loved to play chess and later set up the first British Chess Club. His passion was to create maths problems and publish his puzzles in the local paper. As he wasn't very successful at school, Henry left early to work in an office. He continued to publish his puzzles calling himself "The Sphinx", after a famous old Greek puzzler.

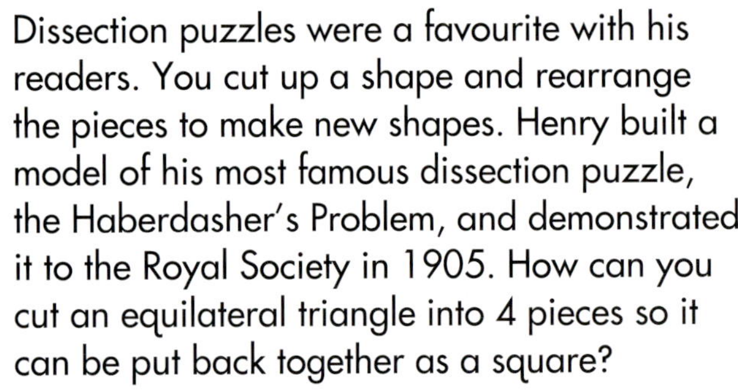

Dissection puzzles were a favourite with his readers. You cut up a shape and rearrange the pieces to make new shapes. Henry built a model of his most famous dissection puzzle, the Haberdasher's Problem, and demonstrated it to the Royal Society in 1905. How can you cut an equilateral triangle into 4 pieces so it can be put back together as a square?

Henry enjoyed playing ball games like billiards, bowling and croquet. These games require you to solve problems with angles and he was very good at this.

SPOTLIGHT on a famous Problem Solver

Henry liked to write a real-life story for each puzzle. Puzzle 74 in *The Canterbury Puzzles* shows a chessboard broken into 12 pieces by some rowdy knights. You have to find a way to reassemble it.

```
   S E N D
 + M O R E
 ---------
 M O N E Y
```

Henry also loved to create cross number puzzles and his first was published in 1926. He invented letter addition puzzles, where each letter represents a different digit.

He also invented number addition puzzles using all the digits from 1 – 9. Can you discover another way to do this?

```
   1 9 2
 + 3 8 4
 -------
   5 7 6
```

No-one has ever counted how many problems Henry created. And although he doesn't have a stamp, or a crater on the moon, or a computer program named after him, Henry published 9 books of puzzles which you can still buy today. One book alone has 536 curious problems and puzzles.

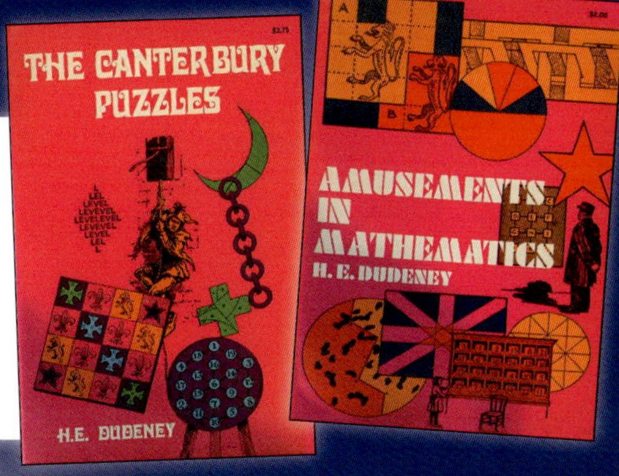

What can you do to solve maths problems like Henry?

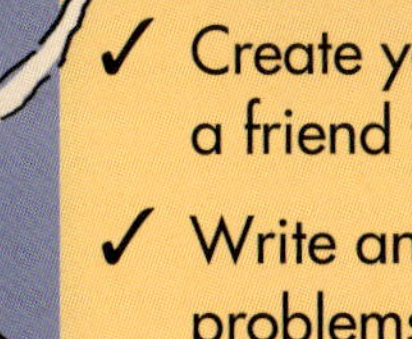

- ✓ Create your own problems for a friend to solve.
- ✓ Write and illustrate a book of problems and their solutions.
- ✓ Investigate a variety of brain-teasers.

Eliminate it

When you read a word problem, sometimes there is text that matters as well as text that doesn't matter. To help solve your problem, try to ignore this extra information or eliminate it from your problem.

Gran's money

Gran gave $45 to each of her 6 grandchildren.

Each grandchild is 1 year younger than the one before them.

How much did she give her grandchildren altogether?

In this story, the age of each grandchild doesn't matter. This is extra text. You can cross it out.

Gran gave $45 to each of her 6 grandchildren.

~~Each grandchild is 1 year younger than the one before them.~~

How much did she give her grandchildren altogether?

Cross out unnecessary information. It may distract your thinking.

This is now a simple 1-step multiplication problem.

6 × $45 = $270

Gran spent $270 on her grandchildren.

Look at the information in this next story.

The grandchildren

Gran has 6 grandchildren. Each grandchild is 1 year younger than the one before them.

For Christmas, she gave the oldest grandchild $60. She gave $10 less to the second oldest. She kept giving $10 less to the next child until she reached the youngest.

How much money did Gran give altogether?

In this story, the age of each grandchild does matter.

All the text is important. It all helps you work out your solution. There is no text to cross out.

This is a multi-step problem where you add six numbers.

$60 + $50 + $40 + $30 + $20 + $10 = $210

Gran spent a total of $210 on her grandchildren.

Harry's fish tanks

Harry has 2 fish tanks.
One tank is red and the other tank is blue.

He has 3 types of fish – mollies, goldfish and tetras.
The goldfish eat the most food.

Harry wants to catch the tetras to give them to his friend.

Which tank gives him a better chance of catching tetras?

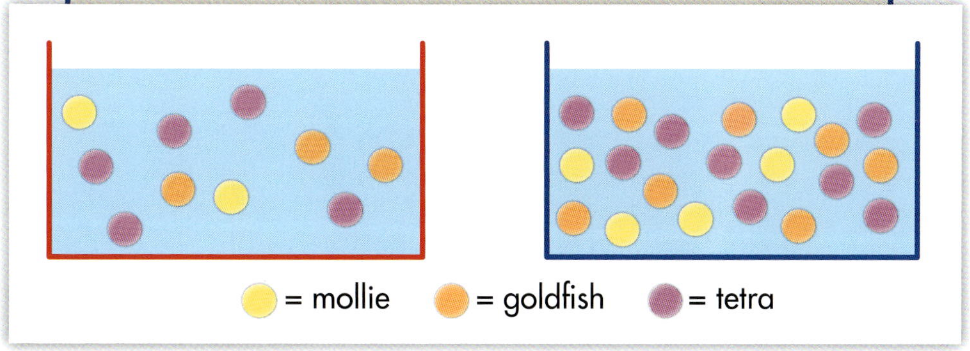

The race

Harry, Barry and Larry ran a race.
Harry is a year younger than Barry.
Larry has dark hair.
Barry came just ahead of Harry.
The person who came first has blond hair.
Larry is Harry's brother.

Who won the race?

Read it again

Understand it

Three boys run a race. The clues tell you who came first.

Select a strategy

There seems to be information that's not important. I'll try the **Eliminate it** strategy.

Work it out

- Age doesn't matter.
  ~~Harry is a year younger than Barry.~~
- Hair colour is mentioned twice. The fact that Larry has dark hair is probably important.
- The fact that they are brothers is not part of the problem.
  ~~Larry is Harry's brother.~~
- The problem now looks like this:
  Harry, Barry and Larry ran a race.
  Larry has dark hair.
  Barry came just ahead of Harry.
  The person who came first has blonde hair.
  Who won the race?

I can now use the **Make a model** strategy. I'll write their names on paper then rearrange them until all the clues match.

1	2	3
Barry	Harry	Larry

Check & reflect

Barry won the race. All the clues match. The information about Larry with dark hair was important.

Crossing out information that doesn't fit the facts is a useful strategy for solving a multiple choice problem. This problem usually shows 4 possible answers and only one answer is correct.

Banana boxes

I have 6 boxes.
Each box contains the same number of bananas.

Circle the total number of bananas.

A 85 **B** 90 **C** 95 **D** 100

Work it out

- The answer is a multiple of 6 as it doesn't say there are any bananas left over.
- 6 × 10 = 60 and 60 + 25 = 85 and 25 is not a multiple of 6 so 80 can't be a multiple of 6. Cross that answer out.
- 60 + 30 = 90 and 30 is a multiple of 6 so 90 is a multiple of 6.
- 95 is only 5 more so that's not a multiple of 6. I can cross 95 out.
- 100 is 10 more and that's not a multiple of 6 either. I can cross 100 out too.

Check & reflect

The only multiple of 6 is 90. There must be 90 bananas, even though it doesn't say how many bananas are in each box.

Remember to avoid distractions. This took up to 5 actions to solve. You need to keep the ball rolling!

Garden edges

Jill is worried she won't have enough edging to put around her new garden bed. She likes all 4 of her designs. Which one has the smallest perimeter?

Garden 1 Garden 2 Garden 3 Garden 4

Work it out

I need to count up the units of perimeter in each garden shape. Perimeter is the length around the outside edge. I think Garden 1 has the smallest perimeter but I need to check.

- Garden 1 has 20 units.
- Garden 2 has 20 units too.
- Garden 3 has only 18 units. I can cross off the first 2 as already this perimeter is smaller.
- Garden 4 has 20 units.

Check & reflect

My estimate wasn't correct. Garden 3 has the smallest perimeter. If Jill is worried about garden edges then this is the best design for her.

I wonder if this shape also has the smallest area?

- Garden 1 has an area of 13 square units.
- Garden 2 has an area of 11 square units, so it's not Garden 1.
- Garden 3 has an area of 12 square units, so it's not Garden 3.
- Garden 4 has an area of 16 square units.

It's not true that the shape with the smallest perimeter has the smallest area. Garden 2 has the smallest garden area.

Be patient and don't expect an instant answer.

Another way to **Eliminate it** is to check for hidden assumptions. Too often our brain jumps to conclusions that are not correct.

Tony's pocket

Tony has two coins in his pocket.
They add to 70c.
One of them is not a 20c piece.

What are they?

Most people are unable to solve this problem. The only way two coins can add to 70 cents is that one is a 50c coin and one is a 20c coin.

But the problem specifically says that one of the coins is NOT a 20c one.

Can you work it out?

Of course! Here are the two coins in Tony's pocket.

The 50c coin is not a 20c coin.

Tony has a 50c and a 20c coin in his pocket.

No-one said you couldn't do this.

You may be blocking your answer even though no-one told you to do this. Try asking a friend to help you solve it.

Some people think problems like this are a trick. But it is your brain playing the trick, not the actual question. Your brain jumps to the wrong conclusion.

Six oranges

There are 6 oranges in this bag.
How can you give 6 children an orange each and still have an orange left in the bag?

Again, most people find this impossible to solve. There are 6 oranges and 6 people so how can one orange be left in the bag?

Can you work it out?

Of course! Just give the last person their orange in the bag.

No-one said you couldn't do this.

Six coins

Move one coin so that both the row and column have the same number of coins.

Can you work it out?

Of course! Just put the extra coin on top of the coin in the centre of the row.

No-one said you couldn't do this.

You need to eliminate possible misunderstandings.

Another way we jump to the wrong conclusion is when we see numbers in a word problem. We sometimes have serious misconceptions about what numbers mean. This is one of the most famous examples.

The farmer

There are 125 sheep and 5 dogs in a flock. How old is the farmer?

Believe it or not, three out of four students think they can calculate the farmer's age using 125 and 5.

125 + 5 or **125 – 5** or **125 × 5** or **125 ÷ 5**

The farmer's age has absolutely nothing to do with how many sheep or dogs he owns. He could be many different ages. There is no known answer to this problem.

These number misconceptions can be found in a wide range of problems. We need to eliminate these misunderstandings before we can be a successful problem solver.

Eating ice-creams

2 children eat 2 ice-creams in 2 minutes.
How long will it take 5 children to eat 5 ice-creams?

The first thing most people think when they see this problem is that 1 child eats one ice-cream in 1 minute. So 5 children will eat 5 ice-creams in 5 minutes.

Do you agree this thinking is correct?

If 2 children take 2 minutes to eat 2 ice-creams, 1 child still takes 2 minutes. Five children will take 2 minutes to eat 5 ice-creams.

The number of children doesn't matter, they each take 2 minutes to eat 1 ice-cream.

- 50 children will take 2 minutes to eat 50 ice-creams.
- 1000 children will take 2 minutes to eat 1000 ice-creams.

Giraffe smells

A giraffe can smell something 250 m away.
How far away can 2 giraffes smell?
How far away can 1000 giraffes smell?

Emmy Noether

Who said algebra isn't fun?

Emmy Noether was one of the greatest female mathematicians in history. She became an expert in algebra and taught people to think in new ways about it. Imagine all the mathematical problems involved in this process.

Emmy was born in Germany in 1882 and died in America in 1935. Her dad was a famous mathematician at the local University. He taught her to love mathematics and her favourite problems were always about algebra.

As a young girl Emmy was a very good dancer, was quick to learn French and English and was quick to solve brain-teasers. All her life she loved working out puzzles and riddles.

After getting her university degree, Emmy wanted to teach at University like her dad but most men at that time did not like the idea of female professors. Eventually she became a famous University teacher but she was quite eccentric. She talked very loudly and quickly as her mind was full of ideas about algebra and symmetry. She was devoted to mathematics.

SPOTLIGHT on a famous Problem Solver

Emmy created *Noether's Theorem* which transformed the way we think about the universe. She wrote lots of important papers about algebra and mathematical rings. She also liked elimination theory where you remove unwanted information from an equation.

Asteroid Noether and crater 7001 Noether on the far side of the moon are both named after Emmy.

In 1982, 100 years after she was born, the Emmy Noether school in her home town was opened.

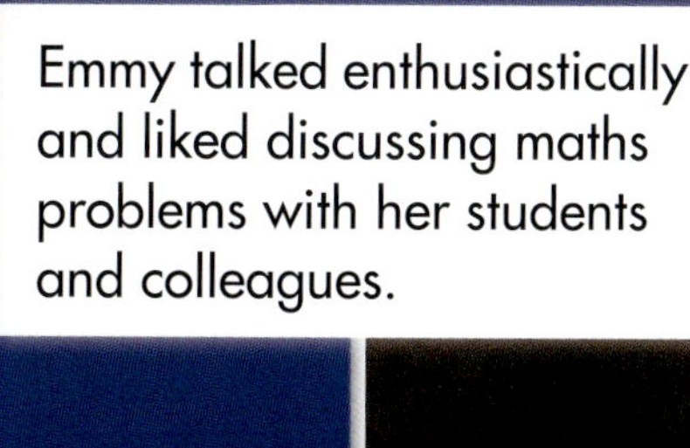

Emmy talked enthusiastically and liked discussing maths problems with her students and colleagues.

- ✓ Enjoy solving brain-teasers.
- ✓ See algebra as an important part of mathematics.
- ✓ Enjoy talking and writing about parts of maths that inspire you.

TYPES OF PROBLEMS

1 step

One-step problems are the simplest problems. There is only one action before your problem is solved. And many aren't really problems but procedures.

Termites

17% of the mass of all land animals is termites. What percentage is **not termites**?

The total mass is 100%.
You know 100 – 17 = 83.
So 83% of all land animals are **not termites**.

Russia

Russia is twice the size of Brazil.

If the area of Brazil is 8.5 million square kilometres, what size is Russia?

Russia = 2 × 8.5
Russia has an area of 17 million square kilometres.

Budgies

The average mass of a budgerigar is 35 g. The total mass of Olivia's budgies is 200 g. How many budgies might Olivia have?

200 ÷ 35 = 5.7
Olivia probably has 6 budgies.

You know exactly what maths to do in a 1-step problem.

2 steps

Two-step problems need two actions before you can solve them. You need twice as much patience.

What am I?

3 x [girl] = 18  [girl] + [boy] = 15  [boy] = ?

- Your 1st action is to work out what  represents.

   = 18 so  = 18 ÷ 3 = 6

- Your 2nd action is to work out what  represents.

6 +  = 15 so  = 15 − 6 = 9

 = 6 and  = 9

Lily's teapot

Lily's teapot holds $3\frac{1}{2}$ cups of tea.
If she fills it 4 times, how many people can each have 2 cups of tea?

- Your 1st action is to find 4 groups of $3\frac{1}{2}$.
  Add this mentally: **$3\frac{1}{2}$**, **7**, **$10\frac{1}{2}$**, **14**.
  That's **14** cups of tea.
- Your 2nd action is to find how many groups of 2 in 14 cups? That's **7**.

So 7 people can have 2 cups of tea each.

Bacteria

There are 50 million bacteria in 1 cubic centimetre of soil.
How many bacteria in 1 cubic metre of soil?

- Your 1st action is to work out how many cubic centimetres in a cubic metre.
  100 × 100 × 100
  = 1 million
- Your 2nd action is to multiply.
  1 million × 50 million
  = 50 trillion

There are 50 000 000 000 000 bacteria in one cubic metre of soil.

More than 2 steps

Most problems you meet in mathematics will need more than two actions to solve them. You have to stay patient, focused and calm. These are REAL problems. You don't know the answer straight away.

Some problems look quite simple – like this next one. They use facts you should already know but you need to do quite a bit of logical thinking. Remember to keep going. Don't give up.

Times

How many minutes in 40% of an hour?

- Step 1: 1 hour is 60 minutes.
- Step 2: 10% = 60 ÷ 10 = 6
- Step 3: 40% = 4 × 6 = 24

So 40% of an hour is 24 minutes.

Carpet area

Kevin has a customer who wants him to carpet a shop floor.

She gave him this diagram. What is the total area?

Scale ⊢⊣ = 5 m
10 m
25 m
20 m
5 m
10 m

You can break this shape up into 3 areas. Even though some measurements are missing you can work it out from the scale.

Scale ⊢⊣ = 5 m
10 m
25 m
20 m
5 m
10 m

- Step 1: 25 × 10 = 250
- Step 2: 10 × 20 = 200
- Step 3: 5 × 10 = 50
- Step 4: 250 + 200 + 50 = 500

The total carpet area is 500 square metres.

Solve a simpler problem was a faster strategy to use here.

Another way to solve this is to see that each square on this grid is 5 × 5 or 25 m^2. There are 20 squares like this.

- The total area is 20 × 25 which is the same as 10 × 50 or 500 m^2.
- That's only 2 steps.

Multiple choice

A multiple choice problem is one where you select the best answer from 2 or more possible solutions. Read each solution and consider if it fits the problem. **Eliminate it** is a great strategy to use with this sort of problem. As soon as you find a solution that doesn't work, cross it out.

Measurements

Fran puts 3 apples on this scale.
The scale measures in kilograms.
About how heavy is one apple?

A 20 g **B** 200 g **C** 400 g **D** 600 kg

What measurement does the scale show?
You can't begin to work out the correct answer before you know this.

- The scale reads 0.582.
  What unit does this represent? Kilograms.
  And 0.582 kg is almost 600 g.

Look at your 4 choices.

- Can you see an answer you think fits straight away? Answer D says 600 kg. Is this what you want?

Go back and read the question.

- You want one apple, not three.
  You need 600 g ÷ 3 not 600 kg ÷ 3.
- It looks like Answer B is correct. Each apple has a mass of about 200 g.

Check the other solutions.

- Is 20 g a reasonable solution?
  No: it is way too small. Cross it out.
- Is 400 g a reasonable answer? No: that's the approximate mass of 2 apples. Cross it out.
- Is 600 kg a reasonable solution? No: that's way too big. Cross it out. It was put in to try and trick you as you know the scale is measured in kilograms.

Multiple-choice questions are often used in standardised tests, market research and even when you vote for a politician. They are easy for teachers or a computer to mark but in real-life you don't meet many problems like this.

Open ended

Open-ended problems have more than one solution.
As long as you can find at least one solution that works then you are "correct".

How much juice?

Three containers together contain 2000 mL of juice.
How much juice is in each container?

There are so many possible answers.
Which ones should you discover?
As long as the sum of your 3 numbers is 2000 then your solution is a correct one.
No one solution is better than another.

How many solutions should you find? In an open problem try to find at least 2 different answers.

788 + 565 + 677 = 2000
or
555 + 89 + 1356 = 2000

If you like trying, perhaps you could list even more solutions. If you had nothing better to do you could spend all day and night thinking about it. You could even list all possible combinations of 3 numbers that add to 2000. Phew!

Believe it or not, this is how some crazy mathematicians spend their days and nights!

In 2016 Michiel Jansen and Jens Kruse Andersen calculated the largest gap between 2 prime numbers. The difference was 3 311 852.

Explain this!

Give 3 different explanations for this picture.

This is an open problem so any solution that fits is acceptable.

- A hole in the ground
- An umbrella from above
- A ball at the beach

What do you think this picture represents?

Puzzles

Puzzles are just for fun. Read them in a light-hearted way.
They often contain silly information so don't take them seriously.

Pancakes

Sally and Lucy cook 4 pancakes. They put them in 2 rows and 2 columns.

They hide a digit card 1–4 under each pancake.

Column 1 adds to more than twice Column 2.
Row 2 digits are both odd.
The diagonals have the same sum.

Which digit is under each pancake?

Break it into smaller parts is a useful strategy here.

Column 1 must have 4 and 3.
Column 2 must have 1 and 2.

3	2
4	1

Row 2 digits must have 3 and 1 (as they are both odd).
Row 1 must have 4 and 2 (as they are both even).

Check by adding the diagonals.

Yes: they both add to 5.

Grid puzzles

Grids show you an effective way to use puzzle clues. Clues are puzzle facts. When you know one fact, you actually know much more. The grid reminds you about this.

Think like a detective.

If 2 people have a different name and one of them is called May, the other person is NOT May. It sounds crazy but this can be very helpful, especially to a good detective.

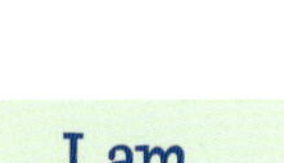

May	Tom
✓	✗

If 2 people are doing 2 different jobs and one person is a Nurse, then the other person is NOT a Nurse.

Teacher	Nurse
✗	✓

This strategy helps you sort information.

Favourite films

Jack and Jill like movies.
Jack hates horror films.
Can you match the person to their favourite films?

	Jack	Jill
Horror films	✗	
Comedy		

In a puzzle, don't worry about what happens in real life where both people might hate horror films.

Fill in just one fact in the grid and 4 facts are revealed.

	Jack	Jill
Horror films	✗	✓
Comedy	✓	✗

Jack likes comedy but Jill doesn't.
Jill likes horror films but Jack doesn't.

Solve even more complex puzzles by adding a third column and row to a grid.

Boris, Bev and Betty go to the park. Boris rides his skateboard. Betty doesn't ride a bike.

Can you match each person to their transport?

You are told 2 facts.

	Bike	Skateboard	Walk
Boris		✓	
Bev			
Betty	✗		

But when you put this information in the grid you actually know much more. Boris rides his skateboard, but NOT the bike and NOT walk. So put a ✗ in those two columns.

	Bike	Skateboard	Walk
Boris	✗	✓	✗
Bev			
Betty	✗		

If you look in the Bike column, you see that Bev must ride the bike, as that space is empty. So put a ✓ there. But now you know Bev doesn't use the skateboard or walk either, so you can put a ✗ in those columns.

	Bike	Skateboard	Walk
Boris	✗	✓	✗
Bev	✓	✗	✗
Betty	✗		

Betty must walk as the space in that column is empty. Put a ✓ there and a ✗ in the empty space in the Skateboard column.

	Bike	Skateboard	Walk
Boris	✗	✓	✗
Bev	✓	✗	✗
Betty	✗	✗	✓

So Boris rode his skateboard to the park, Bev rode her bike and Betty walked.

From just 2 facts we actually worked out 9 facts by using a grid.

Use the positive and negative information to solve your puzzle. If you know a ✓ fact, you then know some ✗ facts too.

The beach trip

Try this

Harry goes to the beach with his sister, mum and gran. Mum takes his little sister Jackie in a stroller. Gran's name is not Jenny.

Can you match everyone to their right name?

	Sister	Mum	Gran
Jenny			
Judy			
Jackie			

Challenge

Charlie owns 3 dogs called Bella, Jax and Daisy.
Can you match each dog to its colour and favourite activity?
The white dog loves to dig holes. Jax loves to run. Daisy is brown.

	Brown	White	Spots	Run	Catch balls	Dig holes
Bella						
Jax						
Daisy						
Run						
Catch balls						
Dig holes						

Sudokus

Sudokus are a popular grid puzzle with puzzlers all over the world. In a Sudoku puzzle, you place the digits 1 – 9 on a 9 × 9 grid. You don't add or subtract them, but write them down according to these rules:

- Every row contains the digits 1 – 9.
- Every column contains the digits 1 – 9.
- Each small 3 × 3 block contains the digits 1 – 9.

Sudokus with a 9 × 9 grid have 81 numbers to think about. You need plenty of patience and definitely no distractions. To get you started, some digits are already filled in for you.

- A famous Swiss mathematician, Leonhard Euler, invented this number puzzle in 1782.
- Centuries later Howard Garns published one in New York in 1979.
- They became a craze in Japan In 1984.
- Wayne Gould created a computer program to mass produce Sudokus in 2003.
- There are **6 670 903 752 021 072 936 960** different ways to fill in a Sudoku grid.

In 2008, a $1 million Australian trial had to be abandoned when 5 out of 12 jurors were secretly solving Sudoku puzzles rather than listening to evidence.

Smaller Sudokus are fun to solve too.

Place the digits 1 – 4 on this 2 × 2 grid according to these rules:

- Every row contains the digits 1 – 4.
- Every column contains the digits 1 – 4.
- Each small 2 × 2 block contains the digits 1 – 4.

2			
		1	2
			4
3			

2			
4	3	1	2
			4
3			

Row 2 is missing 3 and 4. They belong in those 2 empty spaces. If you look at Column 1, it already has a 3, so the 3 in Row 2 must be in the 2nd space and the 4 must go in the 1st space.

Column 1 is missing a number. It must be 1.

2			
4	3	1	2
1			4
3			

2			
4	3	1	2
1	2	3	4
3			

Row 3 is missing 2 and 3. Column 2 already has a 3, so it must go in the 3rd space and 2 in the 2nd space.

Column 2 is missing 1 and 4. It's easy to see where they go. The 2 × 2 block at the top left is missing 1. And the 2 × 2 block at the bottom left is missing 4.

2	1		
4	3	1	2
1	2	3	4
3	4		

2	1		
4	3	1	2
1	2	3	4
3	4	2	1

The bottom row is missing 2 and 1. Column 3 already has 1 so it must go in the 4th space and 2 in the 3rd space.

You've almost finished this puzzle. The top row is missing 3 and 4. Can you work out where they go?

2	1	4	3
4	3	1	2
1	2	3	4
3	4	2	1

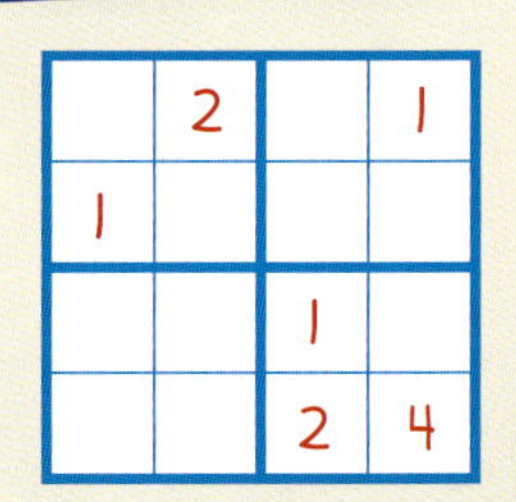

	2		1
1			
		1	
		2	4

- Make your eyes track along a row to look for the digits 1 – 4.
- Make your eyes track up and down a column to look for the digits 1 – 4.
- Make your eyes track around and around in the smaller blocks to look for the digits 1 – 4.

Letter number puzzles

Henry Dudeney invented these addition puzzles. Alphabet letters replace digits. And each letter represents one digit from 0 – 9. But which one?

In this puzzle there are 7 letters, F I M N S U W, that represent 7 digits. Three digits from 0 – 9 are NOT used. **Guess and check** is a useful starting strategy.

```
   S U N
 + F U N
 -------
 S W I M
```

Looking at the place value, S is probably 1. And as there is a trade to the 1000s, F is probably 9. Let's guess that **S = 1** and **F = 9**. Let's also guess that **N = 4**. If this is true then **M** must be **8**.

```
   1 U 4
 + 9 U 4
 -------
 1 W I 8
```

So far, so good. U can't be 1 as that is already taken, and it can't be 2 as that makes 4 and we are guessing **N = 4**. What if **U = 3**? So now it looks like this:

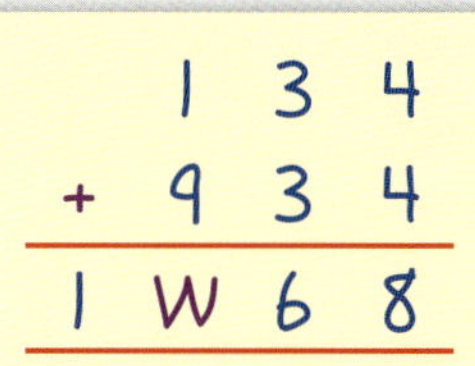

Try this

And if we make **W = 0** then it is all correct:

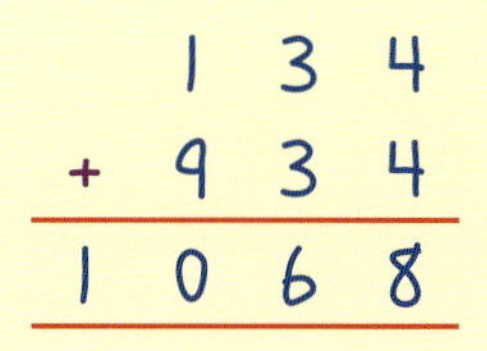

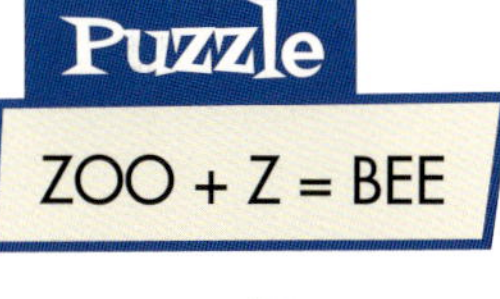

That was a lucky guess. I wonder if there are other possibllities?

I will leave it up to you to guess and check with another combination. The good news is that there are plenty of other possible solutions. See page 161 for 6 more examples.

Challenge

Chloe used the digits 0 – 9 to solve this puzzle. Each alphabet letter represents a different digit. Her clues are E = 5, A = 1 and S = 2. Can you discover the rest?

Types of problems - summary

Let's look at how the word story changes according to the type of problem you want to solve.

1 step

A return airfare to Bali costs $938. How many tickets does Claire buy if she spends $6566?

Multiple choice

A return airfare to Bali costs $938. Estimate the total cost if Claire buys 4 tickets.

A 2000 **B** $3000 **C** $4000 **D** $5000

2 steps

A return airfare to Bali costs $938. Claire's holiday budget is $5000. If she buys 2 tickets, how much is left for other holiday expenses?

Open ended

A return airfare to Bali costs $938. A child's airfare costs $440. How many tickets does Claire buy if she spends less than $5000 on return tickets?

Puzzle

A return airfare to Bali costs $938. Claire buys more tickets than Ness. Ness buys 2 fewer tickets than Bev. Together they spend $5628. How many tickets do they each buy?

More than 2 steps

A return airfare to Bali costs $938. A child's airfare costs $440. How much does Claire pay for 4 adult and 3 child tickets?

Challenge

Use this ferry timetable to create your own set of maths problems based on the 6 different types.

	Circular Quay	Darling Harbour	Cockatoo Island	Drum-moyne	Huntleys Point	Chiswick	Abbots-ford
Time	12:07	12:20	12:28	12:33	12:38	12:41	12:45

USEFUL MATHS FACTS

100s Chart

1	2	3	4	5	6	7	8	9	10
11	12	13	14	15	16	17	18	19	20
21	22	23	24	25	26	27	28	29	30
31	32	33	34	35	36	37	38	39	40
41	42	43	44	45	46	47	48	49	50
51	52	53	54	55	56	57	58	59	60
61	62	63	64	65	66	67	68	69	70
71	72	73	74	75	76	77	78	79	80
81	82	83	84	85	86	87	88	89	90
91	92	93	94	95	96	97	98	99	100

Place Value Chart

This shows the population of Australia in July 2016.

10 000 000	1 000 000	100 000	10 000s	1000s	100s	10s	1s
Ten Millions	M	HT	TT	Th	H	T	O
☺☺	☺☺☺☺	☺☺☺		☺☺☺☺☺☺☺☺☺	☺☺☺	☺☺☺	
2	4	3	0	9	3	3	0

Roman Numerals

The ancient Romans used these symbols to record their numbers.

1	5	10	50	100	500	1000
I	V	X	L	C	D	M

They placed a small bar over the letter to record numbers 1000 × larger.

5000	10000	50000	100000	500000	1000000
$\overline{V}$	$\overline{X}$	$\overline{L}$	$\overline{C}$	$\overline{D}$	$\overline{M}$

Place value beyond 1000000

Number name	Number	Multiples of 10	Powers of 10
million	1000000	10 × 10 × 10 × 10 × 10 × 10	10^6
billion	1000000000 (1000 million)	10 × 10 × 10 × 10 × 10 × 10 × 10 × 10 × 10	10^9
trillion	1000000000000 (1 million million)	10 × 10 × 10 × 10 × 10 × 10 × 10 × 10 × 10 × 10 × 10 × 10	10^{12}
quadrillion	1000000000000000 (1 billion million)	10 × 10 × 10 × 10 × 10 × 10 × 10 × 10 × 10 × 10 × 10 × 10 × 10 × 10 × 10	10^{15}

Addition & Subtraction

+/-	0	1	2	3	4	5	6	7	8	9	10
0	0	1	2	3	4	5	6	7	8	9	10
1	1	2	3	4	5	6	7	8	9	10	11
2	2	3	4	5	6	7	8	9	10	11	12
3	3	4	5	6	7	8	9	10	11	12	13
4	4	5	6	7	8	9	10	11	12	13	14
5	5	6	7	8	9	10	11	12	13	14	15
6	6	7	8	9	10	11	12	13	14	15	16
7	7	8	9	10	11	12	13	14	15	16	17
8	8	9	10	11	12	13	14	15	16	17	18
9	9	10	11	12	13	14	15	16	17	18	19
10	10	11	12	13	14	15	16	17	18	19	20

doubles (highlighted: the diagonal 0, 2, 4, 6, 8, 10, 12, 14, 16, 18, 20)

+/-	0	10	20	30	40	50	60	70	80	90	100
0	0	10	20	30	40	50	60	70	80	90	100
10	10	20	30	40	50	60	70	80	90	100	110
20	20	30	40	50	60	70	80	90	100	110	120
30	30	40	50	60	70	80	90	100	110	120	130
40	40	50	60	70	80	90	100	110	120	130	140
50	50	60	70	80	90	100	110	120	130	140	150
60	60	70	80	90	100	110	120	130	140	150	160
70	70	80	90	100	110	120	130	140	150	160	170
80	80	90	100	110	120	130	140	150	160	170	180
90	90	100	110	120	130	140	150	160	170	180	190
100	100	110	120	130	140	150	160	170	180	190	200

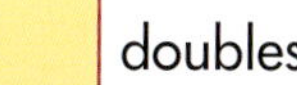

doubles

+/-	0	100	200	300	400	500	600	700	800	900	1000
0	0	100	200	300	400	500	600	700	800	9000	1000
100	100	200	300	400	500	600	700	800	900	1000	1100
200	200	300	400	500	600	700	800	900	1000	1100	1200
300	300	400	500	600	700	800	900	1000	1100	1200	1300
400	400	500	600	700	800	900	1000	1100	1200	1300	1400
500	500	600	700	800	900	1000	1100	1200	1300	1400	1500
600	600	700	800	900	1000	1100	1200	1300	1400	1500	1600
700	700	800	900	1000	1100	1200	1300	1400	1500	1600	1700
800	800	900	1000	1100	1200	1300	1400	1500	1600	1700	1800
900	900	1000	1100	1200	1300	1400	1500	1600	1700	1800	1900
1000	1000	1100	1200	1300	1400	1500	1600	1700	1800	1900	2000

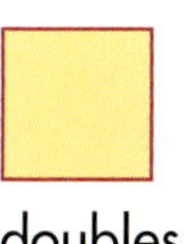

doubles

Multiplication and Division Grids

×/÷	0	1	2	3	4	5	6	7	8	9	10
0	0	0	0	0	0	0	0	0	0	0	0
1	0	1	2	3	4	5	6	7	8	9	10
2	0	2	4	6	8	10	12	14	16	18	20
3	0	3	6	9	12	15	18	21	24	27	30
4	0	4	8	12	16	20	24	28	32	36	40
5	0	5	10	15	20	25	30	35	40	45	50
6	0	6	12	18	24	30	36	42	48	54	60
7	0	7	14	21	28	35	42	49	56	63	70
8	0	8	16	24	32	40	48	56	64	72	80
9	0	9	18	27	36	45	54	63	72	81	90
10	0	10	20	30	40	50	60	70	80	90	100

×/÷	0	10	20	30	40	50	60	70	80	90	100
0	0	0	0	0	0	0	0	0	0	0	0
1	0	10	20	30	40	50	60	70	80	90	100
2	0	20	40	60	80	100	120	140	160	180	200
3	0	30	60	90	120	150	180	210	240	270	300
4	0	40	80	120	160	200	240	280	320	360	400
5	0	50	100	150	200	250	300	350	400	450	500
6	0	60	120	180	240	300	360	420	480	540	600
7	0	70	140	210	280	350	420	490	560	630	700
8	0	80	160	240	320	400	480	560	640	720	800
9	0	90	180	270	360	450	540	630	720	810	900
10	0	100	20	300	400	500	600	700	800	900	1000

×/÷	0	10	20	30	40	50	60	70	80	90	100
0	0	0	0	0	0	0	0	0	0	0	0
10	0	100	200	300	400	500	600	700	800	900	1000
20	0	200	400	600	800	1000	1200	1400	1600	1800	2000
30	0	300	600	900	1200	1500	1800	2100	2400	2700	3000
40	0	400	800	1200	1600	2000	2400	2800	3200	3600	4000
50	0	500	1000	1500	2000	2500	3000	3500	4000	4500	5000
60	0	600	1200	1800	2400	3000	3600	4200	4800	5400	6000
70	0	700	1400	2100	2800	3500	4200	4900	5600	6300	7000
80	0	800	1600	2400	3200	4000	4800	5600	6400	7200	8000
90	0	900	1800	2700	3600	4500	5400	6300	7200	8100	9000
100	0	1000	2000	3000	4000	5000	6000	7000	8000	9000	10000

Fractions of a Circle and a Rectangle

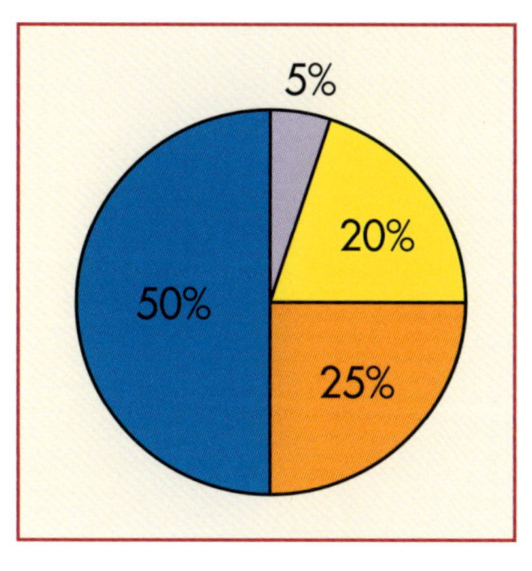

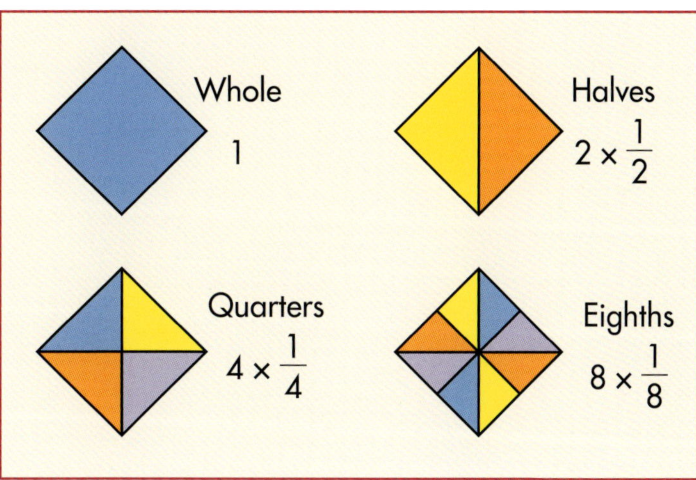

Decimal Place Value Chart

The length of the Darling River is **1472.05** km.

1000s	100s	10s	1s	•	$\frac{1}{10}$	$\frac{1}{100}$
1	4	7	2	•	0	5

Percentages

This table shows multiples of 10% with their equivalent fraction and decimal.

Percentages	Fractions	Decimals
100%	$\frac{100}{100}$	1.0
90%	$\frac{90}{100}$ $\frac{9}{10}$	0.9
80%	$\frac{80}{100}$ $\frac{8}{10}$ $\frac{4}{5}$	0.8
70%	$\frac{70}{100}$ $\frac{7}{10}$	0.7
60%	$\frac{60}{100}$ $\frac{6}{10}$ $\frac{3}{5}$	0.6
50%	$\frac{50}{100}$ $\frac{5}{10}$ $\frac{2}{4}$ $\frac{1}{2}$	0.5
40%	$\frac{40}{100}$ $\frac{4}{10}$ $\frac{2}{5}$	0.4
30%	$\frac{30}{100}$ $\frac{3}{10}$	0.3
20%	$\frac{20}{100}$ $\frac{2}{10}$ $\frac{1}{5}$	0.2
10%	$\frac{10}{100}$ $\frac{1}{10}$	0.1

Other common percentages:

Percentages	Fractions	Decimals
100%	$\frac{100}{100}$	1.0
75%	$\frac{75}{100}$ $\frac{3}{4}$	0.75
25%	$\frac{25}{100}$ $\frac{1}{4}$	0.25

Vertical Column Graph

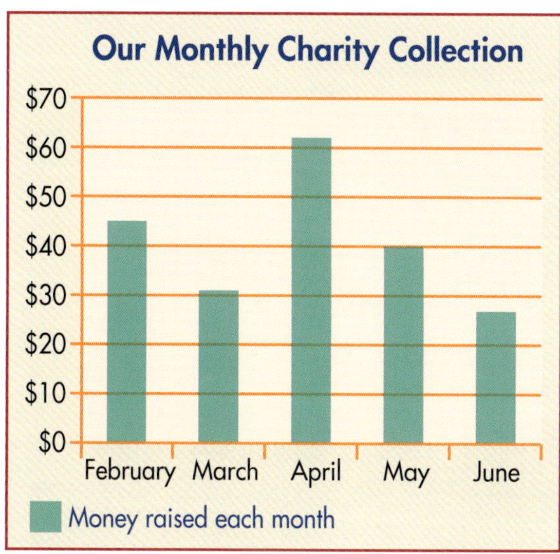

Horizontal Column Graph

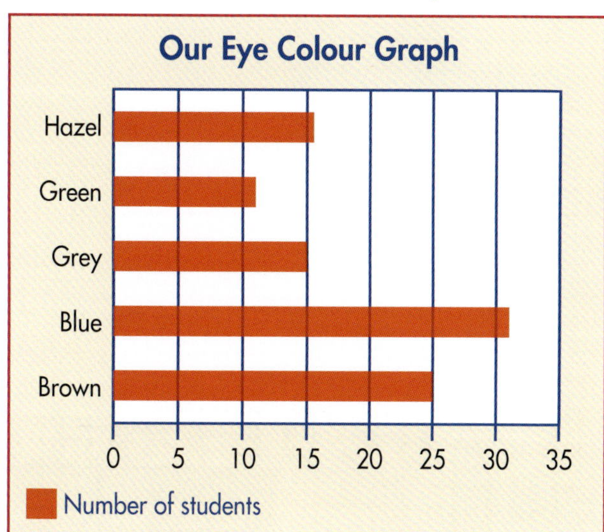

Picture Graph

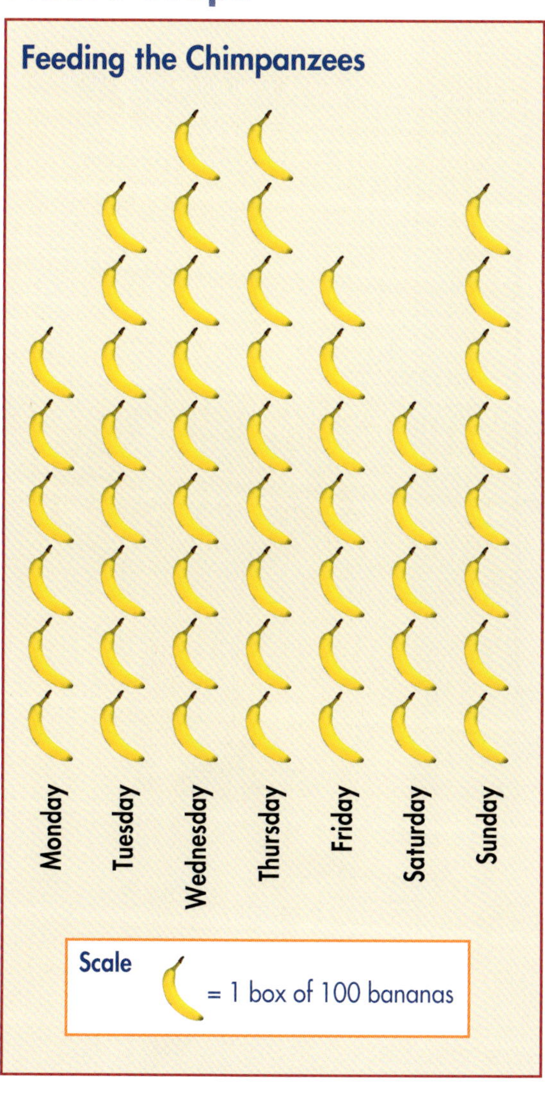

Line Graph

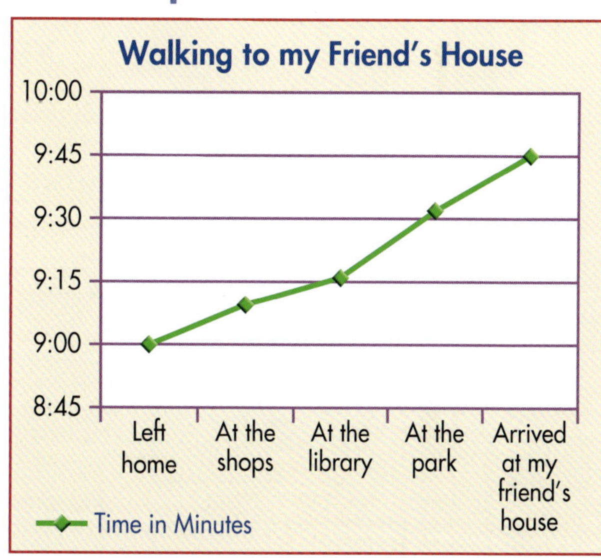

Pie Graph

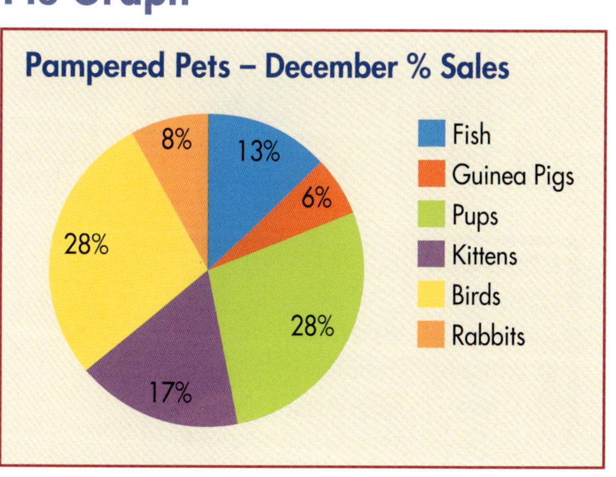

Scale Maps

Sometimes you need more details than a sketch map. You need all the street names, approximate distances and which direction to turn.

An accurate map can help you measure distances. When you use a grid overlay, a **scale** is used to help you know the size of everything.

Scale: 1 cm on the grid might represent 10 metres in real life.

A map **legend** tells you what the symbols on your map mean.

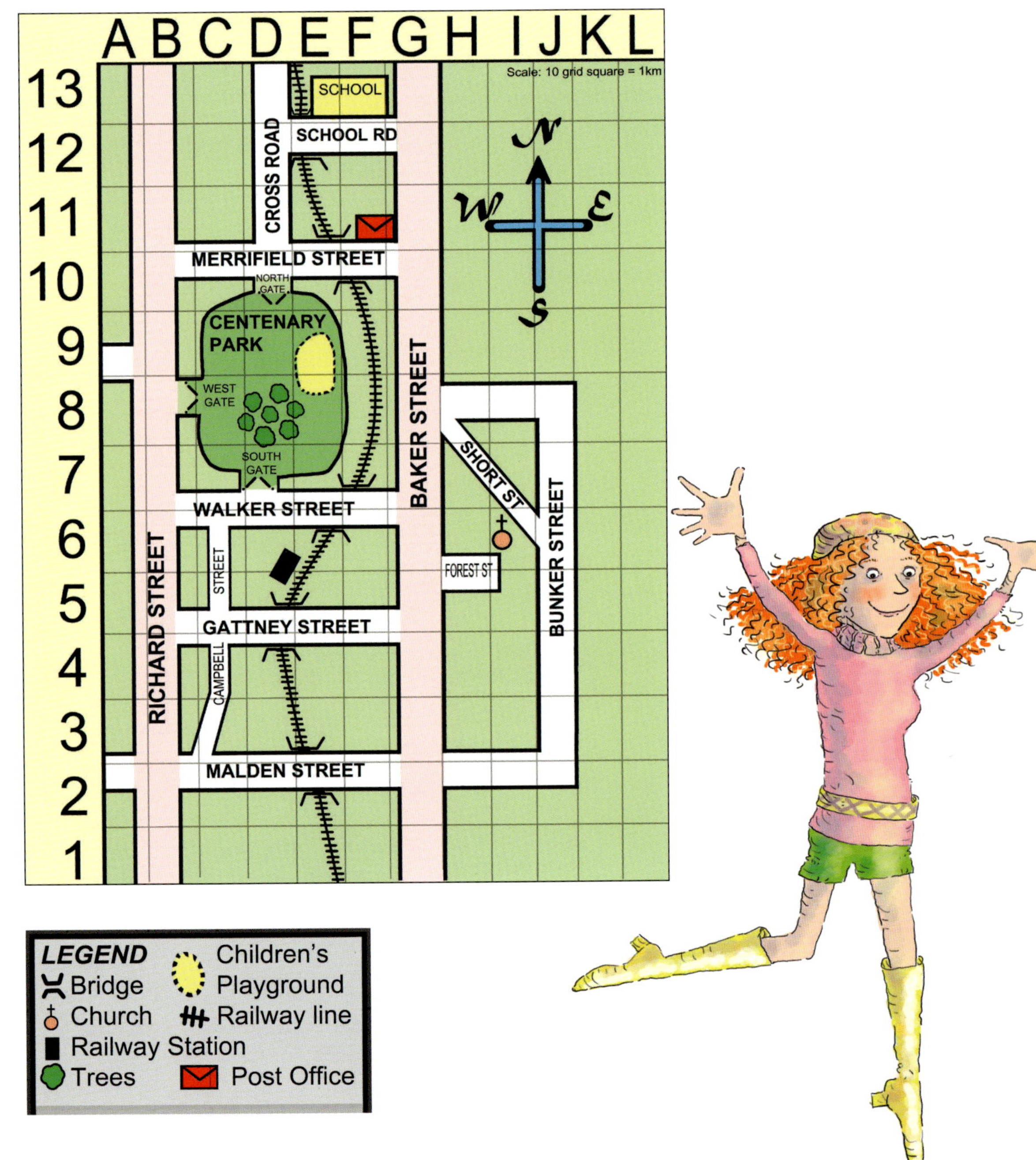

Polygon Overview

Number of sides	Real life example	Name of shape	Irregular	Regular
3		**triangle**	scalene isosceles right-angled	equilateral
4		**quadrilateral**	trapezium parallelogram oblong rhombus	square
5		**pentagon**	irregular pentagon	regular pentagon
6		**hexagon**	irregular hexagon	regular hexagon
7		**septagon**	irregular septagon	regular septagon
8		**octagon**	irregular octagon	regular octagon
9		**nonagon**	irregular nonagon	regular nonagon
10		**decagon**	irregular decagon	regular decagon

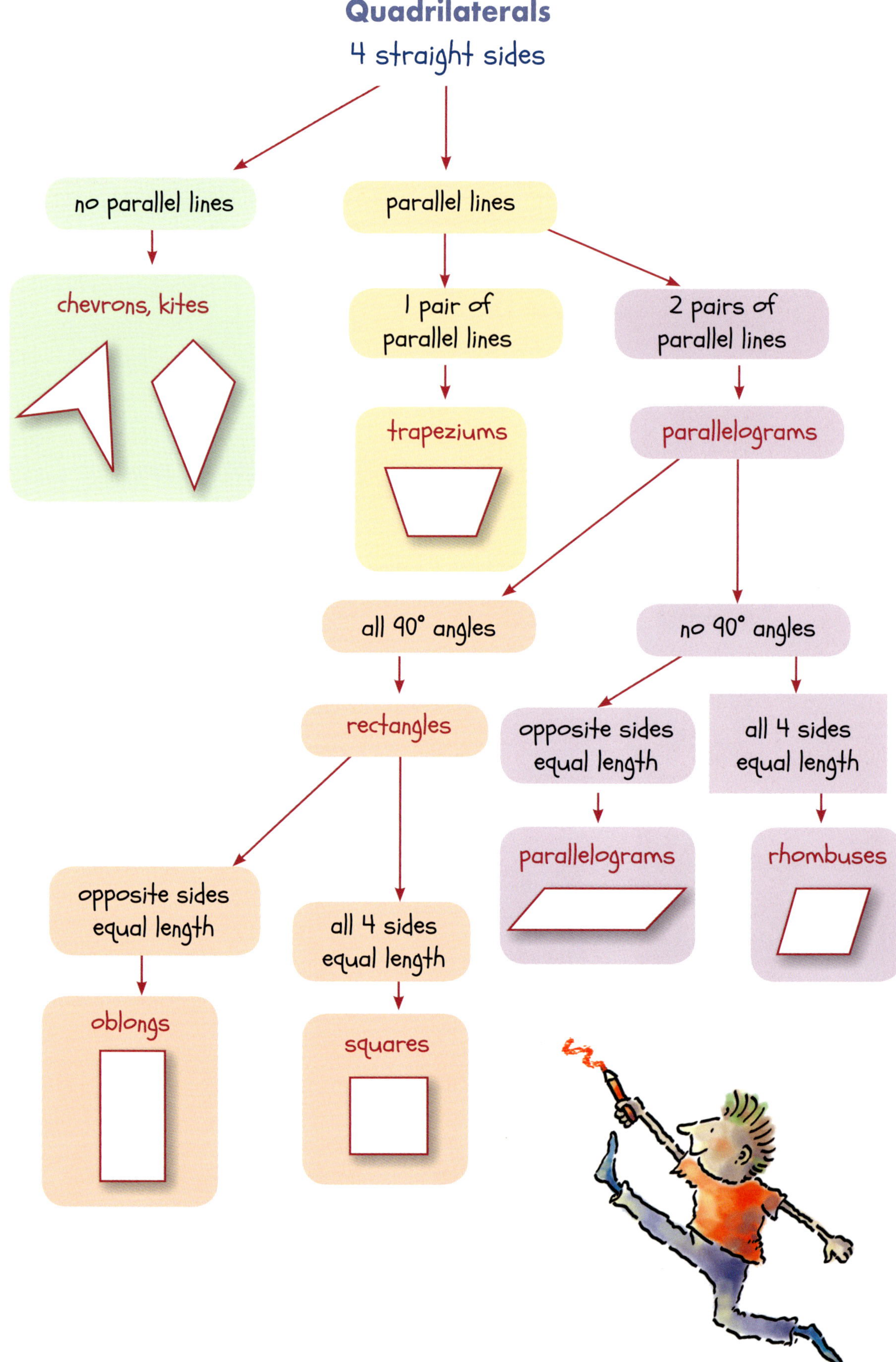
Quadrilaterals
4 straight sides
no parallel lines
parallel lines
chevrons, kites
1 pair of parallel lines
2 pairs of parallel lines
trapeziums
parallelograms
all 90° angles
no 90° angles
rectangles
opposite sides equal length
all 4 sides equal length
parallelograms
rhombuses
opposite sides equal length
all 4 sides equal length
oblongs
squares

Flips

A flip creates a mirror image or **reflection** of the original shape or design. A flip can be in any direction.

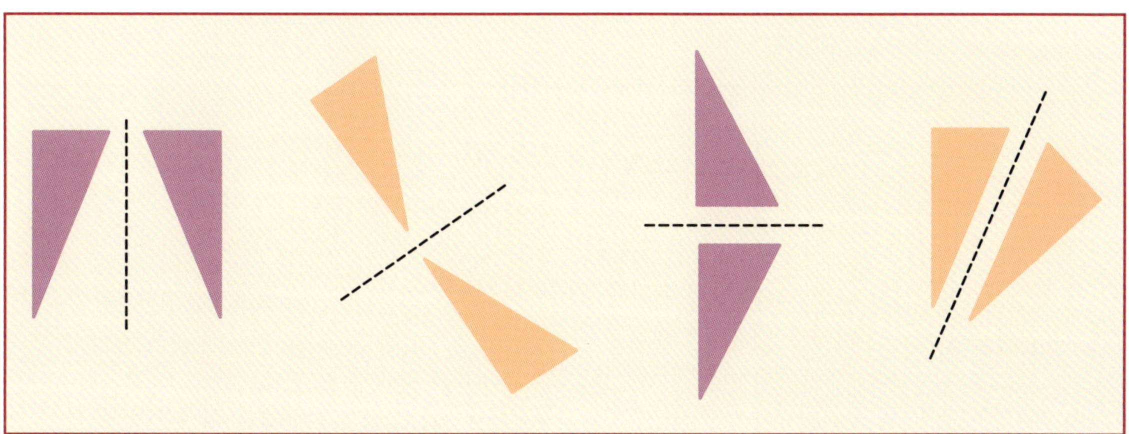

The second shape is now facing in the opposite direction to the first shape. You have created a new shape or part of a pattern. Your pattern is now **symmetrical**.

Translations or Slides

To make a slide pattern, keep taking an exact copy of your first shape or design and slide it without flipping it or turning it. This is called a **translation**. You have created a new shape or part of a pattern.

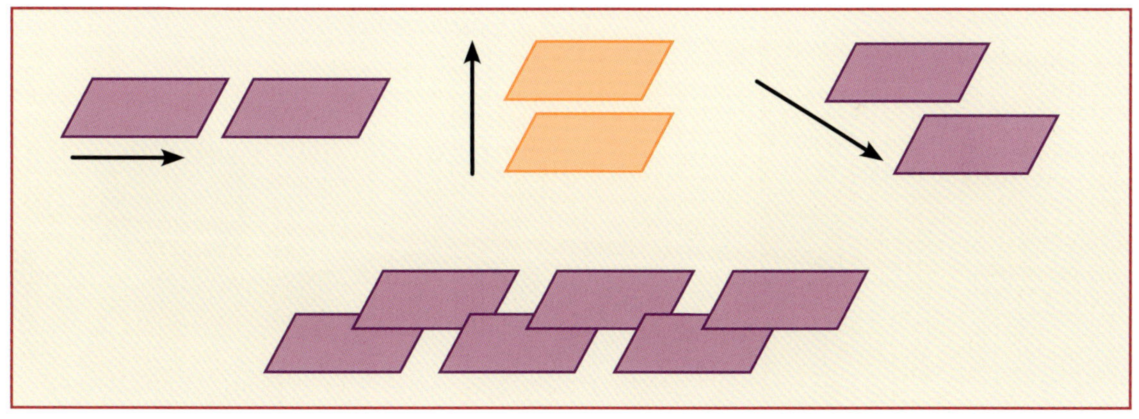

Rotations or Turns

Imagine you are standing in the middle of a circle. You can spin your body **clockwise** or **anti-clockwise**. You can turn a quarter of the way around, halfway around, three-quarters of the way around or all the way around. Angles measure how far you turn.

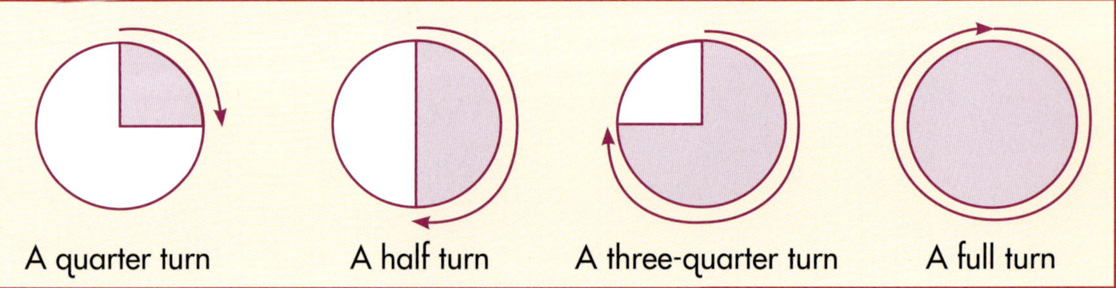

To make a rotation pattern, turn shapes or designs around a point and copy them in the new position.

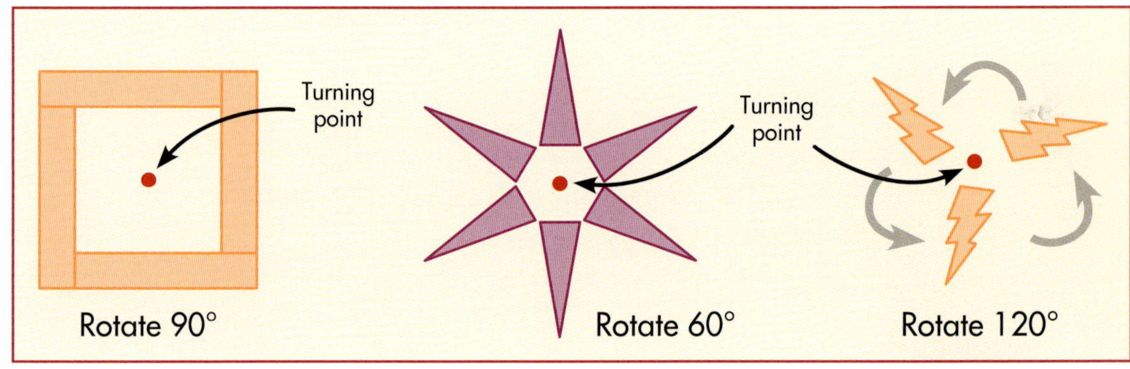

A 180° Protractor

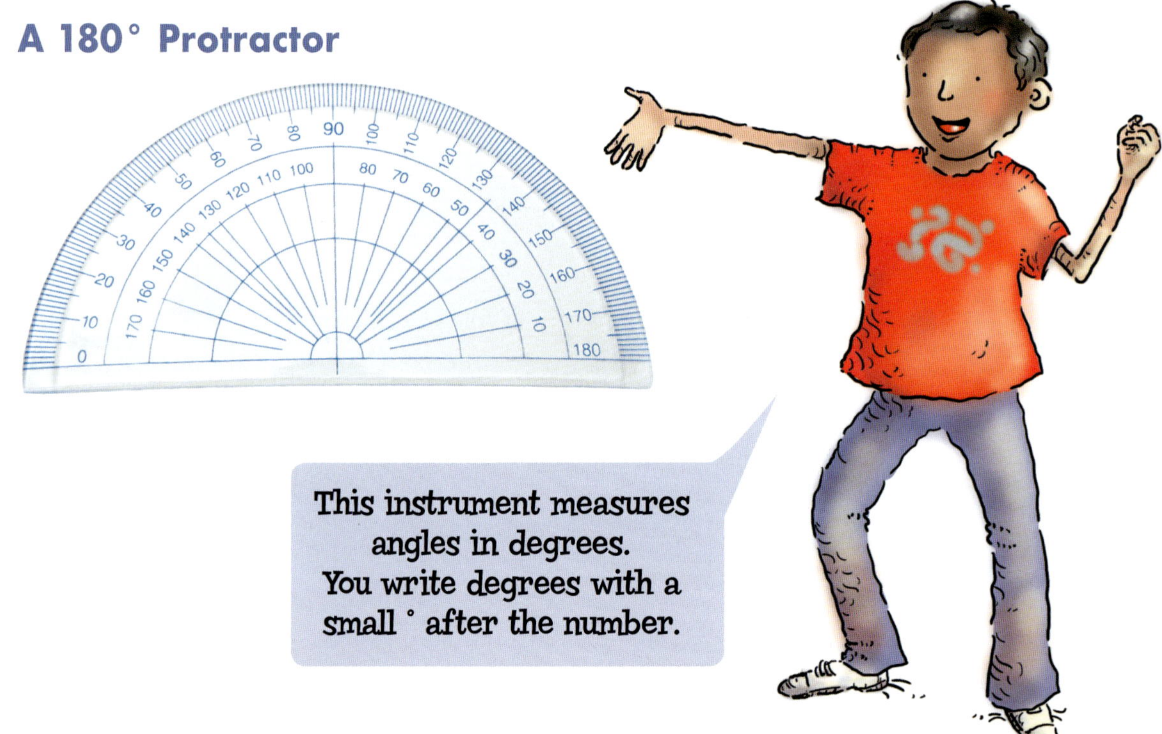

Types of Angles

Name of angle	Description	Example*	Real-life example
Acute (less than a quarter turn)	More than 0°, less than 90°	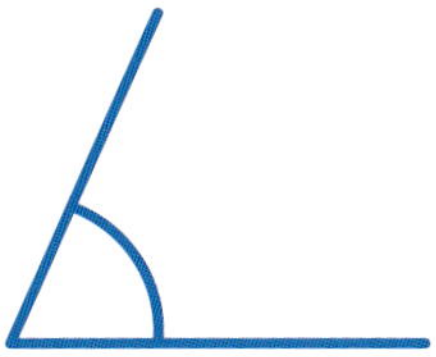	
Right (quarter turn)	Exactly 90° (draw a small square at the vertex to show it is exactly 90°)	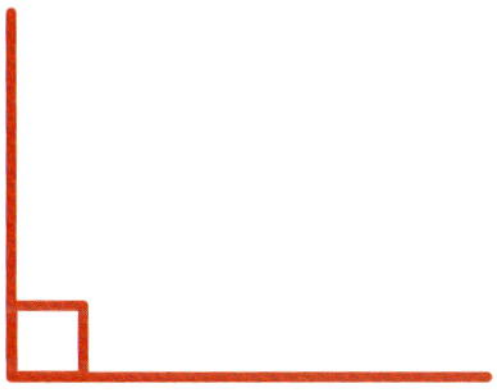	
Obtuse (more than a quarter turn)	More than 90°, less than 180°	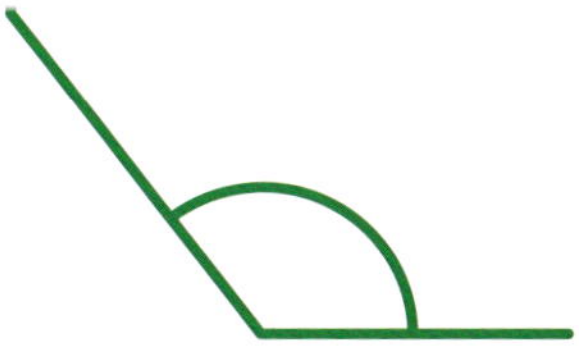	
Straight (half turn)	Exactly 180°		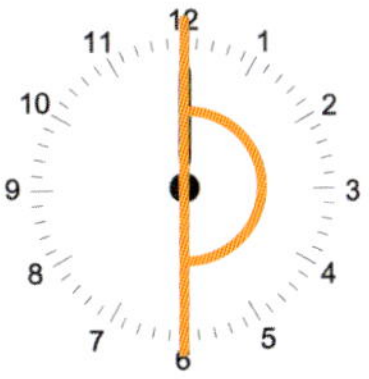
Reflex (more than a half turn)	More than 180°, less than 360°		
Revolution (full turn)	Exactly 360°		

* Each angle has a small curved line near the vertex to highlight the angle

Compass Points

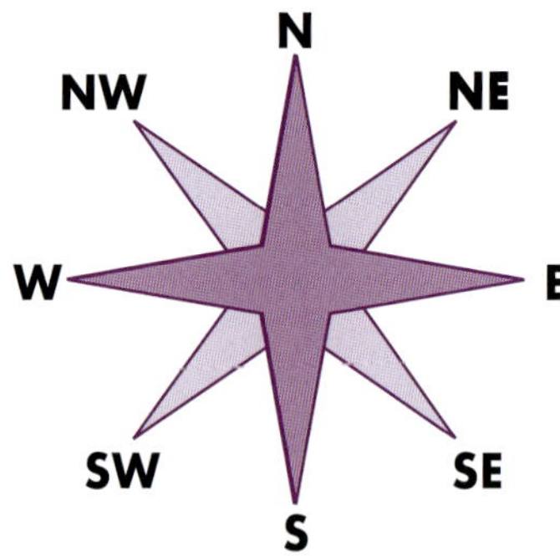

Prisms

Prisms have flat faces with no curved surfaces. They have two identical (same shape and size) faces at the ends (or bases) and the faces that join up these two bases are parallelograms.

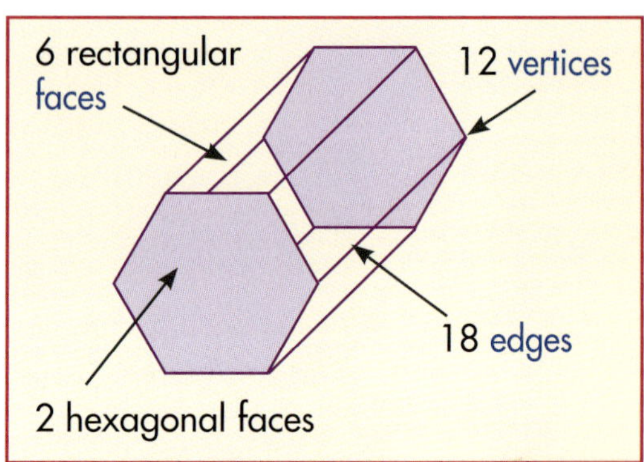

You name a prism by the shape of its base. The corners of a solid are called vertices.

A drawing of a triangular prism looks different from **different viewing angles**.

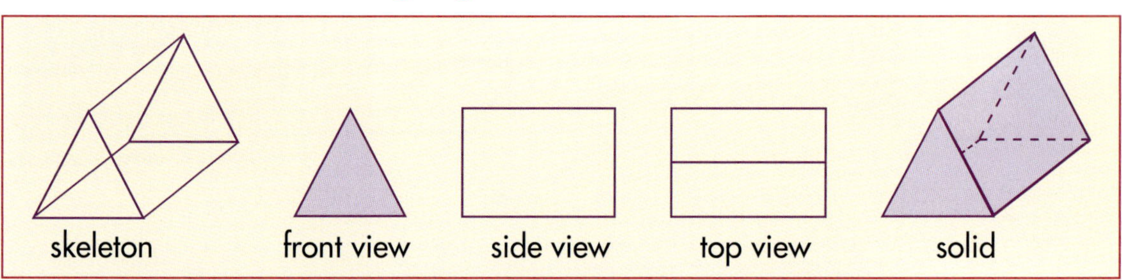

Prism	Base shape	Number of faces	Number of vertices	Number of edges
Rectangular		6	8	12
Pentagonal		7	10	15
Hexagonal		8	12	18
Octagonal		10	16	24

Pyramids

Pyramids are not prisms. You describe pyramids by their base. But unlike prisms, pyramids have only one base.

Pyramids have triangular faces, not rectangular ones like prisms. These triangular faces always meet at one point, one apex or vertex.

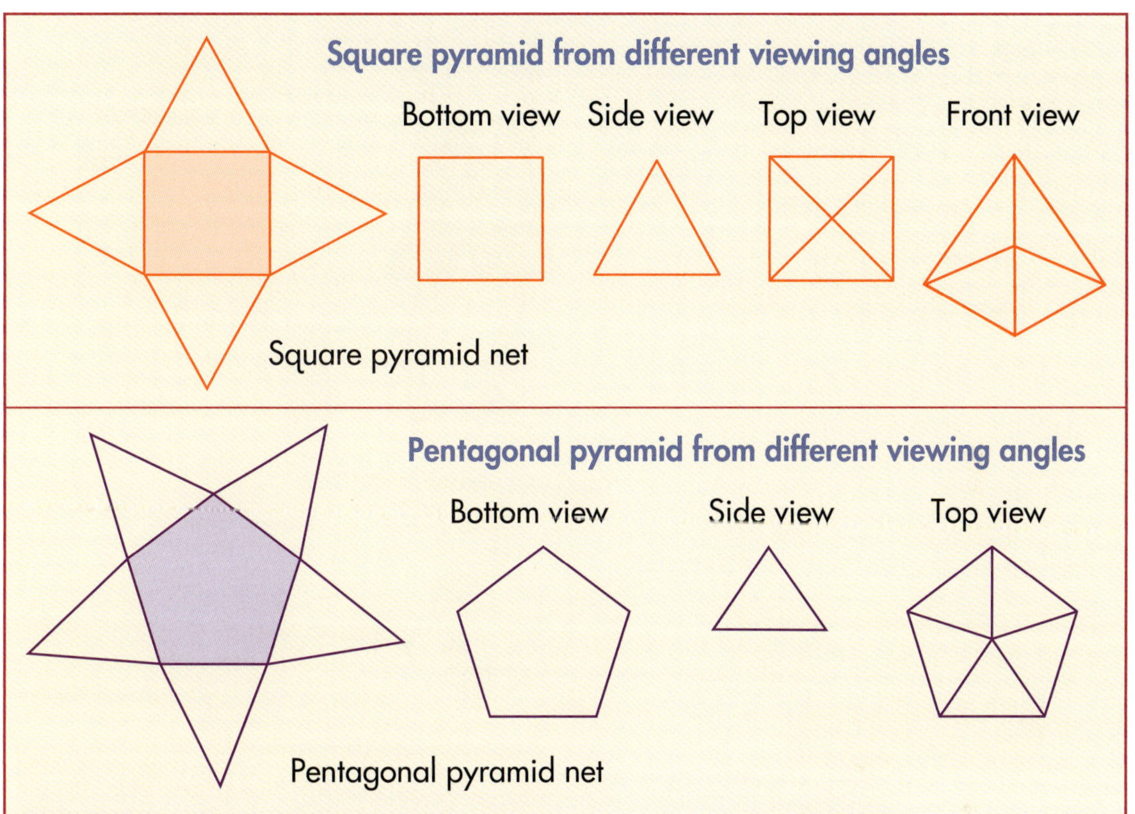

Pyramid	Base shape	Number of faces	Number of vertices	Number of edges
Rectangular	(rectangle)	5	5	8
Pentagonal	(pentagon)	6	6	10
Hexagonal	(hexagon)	7	7	12
Octagonal	(octagon)	9	9	16

Measurement

Length facts

1 mm = 0.1 cm

10 mm = 1 cm

100 mm = 10 cm

1000 mm = 100 cm

1 cm = 0.01 m

10 cm = 0.1 m

100 cm = 1 m

1000 cm = 10 m

10 000 cm = 100 m

100 000 cm = 1000 m

1000 m = 1 km

Area facts

1 square centimetre
= 1 × 1 cm
= 1 cm^2

1 square metre
= 100 × 100 cm
= 10 000 cm^2

1 hectare
= 100 × 100 m
= 10 000 m^2

Mass facts

1 g = 0.001 kg

10 g = 0.01 kg

100 g = 0.1 kg

1000 g = 1 kg

1000 kg = 1 tonne

Volume & capacity facts

1 × 1 × 1 cm = 1 cubic centimetre
= 1 cm^3

10 × 10 × 10 cm = 1000 cm^3

100 × 100 × 100 cm = 1 million cm^3
= 1 cubic metre
= 1 m^3

1 mL = 0.001 L

10 mL = 0.01 L

100 mL = 0.1 L

1000 mL = 1 litre = 1 L

Time

Number of days in a month		
28/29 days	**30 days**	**31 days**
February	April	January
	June	March
	September	May
	November	July
		August
		October
		December

24-hour and 12-hour Time

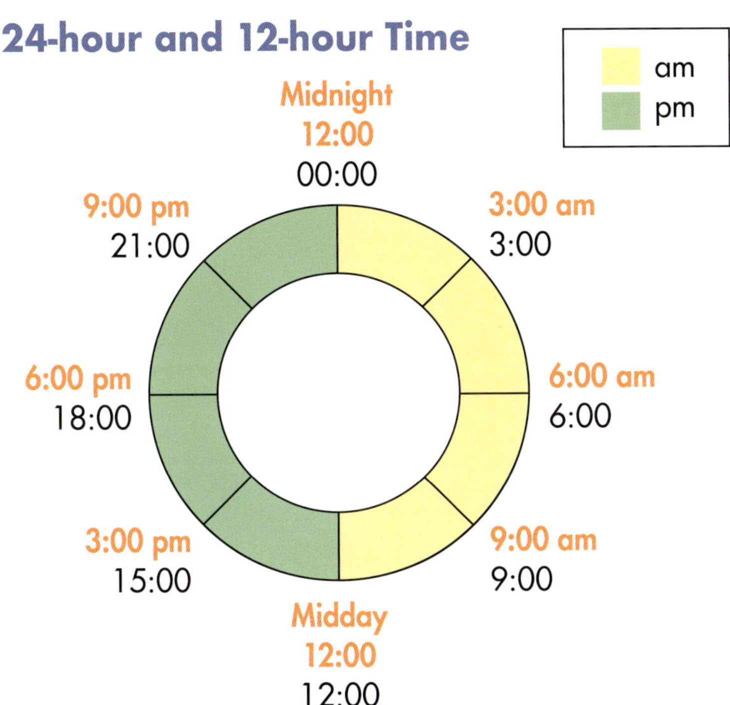

24-hour clock	12-hour clock
00:00	12:00 midnight
01:00	1:00 am
02:00	2:00 am
03:00	3:00 am
04:00	4:00 am
05:00	5:00 am
06:00	6:00 am
07:00	7:00 am
08:00	8:00 am
09:00	9:00 am
10:00	10:00 am
11:00	11:00 am
12:00	12:00 midday
13:00	1:00 pm
14:00	2:00 pm
15:00	3:00 pm
16:00	4:00 pm
17:00	5:00 pm
18:00	6:00 pm
19:00	7:00 pm
20:00	8:00 pm
21:00	9:00 pm
22:00	10:00 pm
23:00	11:00 pm

Selected Try This and Challenge Answers

Page 12 Try this: The birthday

There are 3 more days to the end of March, then 16 days to your friend's birthday. So that's 3 + 16 = 19 days. If you imagine counting on from the pale grey number at the bottom right of the March calendar, then 3 April will be a Sunday, the start of the next invisible row at the bottom. Keep imagining this count until you reach 16. You land on a Saturday, so 16 April 2016 must be a Saturday.

Page 16 Try this: Staircase

The staircase has 8 faces.

Page 16 Challenge: Reading a map

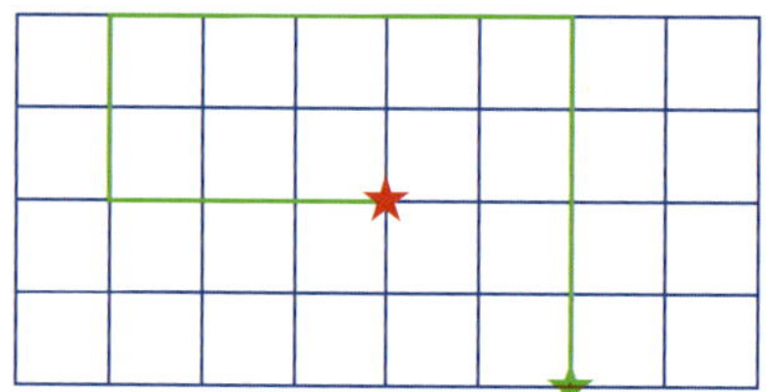

Page 18 Try this: Finished model

Page 22 Try this: Josh's hexagon

Move 4 sticks to create 3 triangles.

Page 31 Try this: Unit shapes

There are several ways to show 3 units:

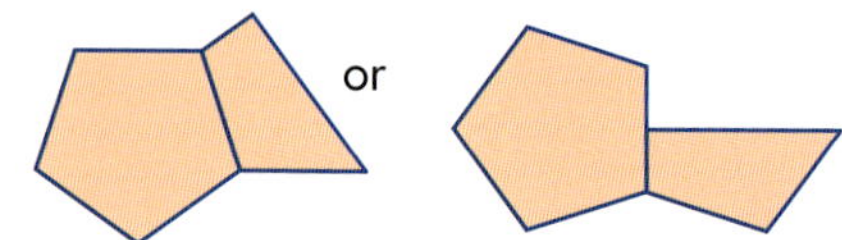

Page 33 Try this: ABC jumps

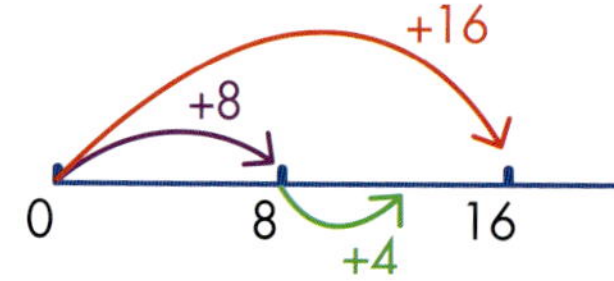

Kangaroo B jumped 8 + 4 times. That's 12 jumps.

Page 34 Try this: Birthday

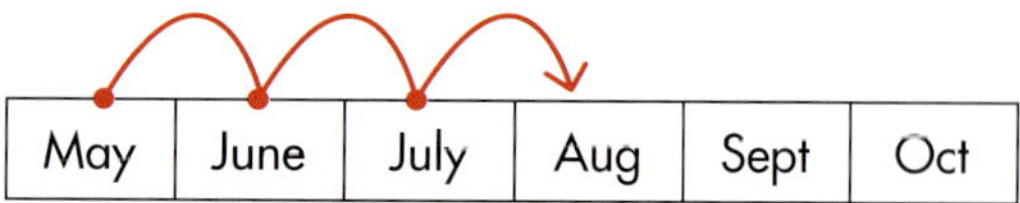

3 months after May is August.

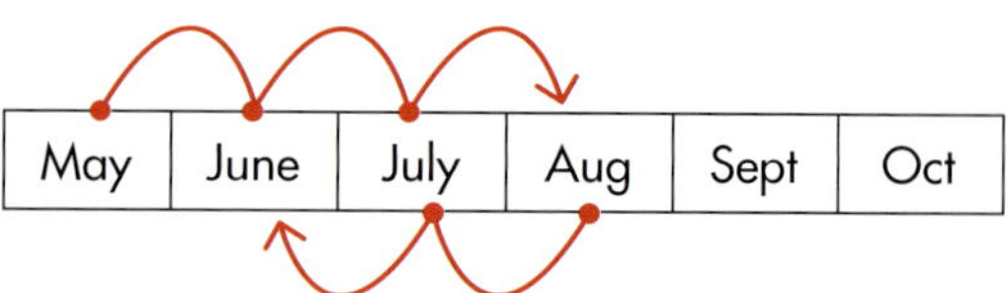

2 months before August is June. Omar's birthday must be in June.

Page 36 Try this: 18 units

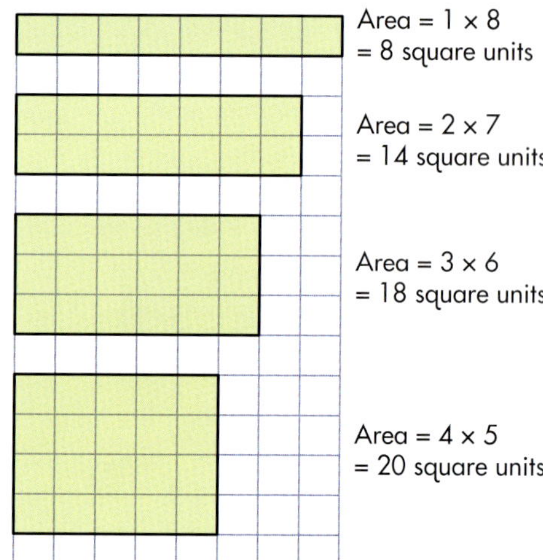

The largest area Farmer Holly can enclose with 18 units of fencing is 4 × 5 or 5 × 4 units. That's 20 square units of area.

Page 49 Challenge

Five shearers take 1 hour to shear 100 sheep. One shearer takes 1 hour to shear one fifth of the sheep (20 sheep). Two shearers in 1 hour will shear 2 × 20 sheep – that's 40 sheep.

Number of shearers	Time in minutes	Number of sheep
5	60	100
1	60	100 ÷ 5 = 20
2	60	40
2	120	80
2	30	20

Two shearers take 120 + 30 minutes to shear 80 + 20 sheep. That's 150 minutes to shear 100 sheep. There are 60 minutes in an hour. That's 2 hours and 30 minutes.

Page 56 Try this: Spring Boat Races

For example:

- There were 50 more boats racing in September than October.
- Twenty-five fewer boats raced in October than November.
- September was the most popular time for racing.
- The total number of boats racing in Spring was (5 × 25) + (3 × 25) + (4 × 25). That's 125 + 75 + 100 or a total of 300 boats.

Page 56 Challenge

For example:

- Tomatoes are the most popular fruit grown worldwide. I estimate the proportion as about 30%.
- About 25% or a quarter of these fruits are bananas.
- About the same amount of oranges and apples are grown each year. It looks like there are slightly more apples.
- Watermelon is the least popular of these 5 fruits as it looks like about 10%.

The graph below shows the actual proportions. As long as you suggested an approximate proportion, you are correct.

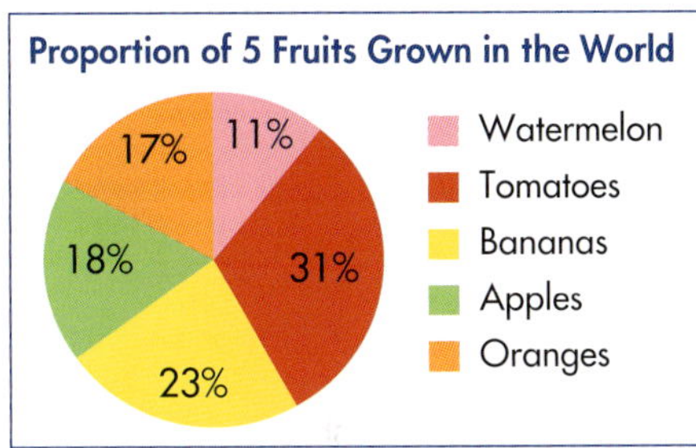

Page 65 Try this: Ticket sales

Use Guess and check until you find the right combination. Or break it into smaller parts. 440 – 66 = 374. 374 ÷ 2 = 187. 187 + 66 = 253. Duffy sold 187 tickets and Bev sold 253 tickets.

Page 67 Try this: How many Zercks?

Use Guess and check until you discover an answer that works. Or Visualise it. If all creatures are Zeds, that's 11 × 3 = 33 legs (10 legs too few). Zercks have 2 extra legs. The missing 10 legs must belong to 5 Zercks. If all creatures are Zercks, that's 11 × 5 = 55 legs. That's 12 legs too many. Zeds have 2 fewer legs. Those extra 12 legs must belong to 6 Zeds. There are 6 Zeds and 5 Zercks.

Page 70 Try this: 12 sticks

Page 70 Try this: Make it true

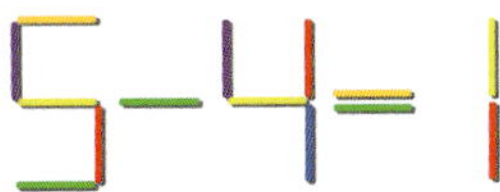

Page 70 Challenge

You can make many larger numbers. e.g.

I think the highest number you can make is:

Page 72 Try this: Add to 9

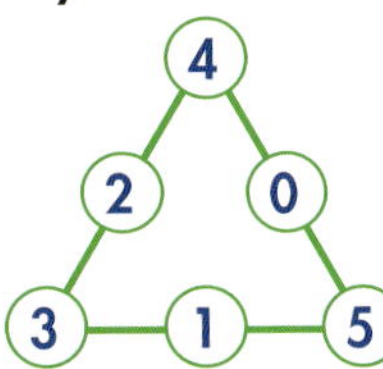

Page 73 Try this: Draw this triangle

Page 78 Try this: Water use

- Ali uses 80 more litres than Imran. 265 – 80 = 185
- Ali and Imran each use half this extra amount in a day. Half of 185 = 92.5.
- Imran uses 92.5 L and Ali uses 92.5 plus the extra 80 L. That's 92.5 + 80 = 172.5 L.
- Ali uses 172.5 L. Check by adding up mentally. 92.5 + 172.5 = 92 + 173 = 90 + 175 = 265.

Page 78 Challenge

36 – 8 = 28. 28 ÷ 2 = 14. Mum makes 14 berry muffins and 14 + 8 banana muffins. That's 22 banana muffins.

Page 84 100-sided polygon

You can draw (100 – 3) diagonals from one corner of a 100-sided polygon. That's 97 diagonals.

Page 90 Try this: Max's money

Work backwards:
$225 – $76 – $88 = $149 – $88 = $61.
Or $76 + $88 = $164. $225 – $164 = $61.
Grandma gave Max $61.

Page 101 Try this: Mystery rule

The mystery rule is "add 15"

Number	2	5	8	10	12	15	20	50	75	100
+15	17	20	23	25	27	30	35	65	90	115

Page 101 Challenge

If this tricked you don't worry. Notice the numbers get larger as the pattern continues. It probably involves multiplication. Think of all your tables facts and see if that gives you a clue.

1x, 2x, 3x don't get you anywhere. And 4x is not large enough either. Try 5x. Can you spot anything now? The mystery rule is multiply by 5 then subtract 1.

Number	1	2	3	4	5	6	7	8	9	10
5 × then –1	4	9	14	19	24	29	34	39	44	49

Page 103 Try this: 100s patterns

Here are some 100s chart patterns: Each column increases by 10 as you go down. Each row increases by 1 as you go across.

2s pattern (all the multiples of 2 are coloured green)

1	2	3	4	5	6	7	8	9	10
11	12	13	14	15	16	17	18	19	20
21	22	23	24	25	26	27	28	29	30
31	32	33	34	35	36	37	38	39	40
41	42	43	44	45	46	47	48	49	50
51	52	53	54	55	56	57	58	59	60
61	62	63	64	65	66	67	68	69	70
71	72	73	74	75	76	77	78	79	80
81	82	83	84	85	86	87	88	89	90
91	92	93	94	95	96	97	98	99	100

4s pattern (all the multiples of 4 are coloured blue)

1	2	3	4	5	6	7	8	9	10
11	12	13	14	15	16	17	18	19	20
21	22	23	24	25	26	27	28	29	30
31	32	33	34	35	36	37	38	39	40
41	42	43	44	45	46	47	48	49	50
51	52	53	54	55	56	57	58	59	60
61	62	63	64	65	66	67	68	69	70
71	72	73	74	75	76	77	78	79	80
81	82	83	84	85	86	87	88	89	90
91	92	93	94	95	96	97	98	99	100

8s pattern (all the multiples of 8 are coloured purple)

1	2	3	4	5	6	7	8	9	10
11	12	13	14	15	16	17	18	19	20
21	22	23	24	25	26	27	28	29	30
31	32	33	34	35	36	37	38	39	40
41	42	43	44	45	46	47	48	49	50
51	52	53	54	55	56	57	58	59	60
61	62	63	64	65	66	67	68	69	70
71	72	73	74	75	76	77	78	79	80
81	82	83	84	85	86	87	88	89	90
91	92	93	94	95	96	97	98	99	100

3s pattern (all the multiples of 3 are coloured yellow)

1	2	3	4	5	6	7	8	9	10
11	12	13	14	15	16	17	18	19	20
21	22	23	24	25	26	27	28	29	30
31	32	33	34	35	36	37	38	39	40
41	42	43	44	45	46	47	48	49	50
51	52	53	54	55	56	57	58	59	60
61	62	63	64	65	66	67	68	69	70
71	72	73	74	75	76	77	78	79	80
81	82	83	84	85	86	87	88	89	90
91	92	93	94	95	96	97	98	99	100

6s pattern (all the multiples of 6 are coloured orange)

1	2	3	4	5	6	7	8	9	10
11	12	13	14	15	16	17	18	19	20
21	22	23	24	25	26	27	28	29	30
31	32	33	34	35	36	37	38	39	40
41	42	43	44	45	46	47	48	49	50
51	52	53	54	55	56	57	58	59	60
61	62	63	64	65	66	67	68	69	70
71	72	73	74	75	76	77	78	79	80
81	82	83	84	85	86	87	88	89	90
91	92	93	94	95	96	97	98	99	100

9s pattern (all the multiples of 9 are coloured red)

1	2	3	4	5	6	7	8	9	10
11	12	13	14	15	16	17	18	19	20
21	22	23	24	25	26	27	28	29	30
31	32	33	34	35	36	37	38	39	40
41	42	43	44	45	46	47	48	49	50
51	52	53	54	55	56	57	58	59	60
61	62	63	64	65	66	67	68	69	70
71	72	73	74	75	76	77	78	79	80
81	82	83	84	85	86	87	88	89	90
91	92	93	94	95	96	97	98	99	100

odd numbers (all the odd numbers are coloured pink)

1	2	3	4	5	6	7	8	9	10
11	12	13	14	15	16	17	18	19	20
21	22	23	24	25	26	27	28	29	30
31	32	33	34	35	36	37	38	39	40
41	42	43	44	45	46	47	48	49	50
51	52	53	54	55	56	57	58	59	60
61	62	63	64	65	66	67	68	69	70
71	72	73	74	75	76	77	78	79	80
81	82	83	84	85	86	87	88	89	90
91	92	93	94	95	96	97	98	99	100

The digits for each number in this diagonal **add to 10**.

1	2	3	4	5	6	7	8	9	10
11	12	13	14	15	16	17	18	19	20
21	22	23	24	25	26	27	28	29	30
31	32	33	34	35	36	37	38	39	40
41	42	43	44	45	46	47	48	49	50
51	52	53	54	55	56	57	58	59	60
61	62	63	64	65	66	67	68	69	70
71	72	73	74	75	76	77	78	79	80
81	82	83	84	85	86	87	88	89	90
91	92	93	94	95	96	97	98	99	100

Page 105 Try this: Continue the pattern

$1 \times 9 + 2 = 11$
$12 \times 9 + 3 = 111$
$123 \times 9 + 4 = 1111$
$1234 \times 9 + 5 = 11111$
$12345 \times 9 + 6 = 111111$
$123456 \times 9 + 7 = 1111111$
$1234567 \times 9 + 8 = 11111111$
$12345678 \times 9 + 9 = 111111111$
$123456789 \times 9 + 10 = 1111111111$

The rule is the part has the same number of counting numbers in order.

You multiply these by 9 and then add 1 more than the part number.

So the 9th part will be the first 9 counting numbers $\times 9 + (9 + 1)$.

The 9th part of this pattern is $123456789 \times 9 + 10 = 1111111111$.

The fast way is to see that the answer is always the same number of ones as the part number. So the answer to the 9th part number will be nine 1s or 111111111.

Page 106 Try this: Pascal's patterns

Here are some of the patterns hiding in Pascal's Triangle:

If you add the numbers in each row the sum is double the sum of the row above.

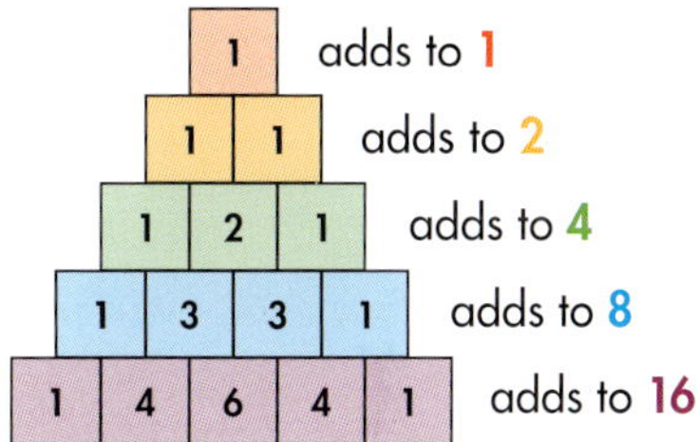

On this 2nd diagonal, the square of each number equals the sum of the 2 numbers beside it in the 3rd diagonal.

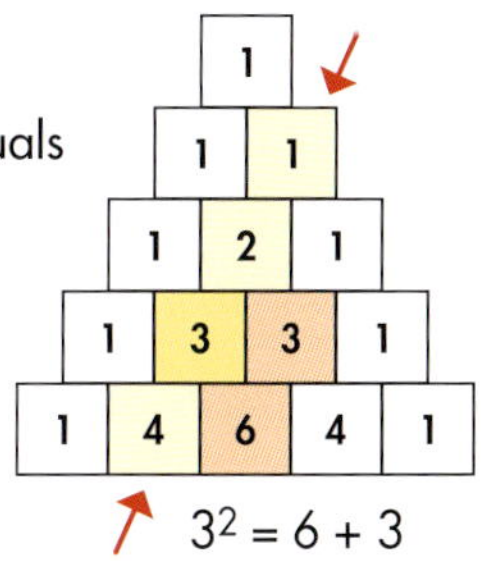

Page 106 Challenge

Here are some of Ramanujan's amazing addition sums.

Each column adds to 139.

22	12	18	87
88	17	9	25
10	24	89	16
19	86	23	11

Each row adds to 139.

22	12	18	87
88	17	9	25
10	24	89	16
19	86	23	11

Each diagonal adds to 139.

22	12	18	87
88	17	9	25
10	24	89	16
19	86	23	11

These all add to 139 too:

22	12	18	87
88	17	9	25
10	24	89	16
19	86	23	11

22	12	18	87
88	17	9	25
10	24	89	16
19	86	23	11

22	12	18	87
88	17	9	25
10	24	89	16
19	86	23	11

Page 108 Try this: Ness's shape

Shape A

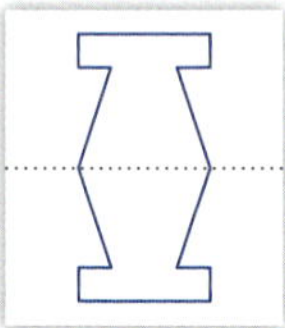

Page 109 Challenge

These examples repeat when they are rotated 90°.

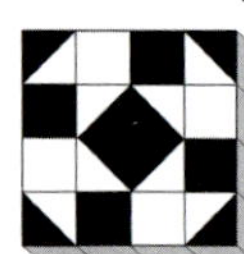

These examples repeat when they are rotated 180°.

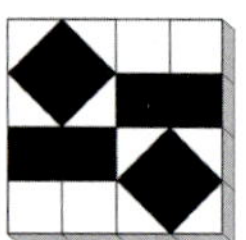

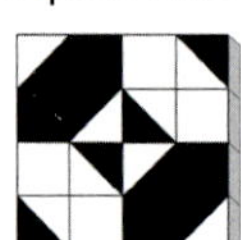

There is no line symmetry in patterns A, B or C.

Page 111 Spotlight on Henry Dudeney

	S	E	N	D
+	M	O	R	E
M	O	N	E	Y

	9	5	6	7
+	1	0	8	5
1	0	6	5	2

	1	9	2
+	3	8	4
	5	7	6

	2	1	9
+	4	3	8
	6	5	7

Page 113 Try this: Harry's fish tanks

Eliminate the extra text by crossing it out.

Harry has 2 fish tanks. ~~One tank is red and the other tank is blue.~~

He has 3 types of fish – mollies, goldfish and tetras.

~~The goldfish eat the most food.~~

Harry wants to catch the tetras to give them to his friend.

Which tank gives him a better chance of catching tetras?

Tank 1 has 10 fish and 5 fish are tetras.

5 out of 10 is the same as a half.

$5/10 = 1/2$

Tank 2 has 20 fish and 8 are tetras.

8 out of 20 is less than a half.

$8/20 = 4/10 = 2/5$

Harry has a better chance catching tetras in Tank 1.

Page 119 Try this: Giraffe smells

2 giraffes each smell something 250 m away.
1000 giraffes each smell something 250 m away.

Page 130 Try this: The beach trip

	Sister	Mum	Gran
Jenny	✗	✓	✗
Judy	✗	✗	✓
Jackie	✓	✗	✗

Jackie is Harry's sister, Jenny is his mum and Judy is his Gran.

Page 130 Challenge

	Brown	White	Spots	Run	Catch balls	Dig holes
Bella	✗	✓	✗	✗	✗	✓
Jax	✗	✗	✓	✓	✗	✗
Daisy	✓	✗	✗	✗	✓	✗
Run	✗	✗	✓			
Catch balls	✓	✗	✗			
Dig holes	✗	✓	✗			

Bella is white and loves to dig holes.
Jax has spots and loves to run.
Daisy is brown and loves to catch balls.

Page 132 Try this: Sudoku

4	2	3	1
1	3	4	2
2	4	1	3
3	1	2	4

Page 133 Letter number puzzles

	S	U	N
+	F	U	N
S	W	I	M

	1	2	4
+	9	2	4
1	0	5	8

$$\begin{array}{r} 1\ 2\ 7 \\ +\ 9\ 2\ 7 \\ \hline 1\ 0\ 5\ 4 \\ \hline \end{array} \qquad \begin{array}{r} 1\ 3\ 2 \\ +\ 9\ 3\ 2 \\ \hline 1\ 0\ 6\ 4 \\ \hline \end{array}$$

$$\begin{array}{r} 1\ 3\ 6 \\ +\ 9\ 3\ 6 \\ \hline 1\ 0\ 7\ 2 \\ \hline \end{array} \qquad \begin{array}{r} 1\ 3\ 8 \\ +\ 9\ 3\ 8 \\ \hline 1\ 0\ 7\ 6 \\ \hline \end{array}$$

$$\begin{array}{r} 1\ 4\ 3 \\ +\ 9\ 4\ 3 \\ \hline 1\ 0\ 8\ 6 \\ \hline \end{array}$$

Page 133 Try this: Puzzle

199 + 1 = 200

Page 133 Challenge

5 + 5 = 10 so P = 0.

G must equal 3 as there is a trade to the 100 000s place. H must be 8 or 9.

There is a trade to the 10s column so L and O must be 4, 6, 7 or 8 as they are the only digits left. L ≠ 8 as O can't be 1. L ≠ 7 as O can't be 0. L ≠ 6 as O can't be 9. So L must equal 4 and O = 7. D must equal 6 as 7 + 8 is greater than 14. So R = 8.

A = 1, D = 6, E = 5, G = 3, H = 9, L = 4, O = 7, P = 0, R = 8, S = 2

Page 134 1-step: 6566 ÷ 938 = 7. Claire buys 7 tickets to Bali.

2-step: Step 1: 2 × 938 = 1876.
Step 2: 5000 – 1876 = 3124.
Claire has $3124 left for holiday expenses.

More than 2 steps: Step 1: 4 × 938 = 3752.
Step 2: 3 × 440 = 1320.
Step 3: 3752 + 1320 = 5072.
Claire spends $5072 on 7 return tickets to Bali.

Multiple choice: 938 is closer to 1000 than 0 so round it up to 1000. 4 × 1000 = 4000.
The correct estimate is C: $4000.

Open-ended: Any combination that is less than $5000 is correct. e.g. 2 adult and 2 child fares = 1876 + 880 = 2756; 4 adult fares = $3752 (it doesn't say you have to buy a child's fare);
3 adult and 4 child return airfares cost 2814 +1760 = 4574.

Puzzle: 5628 ÷ 938 = 6. Together they buy 6 tickets. Ness buys the fewest tickets. Bev buys 2 more tickets than Ness. Ness must buy 1, Claire 2 and Bev 3 tickets.

Page 134 Challenge

You can create 100s of problems.
Here is one suggestion for each type.

1-step: Bev boards the ferry at Darling Harbour. How long is her trip to Abbotsford?
(Answer: 25 minutes)

2-step: Ness catches the same ferry 21 minutes later than Bev. How long is Ness's trip to Abbotsford?
(Answer: Ness must board at Cockatoo Island. The trip to Abbotsford takes 2 + 15 minutes = 17 minutes)

More than 2 steps: What is the longest time between ferry stops on this trip?
(Answer: CQ – DH =13, DH – CI = 8, CI – D = 5, D – HP = 5, HP – C =3, C – A = 4. So the longest time between stops on this trip is 13 minutes from Circular Quay to Darling Harbour)

Multiple choice: Claire catches the ferry 18 minutes after it leaves Darling Harbour.
She boards the ferry at:

A. Cockatoo Island B. Drummoyne
C. Huntleys Point D. Chiswick
(Answer: Huntley's Point)

Open: Ness, Claire and Bev catch the ferry to Abbotsford for a picnic lunch. They all board at different stops. Bev travels the furthest. Claire travels the shortest distance. At which stops do they each board the ferry?
(Answer: There are many possible combinations. Bev could board at Circular Quay, Ness at Darling Harbour and Claire at Cockatoo Island)

Puzzle: Ness, Claire and Bev catch the same ferry to Abbotsford for a picnic lunch. Bev boards 18 minutes before Claire. Ness boards 10 minutes before Claire. Claire travels only 7 minutes before they all get off at Abbotsford. Where does Bev board the ferry?
(Answer: Claire boards at Huntley's Point. Bev boards 18 minutes before this at 12:20. Bev boards at Darling Harbour)

Image credits: All images © Dreamstime except:
p.2 (Andrew Wiles cartoon), © Science Photo Library;
p.3, (Leonardo da Vinci), Creative Commons LACMA 19.4.22;
p.3, (Leonardo's Robot), Photo by Erik Möller. Leonardo da Vinci. Mensch - Erfinder - Genie exhibit, Berlin 2005;
p.10, (Albert Einstein in 1947), Creative Commons: Photographer Orren Jack Turner;
p.40, (Zaha Hadid Portrait 1956), Photograph courtesy Zaha Hadid;
p.40, (Cordoba Mosque Spain), CC Photograph by Timor Espallargas 2004;
p.40, (Zaha Hadid Portrait), Photograph courtesy of Zaha Hadid Architects, CC Zaha_Hadid_Portrait_by_Simone_Cecchetti;
p.41, (Sheikh Zayed Bridge), Abu Dhabi, UAE ,CC Mohammad Khatib 2012;
p.41, (Heydar Aliyev Centre, Azerbaijan), CC Photographer Rossi101, 2012;
p.41, (ZHA Aquatics Centre London), Photograph courtesy Zaha Hada Architects, © Hufton + Crow;
p.42, (Illustration from Margita philosophica 1503 by Gregor Reisch), CC: Houghton Typ 520.03.736 - Margarita philosophica, Harvard University;
p.60, p.106, (Srinivasa Ramanujan [1887–1920]),CC: Srinivasa Ramanujan - OPC - 1;
p.60, (A page from one of Ramanujan's notebooks), DFILES.me Srinivasa Ramanujan Notebooks 6254;
p.61, (Ramanujan at Trinity College, Cambridge), CC: Charles F. Wilson - Ramanujan22.jpg@ www.educ.fc.ul.pt;
p.61, (Statue of Ramanujan in Birla Industrial & Technological Museum), CC Srinivasa Ramanujam bust BITM, Ashlin 2014;
p.61, (Postage stamp celebrating Ramanujan's achievements, 2011), Credit: Brahm Prakash (iStampGallery.com);
p.72, p.110, (Henry Ernest Dudeney [1857–1930]), CC: Henry Dudeney circa 1910;
p.74, (Portrait of Sofia Kovalevskaya, 1868), CC: Zaq1234567890okm;
p.74, (Public Domain: Sophie Kowalevski, 1880), Dahloff of Stockholm Institut Mittag-Leffler;
p.75, (Hubble infrared of Saturn), CC: NASA/E. Karkoschka (University of Arizona) 2007;
p.75, (Kovalevskaya Crater 5024), CC: James Stuby based on NASA image, 2015;
p.75, (Russian postage Stamp with Sofia Kovalevskaya portrait, 1951), CC: Stamp of USSR 1635, Post of USSR;
p.78, (Terry Tao in his UCLA office 2006), Quote with kind permission by Terry Tao, photograph courtesy of the John D. and Catherine T. MacArthur Foundation;
p.81, p.87 (Blaise Pascal portrait), © Science Photo Library;
p.81, (Lithograph showing a portrait of the German mathematician Carl Friedrich Gauss at age 50), CC: Siegfried Detlev Bendixen, published in "Astronomische Nachrichten" 1828;
p.86, p.106, (Blaise Pascal), Etching by J. Henriot after G. Edelinck after F. Quesnel, junior. CCBY Wellcome Library, London, V0004510, ICV No 4715;
p.87, (6-digit calculating machine by Blaise Pascal, 1652), © 2005 David Monniaux Pascals calculator Musee Arts et Metiers Pascaline dsc03869;
p.98, (Portrait of Ada Lovelace as a child), Principal and Fellows of Somerville College, Oxford;
p.98, (Babbage's Analytical Engine 1834-1871), CC: Science Museum London;
p.99 (Textile pattern punch cards), © Science & Society Picture Library;
p.99, (Watercolor portrait of Ada King, Countess of Lovelace 23 years old), CC: Alfred Edward Chalon - Science & Society Picture Library, 1840;
p.99, (Tunnel Boring Machine Ada [fully assembled at Westbourne Park]), © Crossrail Ltd UK;
p.110, (Henry Dudeney's Haberdasher's Puzzle solution with hinged pieces), CC: Yoni Toker Hinged haberdasher, 2008;
p.111, (Puzzle 74), Photograph by Bev Dunbar of Puzzle 74: The Broken Chessboard, Canterbury Puzzles, HE Dudeney, Dover 1958;
p.111, (The Canterbury Puzzles) Photograph by Bev Dunbar of front cover of HE Dudeney's The Canterbury Puzzles, Dover 1979;
p.111, (Amusements in Mathematics), Photograph by Bev Dunbar of front cover of HE Dudeney's Amusements in Mathematics, Dover 1970;
p.120, (Portrait of Emmy Noether), CC: Photographer unknown, before 1910;
p.121, (Noether Crater 5006), CC: Nöther_crater_5006_h3 NASA James Stuby;
p.121, (Emmy Noether in 1930), CC: EmmyNoether MFO3096, photograph by Konrad Jacobs, Erlangen;
p.131, (Leonhard Euler by Jokob Emanuel Handmann), CC: Leonhard Euler, 1753;
p.134, (Sydney Ferry Nicole Livingstone at Circular Quay), CC: Photograph by Hugh Peterswald 2013.